THE
HOMETOWN

Leena Ceraveeni

iUniverse, Inc.
Bloomington

iUniverse books may be ordered through booksellers or by contacting:

iUniverse
1663 Liberty Drive
Bloomington, IN 47403
www.iuniverse.com
1-800-Authors (1-800-288-4677)

Because of the dynamic nature of the Internet, any web addresses or links contained in this book may have changed since publication and may no longer be valid. The views expressed in this work are solely those of the author and do not necessarily reflect the views of the publisher, and the publisher hereby disclaims any responsibility for them.

Any people depicted in stock imagery provided by Thinkstock are models, and such images are being used for illustrative purposes only.

Certain stock imagery © Thinkstock.

Author photograph by Mikaila Adams

ISBN: 978-1-4502-9841-4 (sc)
ISBN: 978-1-4502-9840-7 (ebook)

Printed in the United States of America

iUniverse rev. date: 04/06/2011

CHAPTER 1

"Why do you have luggage?" My father closed the kitchen cabinet at a turtle's pace. The door covered the short glasses, tall glasses, and coffee mugs. He laboriously furrowed his eyebrows in gentle confusion instead of irritation or anger. His fingers were veiny, taut against the drinking glass in hand. His left ring finger looked more like it did when the back swing door of the house smashed it 12 years ago.

I had four black suitcases, two of which were small, that I had purchased from the mall. I had told him I was going shopping. I smiled at my father with immense guilt and a hidden fear so covered up and camouflaged by my audacity. My hands were on top of two of the brand-new suitcases. I dug my right palm into the handle again and again. The price tag sliced my pinky finger.

I typically purchased winter clothes from the clearance racks—fitted wool sweaters and colored corduroys, zip-up fleece hoodies, and crocheted striped glove-hat-and-scarf sets. I also liked to purchase intricately detailed leather purses with short, assertive shoulder straps, and earrings that dangled with subtle elegance while complementing the segments of my neck. But on that evening, I had entered Greenwood Park Mall to buy suitcases for my big move down South in two weeks. I still had to close my Fifth Third

Bank account, visit my sister's grave, and purchase cans of Fix-A-Flat.

I lingered in the beautiful pinewood kitchen in a house that was too spacious for three people, with rooms that were seldom entered and curtains that no one ever pushed to the side spontaneously to gaze through the window. The house would be for two soon.

He stared at me in diluted curiosity, glass in hand, lip wobbling with slim gloominess.

I waited for him to walk to the refrigerator and fill the glass with water.

He stood in a trance instead and smiled uneasily.

"I'm moving to Houston at the end of June," I blurted.

My father treaded the kitchen floor to the family room and stopped where the tile met the carpet. The glass was still in his hand. His feet were bare. His legs looked toned from treadmill commitments forced by high blood pressure and lung problems from decades of smoking. His calves stood out in old fern-colored swimming trunks that had been converted to house shorts. The neckline of his thin white T-shirt was permanently tipped forward. "You're moving to *Houston*? The ... the end of June? It's June now." His voice shook with distress. Scattered syllables of bewilderment projected through the room. "That's in two weeks."

My father crumpled into the wine-colored leather chair in the family room. It matched the sofa and love seat, fringing the walls of the space. His face was plum-colored in the cheeks, with a thick vein colored like a Granny Smith apple pulsating above his eyebrow. My father put the glass down in the coaster on the end table. He didn't look at me.

"I'll be staying with a friend of Eric's. His name is Chad and he works for NASA. He rents his house out to people. He's from Michigan and he went to Purdue with Eric. Five people live there now." I stepped diagonally in front of him. My right hand was wedged between my left thumb and finger as I spoke. "Three girls and two guys," I lied. I was going to be living with five guys but thought mentioning female roommates would sound more comforting to him. I spoke of loose details of my plans, jobs I had been searching for, big-city opportunities, cultural diversity, my restlessness and pursuit of adventure. I heard myself loud and clear, an unstoppable blabbering. "I can't find a … "

"Now, I didn't hear anything you said Mala," my father interrupted. His hands moved back and forth to support his chin. The weight of his authority shifted all over the leather chair. "Now, *what*? You're moving to Houston? And who's Eric?"

"Eric, Dad." I tossed my hands up near my face. "Audrey's brother."

He didn't blink.

"I can't find a job here, Dad." My voice quivered. Slender tears welled up in my dark eyes. "I'm not happy." I held myself together. I hadn't meant to tell him I wasn't happy. I had told him before, in college, when changing my major from physics to English after a semester. He sneeringly said that he hated his job and that it didn't matter—happiness wasn't important.

"You have a job," he said softly.

"I *hate* that job," I growled. I cringed at his reference to my Midwest Bank stint as a career.

"When are you putting in your notice for work?" my father managed to ask.

"I already did," I lied. I didn't tell him that I had walked out on my job and had been loitering around Meijer in the mornings, perusing '80s-rock greatest-hits CDs and counting the ears of corn in the produce section while he got ready for work. I didn't tell him about the gratifying end of my dead-end job. I looked at my father in the chair. I wondered why he wasn't yelling or making negative comments about my decision. I was taken aback by his attitude.

"You *did*?" My father dug his fingers into his scalp, pushing up the chunky black and gray locks on his head.

"I appreciate everything you've done for me," I said. "But it's time for me to go." It was difficult for me to say, as I had never been mushy with my father. Sentiments were rarely expressed except for an occasional "I love you" over the phone and a hug after visits home during my college years.

"You could always go back to school." His voice was the gentlest I had ever heard it. "There are more and more graduates, and they will be competing for the jobs that you want."

"I'm going to find a job in Houston, Dad."

"There's a huge Malayalee population in Houston," he said. "You could find a husband there and you could both move back here. We could all live together in this house. Try to find *our* people when you get there."

"I probably *will* meet more Indian people in Houston," I said, attempting to swerve away from the marriage topic.

"I've been saving up money for your wedding." He occasionally reminded me of the wedding fund. "Do you have money saved up for the move?"

I knew he would ask about money. He was frugal with his six-figure salary as an engineer for Eli Lilly. "Yes, I have money saved up, Dad." I would've had more saved if I wasn't depressed and shopping at Circle Centre every day. "I have enough. I have an interview lined up when I get there."

"I guess if you run out of money and *when* it doesn't work out, you can always come back," he said as he sat back in the chair, tilted his head against his hand, and looked up at me.

I ignored his lack of faith in me. His calm motions and semi-supportive statements had me on edge. I assumed his initial shock would wear off by morning. I nodded with my lips pressed together and avoided eye contact. I knew I would not return. If Houston weren't my city of opportunity, I'd pack up again and drive to Los Angeles.

"Can you wait until Mom gets back?"

"No." I shook my head. "I can't wait any longer." I was job-searching, corresponding with Chad about living arrangements, researching Houston freeways, and pinpointing the best and happening areas to live. I was looking forward to warm, snowless winters with windshields that did not need ice scrapers. I was looking forward to palm trees, ethnically pronounced communities, endless options, and a fresh place where people did not consider my Indian traits to be exotic and unusual.

"We're your parents," he said. "You weren't going to tell us about this major life change? Mom's going to be upset." He stood up. "We need to call her." His arms efficiently waved back and forth as he sauntered past me into the kitchen.

I would have to report the news to my mother soon. I would do it after I folded and flattened my last thin tee in the suitcase for the humid Houston summers or finished packing the box I was shipping to Chad's house. I'd have to tell her that not only was I moving but I would be living over 1,000 miles away from home.

"Let's call her now." The phone numbers of my parents' family and friends were inked in blue and black on white lined paper. It was a fusion of English and Malayalam, with cross-outs and additions that were squeezed in and failed to land on the lines. The list had a crinkle three-fourths of the way down the page, a result of an air-dried spill, and remained on the kitchen counter under a black wall phone. He lifted the handset.

"*Now?*" I was stunned by my father's urgency and his own plans to announce my move. I didn't fight him. I let him exert his authority over me one last time.

"Pick up the other phone," he said, turning halfway around without making eye contact. He dialed the phone with his middle finger. It was a habit I always found awkward. I always wondered why his index finger was not the first choice.

"Oh." My long eyelashes shot up to my eyebrows. "Okay." I naturally entered the study and plopped into the old periwinkle recliner that my father had kept for more than 15 years. The color had faded to a whitish blue in areas. He had moved it to the study recently and had plans to move it back to the living room. He had rearranged the recliner several times over the years in the family room, the living room, and the study. He usually kept it in the family room. It was *his* recliner. He fell asleep in it almost every day with his hand on the remote, pointing at the television. He always awoke when his head slid off his fist. It would take him a brief moment to realize he'd been asleep, and then he'd drift away again.

I smoothed the arm of the recliner with my hand, meticulously routing my fingers through the blended lines of the fabric. I realized I was unsure when I would see the chair again.

"It's ringing Mala *mol*!" His voice was blaring, piercing and abrupt. He coughed, clearing his throat as he always did before answering or making a phone call.

I looked down at the numbers of the Hoosier Lotto ticket on the side table while snatching up the handset. There were small crumbs of dirt between some of the buttons. The bottom left curve of the number 8 was faded. It was the phone that used to be in my bedroom as a teenager. I put it against my right ear and listened to my father as he yelled to my uncle on the line, masses of miles away from Indianapolis. I never understood why they shouted. I could always hear my relatives loud and clear through the excitement in their voices and the movement of their South Indian accents as they summarized their recent life events.

Even though I was American born and raised, with an American accent and American style, a former co-worker had told me I had an Indian accent. It had been a scorching summer morning at Aviation Plus, a west-side postal hub where I worked as a Japanese-beetle catcher during college breaks to prevent damage to crops on the West Coast. I was assigned to LAX with my best friend Audrey. Jackie, our other best friend, had called in sick to go boating at Lake Monroe with her family.

I stood on the small deck of the stairs at the crew door of the airplane with Audrey. I reeked of jet fuel and sweat. Disposable orange earplugs projected from my ears like bird wings in midflap. I gripped my Japanese-beetle catching net unconsciously at my side. The wind blew the pointy depths of my net back and forth against the stairs. Audrey and I had been in the same position for three hours. There were no Japanese beetles for capture. I was paid $17 per hour to do nothing. Working at Aviation Plus was a college student's dream job. My friends and I worked there every summer until graduation.

Audrey's eyes (one green, one blue) were covered with oversize snow-colored sunglasses. Her skin was turning pink even though she applied SPF 50 in my 1994 regal-plum-pearl Acura Vigor every morning on I-465. "I found this old picture of us the other day." She twisted her wrist, rotating her net. "I think it was probably from the third grade. We were wearing our Best Friends Forever necklaces, in front of the basketball hoop on your driveway. We were holding the Hoosier Hysteria teddy bears that my mom made us."

I laughed. "Bring that tomorrow. I *have* to see it." Snippets of short curly hair fluttered around my temples. I was wearing a white Indianapolis Colts T-shirt inside out, with the sleeves rolled into my bra straps, and irregular blue work shorts and generic-brand steel-toe boots from Value City. Hurricanes of sweat plateaued at the back of my neck and beneath my bra cups and circled my shoulders. I had a farmer's tan. I savored a sip from the can of Coke that a pilot had given me for "being so cute with my net."

Audrey waved to her boyfriend, Tom, a ramp worker. His hair was as red as Axl Rose's. The sleeves of his dingy Hanes T-shirt were rolled to his collarbone, unveiling scarlet-on-pale skin. He never wore sunscreen. Tom controlled the loader at the cargo door, sending white USPS cans into the aircraft, obstructing his view of Audrey.

The stairs shook, breaking our hollow stares at the runway. I pressed my hand against the airplane for support and silently criticized my different-sized nails and chipped glossy, coriander-colored polish. Audrey and I looked down at the unattended parked tug and the driver thundering up the stairs. His belly bulged through an Aviation Plus T-shirt with an unraveled hem. He acknowledged us with an accelerated chin tilt and waddled into the cockpit, carrying a compartment-designed clipboard.

Audrey and I looked at each other and laughed.

He returned without the clipboard and stood between us. "Are you a bug catcher?"

"*No*," I replied sarcastically. I erratically waved the net with Japanese-beetle remnants suctioned to the bottom. A carcass fell out.

Audrey turned away to laugh.

He inserted his fingers into and over a hole in his shirt as if he were trying to cover it up. "Catch any bugs today?" It was *the* annoying broken-record question asked by the Aviation Plus employees.

"Oh *yeah*." I rolled my eyes. "They were swarming."

"Really? Wow." He peeked inside the plane. "I rarely see any." He walked down two steps. "You have the most beautiful hair that I have ever seen." He was balding, with a thicker patch of hair on the left side of his head than on the right. The patches were mercilessly matted with sweat. He took off his sunglasses and squinted into the sun. His face was sunburned, with spheres of white around his eyes.

"Thanks." Hair compliments were my favorite. Americans liked my short, curly, neck- and ear-revealing hair, but Indians told me to grow it long and straighten it.

"You girls enjoy gettin' a suntan." The stairs rattled again. He hopped on the tug as if it were a Harley and drove away to SAN.

The USDA staff walked through the ramp area, looking high-profile in their uniforms: tucked-in shirts, knee-length shorts, and baseball caps. Audrey and I waved to our bosses, verifying our day's hard work in heading off five-figure fines for the presence of Japanese beetles.

The weight of the white USPS cans lining the airplane was perfectly distributed to prevent the plane from tipping and ensure a safe takeoff. I watched SEA taxi out. The departure controller directed the pilot, waving the orange traffic batons like a rave kid on ecstasy with glow sticks.

The pilots informed us that they were ready for takeoff and shutting the crew door.

Audrey and I headed inside to separate mail, dragging our nets and ignoring lustful waves from tug drivers and ramp workers. The air in Aviation Plus was suspicious and musty. Aviation Plus was filled with lines of conscienceless conveyer belts and supervisors who used clipboards as a VIP accessory. Lynn from human resources took attendance, clipboard in hand, by circuiting around and checking faces instead of bellowing names.

My sleeve unrolled as I threw my straw-weaved backpack purse and thirst quencher onto the large metal cart used for paperwork, storage, and water bottles. I rolled my sleeve back up into my bra strap, sweat moistening my fingers and swirling around to my triceps.

I took out my earplugs and zoned out while boxes brutally landed on the conveyer belt. I daydreamed about lying around on the couch in my polka-dot tank and shorts pajamas and watching *The Price Is Right*. I was wearing glasses and dozed off during an Indiana Beach or Watson's commercial and missed the showcase showdown. With glasses marks on my face, I was left to forever wonder who won—the college student in a university T-shirt or the Navy SEAL in his stellar uniform.

My eyes slumped down the postal container in front of me. It held miscellaneous packages and boxes of various sizes. A package with teal wrapping paper stood out against the brown cardboard of the other boxes. I heard the sound of packages rampageously launching onto the conveyer belt. It was a joke on senders who label parcels "Fragile" and "Handle With Care." I heard containers unlock all around me. The clanging and crashing made my arms weak and reluctant to do work. Boozing and dancing at Retro Rewind at the Vogue the night before did not help.

The man next to me hurled the boxes from his container. His exertion emphasized my laziness. I recognized him from Japanese-beetle catching. He was a ramp worker who usually sat on his butt and got paid while waiting to load or unload a plane. The ramp workers would come inside to help when the area was overwhelmed with packages.

The hair around his forehead looked damp with sweat. It was short yet sufficient, pitch-black and wavy. I imagined it with dollops of gel. A Jheri-curl transformation popped into my mind.

I observed, through the corner of my eye, his constant glances. Some of his staring was unconcealed but some sneaky. He pretended to watch an airplane taxi out through the open gate when he was actually looking me up and down. I knew he wanted to talk. The conveyer belts came to a screeching halt, overflowed with mail, and created a momentary lack of work.

He hesitated. "Where are you from?" The loud buzzer sounded, indicating the start-up of the conveyer belts. His voice perished as he heaved a wide package onto the conveyer belt. He dusted off his gloved hands and placed them on his hips. The Aviation Plus T-shirt was tucked sprucely into his blue shorts. He was wearing unsoiled steel-toe Caterpillar boots, black with yellow accents and gray and pepper-colored fused laces. His white socks were visible only from a side view. Big, movie-star sunglasses were on his head, pushing about an inch of hair forward. The ear frames were hidden, weaving through his waves. He was a man who prided himself in his blue-collar work appearance.

"You mean what's my ethnic background?" I hated when people asked me where I'm from. It made me feel like a foreigner. I chucked the first package onto the conveyer belt. I regretted the question as the words came out of my mouth. I didn't know why I even asked. I should've known better.

He presented a facial cast of confusion and seemed to find comfort in lifting another oversize box while avoiding my question. "Uh, yeah, that's what I meant."

"I'm Indian." I consumed myself in work, flinging packages one after another. "My parents were born and raised in India."

"I can tell you're Indian." He put the package he was holding back into the container. He moved toward me until we were both standing in front of my postal container. He creepily stared into my eyes. A thin stream of sweat was smeared above his lip. "You have an Indian accent."

I let out one huffed laugh, displeased by his unpersuasive sense of humor.

He was not laughing. "You *do* have an Indian accent." He looked at me as if I were a naive little girl who needed to learn about the birds and the bees or the hazards of sticking utensils in the toaster.

"No ... no, I don't."

"You *do*." He secured his sunglasses as they plunged forward. "You probably don't even notice that you have one. You picked it up from being around your parents. You picked up their Indian accent. I'm sure you sound just like them."

My mouth plummeted while my eyebrows narrowed. I sidestepped him, walking away with no destination and glancing back four times. My steel-toe boots squeaked rhythmically against the abrasive, dirty grounds of Aviation Plus.

*

As soon as my mother addressed us in Malayalam, I sat back in the periwinkle recliner, crossed my legs, and smashed the phone to my ear with the palm of my hand.

"Hi, Mom." I was fidgety, uncrossing and crossing my legs and filing the upper part of my chin with the border of my index finger.

"Hi, Mala!" Her accent sounded richer, an influence of her lengthy trip in India. She was taking care of her dying mother, being with her in Kerala during her final days.

My father would join her in Cochin in less than a week to keep her company, drink Johnny Walker and play 56 with his brothers with an American deck of cards, eat sambar and mango pickle off plantain leaves, toss rupees to beggars on the streets of Ernakulam, and take trips departing from the Alwaye train station. They would fly back to the states together in one month, and when they returned, I would not be at home to greet them.

My mother did not give the delay enough time to process my voice and shouted even louder to me again.

"Hi, Mom!" I said, matching the amplitude I'd heard in her voice.

"Mala's moving to Texas," my father said abruptly. He coughed roughly, freeing his throat yet failing to utter another word.

I cringed at the outburst. I clawed the phone away from my face and gave it a beastly look before holding it back to my ear. I waited on the delay, and as the silence refused to end, I realized that my mother was not talking.

"Oh," she finally said, shattering silence into questions. "So you got a job?"

"No, Mom. I didn't get a job."

"Oh. Some people just aren't smart and have to study subjects in college such as English because they can't be doctors or engineers. You're not a doctor or engineer like your sisters."

I rolled my eyes. "I just want to move."

"Will you be there when I get back?"

"No."

CHAPTER 2

I arrived in Houston on a Wednesday evening. I passed the drive by talking on my cell phone to Audrey and Jackie and my sisters Sara and Jency and listening to my music. Sara's husband, Fred, had installed a CD player in the Vigor as well as a cup holder in the console.

I took one last look at the house I grew up in and started out of the driveway with Poison's *Nothin' but a Good Time* turned up. The drive was a tour through several states, my stage set for self-meditation and reflection and, when I came closer to Texas, a first-time look at refineries and plants on I-10. I wasn't sure what they were but clicked the camera anyway to add to the Texas-move memories taken from the viewpoint of my steering wheel. I took exit 880 to stop at the Texas Travel Info Center at the Louisiana/Texas border. I didn't go inside but snapped a photo of myself in front of the Texas star. I was in Texas and no longer considered a minority.

The Vigor made it to the Lone Star State alive with over 100,000 miles on it. My father handed it down to me when I started my sophomore year of college. It was in good condition after more than a decade, with a synthesis of uninterrupted paint, chipped sections, and a new timing belt, muffler, and brakes. The alarm would go off when I unlocked it, and the antenna clattered up and down. It gave the car charisma. I loved the Vigor, becoming even more attached as it brought me to Texas.

I exited I-45 at NASA Road 1 to get to Chad's house. Several cars cut me off with no turn signal. Houston was hot and humid, but I didn't mind as long as it was not cold. I was only concerned about my neck-revealing curls frizzing in the humidity.

I listened intently to Spanish music blaring from vehicles, admiring the drivers' cultural frankness. I appreciated the emerald-green palm trees with solitary trunks of crosshatch patterns and a man in the Nissan Texas Titan next to me at the horizontal stoplight wearing a wide-rimmed cowboy hat. I didn't know Texas-edition vehicles existed. The words "Lone Star Ambulance" on an emergency vehicle made me laugh, along with the Texas-shaped auto emblems on some cars. There were also license plates from other states on the road. The sights were unseen in my hometown—fresh, different, and necessary. I was instantly seduced.

I pulled into the stretched, T-shaped driveway of Chad's house and noticed one curtain launched to the side and my future landlord peeping through the window. The house looked as it did in the several photos he e-mailed me along with the lease. It was suburban, undisciplined yet complete, with a blend of red and cinnamon-colored bricks naturally discolored in certain areas. Six elongated windows looked out from the front of the house. A shorter, front window was considerably masked by fan-shaped, yellow-hinted palm leaves. The lawn was well kept. The grass, a green as lush as the feathers of a peacock, sketched the driveway and sidewalk. The tops of flourishing, vivid shrubs were severed on point, unable to grow past the windows. A weeping willow, motionless in the core of the yard, did not harmonize with the other pieces of greenery.

Chad approached as I opened the car door. He was clean-cut, soaring in height, wearing a carbon-colored polo shirt tucked into khaki professional pants. His hair was grungy blond, designed to hug his skull. He had wide-open, narrow green eyes of cordiality but not much of a smile to match.

I had not seen a photo of him. Eric offered to e-mail one, but I wanted to be surprised.

He stuck his right hand out. "Hi. I'm Chad."

We had been exchanging e-mails for the past two weeks. I had become apprehensive about the roommate situation at one point and asked if he lets just *anyone* reside in his home. "How do you know they are not crazy?" I had typed. He replied that I was the only roommate he had never met prior to move-in and he normally requires steady employment. "You bypassed those requirements because of a recommendation from Eric."

I followed him through the hinged-open side gate adjacent to the unattached three-car garage. The roof was black, contrasting with the white Corvette that was inside.

Chad made small talk as I adjusted my long, white tank that slinked below a black short-sleeve, hooded sweatshirt with drawstrings of polka-dot ribbon. He asked about the drive and explained that he had been home from work for a while.

The interiors of the gate revealed a spacious back patio. In each corner was a palm tree. I laughed to myself at the sight. I was positive that the palm trees were appealing, a major selling point, and desirous to Chad because of his Midwestern upbringing.

A pristine in-ground swimming pool was enclosed by an ashen fence on the sides, connected by a refined brick wall that matched the color of the house. A hot tub for four, water tranquil, not bubbling, was separated from the pool by a concrete divider of dark blue tiles. Each tile had an off-white square with a dark blue doughnut shape in the center and parsley-green miniature circles in the corners. The same pattern lined the interior of the pool. Flattened, smoothed bricks encircled the hot tub and pool in a single formation against a pebblestone-finished top. A green and white striped lounge chair and plastic pool chairs in beige, white, purple and red were scattered throughout the area, turned in every which way, with beach towels draped over the arms of a few.

I had the feeling my new place was a party house, a hotel for NASA employees, and a host of NASA gatherings.

Chad turned the golden doorknob and pushed forcefully against the back door. He stood to the side, waiting for me to enter.

"Thanks." I took note of the washer and dryer and half-bath as we predictably entered the kitchen.

"Are you thirsty?" Chad watched me take a sip of an almost-empty Mountain Dew bottle from the drive. He opened a cabinet.

My cell phone rang before I could respond. It was Arpita, an Indian girl who worked at Midwest Bank. We were the only two Indian people in a building of 400 employees except for an older Indian woman who began her employment on my last day. Arpita was slender, with bumps for breasts and long, straight black hair cut to one length. We looked nothing alike and rarely went on lunch together, but our co-workers constantly asked if we were sisters or mistook me for Arpita or vice versa.

Arpita was the only person I could stand at Midwest Bank. We bonded, in a blunt encounter in the break room, over similar job circumstances and our shuddering hate for Midwest Bank.

I didn't answer, letting it ring out to voice mail. I wanted to move on to my new city with the past behind me. The phone call gave me a refreshing surge of satisfaction. I was finally free of my dead-end job.

"Not going to answer that? Not anyone important?"

I found it almost intrusive that he asked about my call. "I'll call them later." I turned on the kitchen faucet to fill the glass Chad set out. I poured out the water when I noticed a ring of grime lingering within the brim and lip imprints on one side.

"Is it dirty?" He immediately returned to the cabinet and flipped a glass right side up on the counter. A solid sound emerged on contact.

"Uh. It's fine." I filled one-third of the glass and took a sip, relieved there was no foul taste.

"Well, this is the kitchen, and we usually do our own thing." Chad opened his arms while breezily walking from one end to the other, the kitchen table to the pantry, as if he were selling it to me. "Just make sure you keep it clean if you use it." He opened the refrigerator, leaned in, took no food, and shut the door before I could snatch a peek of my roommates' eating habits. He lodged his left hand in his pants pocket and twisted the other one around as if it were cramped. He stopped when it made a single, light cracking sound. "I eat out about 90 percent of the time."

I blindly followed him out of the kitchen.

"I'll show you your room."

Bottles of Bacardi, Smirnoff, Captain Morgan, Seagram's, generic brandy, boxed wine, tomato juice, shot glasses, cut limes, club soda, Houston Rockets coozies, stacks of red and blue 12-ounce plastic cups, and a yellow mini football helmet, signatures covering it like graffiti, packed the bar on the outskirts of the kitchen.

Heaps of men's dress shoes and sneakers with tied and untied laces, ragged and scuffed uppers, and exhausted and limp outsoles were turned in every direction at the intersection of the kitchen floor and the carpet of the family room.

A fancy big-screen HDTV was angled in the corner next to the fireplace.

"The remotes are also on top of this DVD stand." Chad tapped the remotes in a single motion. "Just make sure you always keep the remotes here when you're done using them."

Half of a black sectional couch with disgruntled cushions, a tan leather love seat, and a maroon recliner with engorged, soft fabric faced the big screen. It was a representation of the contrastive styles of my roommates. It was a guys' house.

My bedroom was the third room down the upstairs hall. It was my first out-of-state room. My first Texas bedroom. Furniture was absent. There were fresh vacuum lines. Indentations from bed rails hollowed out the carpet. The air vents were near the ceiling, unlike in the house I grew up in, where they were in the floors. The ceiling fan whipped around at a warlike speed. Our voices smashed against the white walls.

The shipped package, a Cub Foods box I found in the garage, was next to the door. It was the only space-consumer in the room. I had packed it with a set of pastel-blue bath and hand towels and washcloths from my linen closet. The box also contained a plain white sheet set I had purchased at Value City. I realized my level of paranoia in packing the box at the sight of the excessive layers and crossroads of tape. I looked at the diagonal position of my past address and freshly current address. I no longer lived in Indianapolis, Indiana.

"I have a friend at work. At NASA," Chad emphasized. "He's moving and doesn't want his futon, so he's bringing it over here. We'll put it in your room."

"Thanks." I smiled at Chad, impressed by the hospitality. I had planned on crashing on the couch until I purchased a mattress. I opened the door to the walk-in closet. There wasn't much room for walking but plenty of space for a Vigor load of stuff. I had only two suitcases of clothes and shoes, one suitcase of purses, accessories, photos, goodbye and good luck cards, a small garbage bag of hangers, a laptop, and a carry-on suitcase of shampoos, conditioners, bottles of hair spray, lotions, hair remover for my upper lip, soaps, deodorant sticks, pads, tampons, and toothpaste twin packs.

I also had leftover cheese-flavored crackers, grab-bag chips, salty pretzels, thawed Mountain Dew bottles that I froze the night before the drive, and two empty Starbucks Doubleshot cans. I bought a four-pack of the espresso brew for the drive: two for each day. I trashed the other two cans in my hotel room in Canton, Mississippi.

Chad walked across the room to another door. The bathroom was a bridge to the adjacent bedroom. The lights were on. I assumed it was the carelessness of the roommate in the connecting room. The wasting of electricity bothered me.

I involuntarily breathed in cleaning supplies and noticed the sparkling show of the rectangular counter with double sinks, a floor swept clean of toweled, doused hair, and the spotlessness of the mirror above the sink with a runaway streak across the lower left corner. I knew the bathroom was freshly scoured over, scrubbed, and cleansed for my arrival.

"Sorry, you'll have to share a bathroom with Bob. He's a real slob. Bob the slob." He laughed cleverly as if he had just come up with the rhyming nickname.

It was information I was not interested in learning. I pretended to be enamored with the bathroom, catching glimpses of my roommate's aftershave, uncapped deodorant, tattered bristle toothbrush near the sink closest to *my* bedroom, and a roll of half-size sheets of paper towels with part of a sheet dangling from its perforation. "Slob, I mean Bob does he work with you, too?"

"Yes, everyone that lives here works for NASA. Chad switched off the light. "You should bring your stuff up."

A young man was on the couch. His brown hair was hinted with salmon-colored splashes. I gathered that he was one of my roommates from his cozy, slouchy position, crossed feet on the coffee table, and arm flung over the top of the black sectional couch. He was lanky and tall in a blue and white gingham dress shirt, khaki pants, and white socks revealed by short, cuffed trouser legs. He looked like an all-American boy who drove a Chevy, felt slighted at work, and surfed the Internet all day to rebel. A big bowl of barbecue chips occupied his lap. The TV was loud. Orange crumbs were on the remote. "I'm Matt," he mumbled through a mouthful of food.

In that moment, I realized how much I longed to be alone. I wished I'd stuck to my original plan of booking a hotel room. I convinced myself that I should be open to living with people in my new, big city when I was someone who did not always enjoy the company of other people. I had always been an antisocial person. It was who I was, and I acknowledged my personality after years of trying to blend. My hometown was not a city of diversity. The kids in my white, Catholic grade school were not always the nicest and liked to call me names like Brown Broom and Black Girl.

I had wished I were white during those years. High school was an improvement, but not much, due to an increase in the student body. I was still the only nonwhite student.

Marion Catholic High Preparatory required all freshmen to take Physical Education. My classmates and I ran laps around the track and then walked back to the school to change out of our white Marion Catholic P.E. shirts and green knee-length shorts and into our white or green uniform of collared shirts and khaki pants. The sea of white and green gym-wear was like a Category 1 hurricane accelerating full force at the building. I was sickened by the school spirit and it was only my fourth week of high school. I didn't have a single class with Audrey or Jackie. P.E. was my last class of the day, and I was ready to go home. I had received a disturbing letter during second period from the principal asking for suggestions on how to recruit and attract more minorities to Marion Catholic High Preparatory. At lunch, a table of popular girls had mocked me when I walked by, babbling gibberish loudly as if it were a foreign language. Then they had laughed and pointed and called me Foreign Girl.

"I don't want to go home," said Shannon. She was out of breath, hunched over and coughing. She could barely handle the walk back to the building. Shannon was one of my new high school friends who smoked marijuana, went to raves, wore baggy clothes, talked back to her mother, cursed out her sister for no reason, and got along with her father. She smoked a pack of Marlboro Reds a day and voraciously scarfed down a Sack of 10 from White Castle or Noble Roman's breadsticks when she was high.

The seventh-period study-hall class was outside in front of the building. I was surprised we were offered study hall rather than being subjected to another learning session. Two students were lethargically perched on the front steps. They were a sophomore boy-and-girl duo who hung out with the rich gangbanger wannabes and the popular kids who did drugs. Cliques were the foundation of the school, along with faster-than-the-speed-of-light malicious gossip, tucked-in Marion Catholic emblem shirts, detention for boys with facial hair, pestering for monetary donations, "Jesus loves you" talks, and challenging grading scales.

The girl was flabby in the face, with wavy, buttery toast-colored hair that looked wet and crispy. She always wore a tie-dyed Grateful Dead T-shirt and frayed denim on Jeans Day. I was tempted to ask about her favorite Grateful Dead song to prove she was not a fan and was just following the latest fashion craze.

The boy next to her was Lucas Ward. He had sunken, anemic cheeks with unchanging, bloodshot eyes and slicked-back, disjointed strands of oily hair. Lucas had a reputation for being a celebrated burnout.

My long green shorts rode up in the back as I walked up the steps. My neck was sweaty from my thick, curly hair that had grown out and needed to be cut.

"Indians, ugh," Lucas said loudly while thrusting his upper body forward in disgust.

I gave him a dirty look, finishing it quickly. I imagined his parents as KKK members who got high with their son and shouted "white power" to each other instead of saying "good night" before going to bed.

"Did you *hear* what he said?" Shannon pulled the door open. Stray, jagged hairs from her loose ponytail whisked the sides of her face.

"Yes, I *heard* what he said." I rolled my eyes, annoyed with Shannon.

Shannon's head shook back and forth. "Oh my God!" She was enraged. "What a jerk!" She grabbed the nearest girl by her arm. "Did you hear what Lucas Ward said to Mala?"

The word spread like water through cracked concrete. Shannon bellowed the anti-Indian tale in the girls' locker room over and over as if it had happened to her.

I was spinning within a circle of the white girls. Everyone stared at me in pity. I hated the attention.

Shannon bolted through the locker room. "Did you hear what Lucas Ward said to Mala?"

I started crying. I was angry with Shannon for making a spectacle out of the situation. I was angry about the stares and pity that dissolved into reapplications of deodorant and discussions of after-school plans. They were white girls. They would never experience these racial insults while going about their daily business. They could never identify with me. They would never understand why I wasn't allowed to date or why it was acceptable for my mother to be dependent on my father. They would never understand that placing my parents in a nursing home or calling them by their first names was disrespectful. They would never understand that turning 18 years old did not mean I was in control of my life or would be kicked out of the house.

There was no one at Marion Catholic who looked like me. I was alone. I pulled my clothes out of my locker.

"Hi. I'm Molly." Her P.E. shirt was molded to her chest and stomach with perspiration. She had changed into khaki pants that were so forcefully buttoned that the fabric over the zipper veered to the side. Coach loafers were on her feet. Blond, sloppy-highlighted hair landed at her shoulders, with bangs sliced straight across as if a ruler had been used as a reference point. Her face was like rising dough. Dabs of concealer dried under her eyes, on the right side of her forehead, at the edges of her nostrils, and on the center of her chin. "Muhhhh," she began. "What's your name again?"

"Mala." I didn't make eye contact.

"Just say, 'Well you know what? I was here first, motherfucker!' "

I slammed the locker shut. "I'm not Native American!"

*

I lifted the suitcases from the Vigor and unloaded and dropped them off in my new room while passing Chad and Matt. It bothered me that they didn't offer to help.

"I can get those." Matt stood behind me at the trunk of the car. His gingham dress shirt was untucked, with the top two buttons unleashed. He changed into black flip-flops with woven y-shaped straps. He groaned a little as he lifted the heaviest, largest suitcase from the trunk. He pulled out the handle and wheeled it to the house.

I followed him inside with the laptop.

Matt clenched his teeth. His arms trembled as he carried the suitcase with both hands, practically dragging it two inches above the carpeted stairs.

"It's heavy." I reached for the bottom of the suitcase. "Here, I'll help you."

"Oh no." He pulled it higher away from me. "I got it."

I didn't offer to help with the second-heaviest suitcase. I followed him back to my room with the last of my belongings.

Three guys stood in the kitchen as we stepped back down the stairs. I homed in on them, attempting to figure out which one was Bob the Slob.

"Dude. You must be the new roommate. I'm Jordan." He waved at me even though I was within a few feet of him. He had brownish-black roots in bleached-blond hair drawn back into a ponytail. Bermuda shorts wavered over hairy, death-colored legs.

Carl was standing next to Jordan. He shook my hand while a smile was cemented across his face. He wore light-wash denim, a white polo shirt, and black slip-on Vans with no socks. I wondered what the odds were of having two male roommates with long hair as I noticed Carl's copper-colored ponytail.

I winced when Bob introduced himself. His face was clean-shaven, intensified by an impeccable, sun-kissed complexion and hair that was golden brown like pancakes. He wore gleaming black dress shoes with laces tied in perfect loops, subtly cuffed dress slacks, and a neatly tucked-in collared shirt. All my roommates were white. It felt just like home. I needed to move out of Chad's house.

"We just started heating up this pot of jambalaya from last night," said Carl, his smile becoming even cheesier. "You should eat with us."

I was always up for free food, especially since I was unemployed. "I've never had jambalaya."

They abruptly looked at me and laughed. "You're like the female Chad," said Jordan. "You people from up North. You have no culture."

I laughed. I found it bizarre that he referred to the Midwest as "up North." "So you're all from Houston?"

Jordan stirred the pot and scratched the back of his left knee with his right big toe. "San Antonio." He looked up. "The birds fly down South for the deep dark winter."

The boys weren't fazed by his stoner-like comment.

Carl's smile remained. "I'm from Lafayette." He held a stack of paper plates vertically between his hands, his palm flat against the top plate.

"Lafayette?" I leaned against the table, trying to do something with myself.

"Lafayette, Louisiana."

"Austin," said Matt. "Got my Longhorns season tickets."

I noticed their Southern accents in certain words. "I" sounded more like "ah." There was a shift in vowels. "Who are the Longhorns?"

They all laughed at me. "University of Texas," said Matt. "UT."

"Oh."

Bob sat down at the table, facing my backside. "I'm from Houston. I was born and raised about 10 minutes down the street. My parents live right down the street. I have a lot of my stuff there still. I just picked up my Green Day posters after work to hang in my room."

I shot around. "Oh, I *hate* Green Day. They're not a *real* band."

Chad walked in, pulling down on a white "Don't Mess with Texas" T-shirt he'd changed into, looking comfortable in house shorts and midcalf socks. The shirt looked as if he had just cut the price tag off. He told us he'd eaten Whataburger around 3 o'clock and wasn't hungry.

I had never heard of Whataburger.

"So, Mala, do you know anyone in Houston?" Jordan decreased the heat to low and scooped jambalaya onto a paper plate after one final stir-through.

"Nope. No one." I poured a glass of water from the Brita pitcher on the kitchen counter.

"Oh, you can use that," said Carl, smiling so big that the center of his bottom lip was on the verge of cracking.

"Oh, sorry, I didn't realize the filtered water wasn't for everyone." I waited for my roommates to get their jambalaya before getting a plate.

"Do you have any brothers and sisters?" asked Matt.

"Two sisters."

"How old are they?" Bits of barbecue chips were cornered in Matt's top front teeth.

I was always uncomfortable with this question. "33 and 36." Sara was 33. Jency was 36.

"Wow, they're much older than you."

I was quiet. Sara was 10 years older than me. I rarely mentioned my deceased sister, Krupa, who was between Sara and me.

"What do your parents think of you just packing up and moving down here?" asked Jordan.

I put a piece of rubbery sausage in my mouth. "Oh, you know, they wanted me to stay."

"*So*. What kind of music *do* you like?" asked Bob.

I could tell how offended he was by my Green Day comment. "I like '80s rock."

Bob looked up from his plate. "The *hair* bands?"

"Yup. My older sister Sara was a teenager in the '80s and I worshiped her when I was little. I listened to everything she listened to. I was never into the New Kids on the Block."

Chad laughed. "My little sister had New Kids on the Block bedsheets."

"My sister had this boyfriend that everyone called Dokken because he looked just like Don Dokken." Sara had kept him a secret from our parents because she wasn't allowed to date. She was always "studying at a friend's house." "She named her cat Vai after Steve Vai. I wish '80s rock would make a comeback. The bands today suck. I know there are other people like me, but I just haven't met any other twentysomethings that are into hair bands."

"I don't know any," said Chad. Everyone agreed with him.

*

I unpacked a pair of medium-wash, flare-leg jeans, a white fitted, scoop-neck tee with penny-size armpit stains, an Indiana University Mini 500 trike-race T-shirt, and some other basic pieces. I hung them in my closet while burping up jambalaya and put powder-scented deodorant, a four-blade razor, soap, and 15-ounce bottles of moisturizing shampoo and conditioner to the side to place in the bathroom.

I pushed the air mattress to the corner of the room with my foot. Jordan had inflated it for my first night of sleep in Texas. He was having a couple of friends over who planned on crashing on the couch.

Conversation mixtures, laughter, shouting, and rap music permeated the house as I unpacked. It became louder in a short time. There were more than a couple of friends downstairs.

"Don't you have a new roommate?"

"Where is she?"

"Where's the new roommate?"

The inquiries dissuaded me from going downstairs at first, but I finally joined the party, certain that it would look absurd and preposterous if I did not parade my face and mingle with my roommates' friends. The feeling of obligation bothered me.

It was mostly twentysomethings who were dispersed throughout the family room, kitchen, and living room with red and blue plastic cups. No one was engaged in any reckless and wild drinking games with decks of cards scattered across the table and alcohol dripping to the floor. It was a casual get-together.

I slid my hand down the banister and moved down the stairs in slow-motion footfalls. I noticed, through the window, that the hot tub was at full capacity, with more white, hairy chests than half-naked women. The bulk of the guests stared at me, since the party had been going on for a while and I had just arrived.

Chad was tipsy. "Hey, y'all, this is Mala!"

It was the first time "y'all" had been spoken in my presence. It made *me* laugh but seemed to be part of the regular lexicon to the others in the room, as they were oblivious to the cultural uniqueness of the word. It was especially amusing coming out of the mouth of someone from Michigan.

I heard sporadic introductions and shook the hands of a few guys.

"I'm Anthony. I live next door." He appeared to be about Chad's age, 28. His goatee looked like tumbleweed. He wore a bright orange V-neck Astros jersey with striped sleeves and a dark blue star on the lower left chest. The jersey scrunched up around his midsection. Tapered jeans flattered the tongues of his white high-tops. "So do you have a job?"

"No." I was instantly annoyed. I felt all eyes suddenly shoot to me. I sensed the judgment in their stagnant expressions. I loathed the question. It was *the* question asked of me for one straight year. It was *the* question that I was looking forward to *not* being asked in my new, big city.

"*Well*," Anthony laughed. "What are you going to do?"

I didn't know. And that's what I liked about it. I didn't have a plan. I didn't need one since I had a savings account and a newfound boldness.

"We all work for NASA," said Anthony.

"*Everyone* does?" I spun around to look at the group. "*Everyone* in this room?" I learned that the majority of them were engineers who weren't too pleased with the space program. They complained about co-workers, bosses, and cubicles but appeared to be happy in each other's company.

"You should give me your résumé and I'll give it to NASA HR."

"Oh no." I didn't want his help. "That's okay."

Anthony looked stunned, as did the other guests.

"Why did you move here?" asked a girl at the kitchen table in a towel and Texas-flag bikini top. She wore heavy-duty bifocals too big for her face, with wisps of hair stuck in the corners. She gripped her drinking glass of melted ice cubes in clear liquid, locked her shoulders in midshrug, and leaned forward. A group of girls at the table tore looks into me.

I felt bombarded, ridiculed almost. "I wanted a bigger city with more options and no cold weather." I forced a smiled.

"Why Houston?"

"Chicago was too close and New York and L.A. are too expensive."

"So you just packed up and left your life? You just left your family and friends?"

"Yes."

"You don't know anyone here?"

"No."

"Well, it's good to hang out with someone for once that doesn't work at NASA." She looked around at all the men. "I've done my rounds at NASA, if you know what I mean."

*

I looped a pastel-blue hand towel through the chrome rack on the bathroom door, realizing that no one at the party had asked about my ethnicity. The rumpled, faded care tag flipped upside down. I read the words "100% cotton" as I got ready to brush my teeth and wash my face before my first sleep in Texas.

I slipped my contacts out into a mint-green and white case. The contact-solution bottle cap left an imprint in my left thumb. My travel toothbrush was the most accessible. It was in my roomy road-trip purse with travel-size lotion, toilet-seat covers, and diarrhea caplets. I cleaned each tooth individually, slanting the brush downward against my lower incisors. I flossed thoroughly with generic waxed mint floss and dropped the thread into the trash. An accumulation of wadded-up paper towels was in the trash can. I realized that Bob used paper towels to dry his hands instead of a towel.

I closed my eyes and splashed water on my face, thumbs landing on my cheekbones. A trickle of water proceeded down my right forearm and dripped off my elbow onto the counter. I turned the cleanser bottle upside down to let the residue flow down to the cap. There were only a few squirts left. I had no job lined up and a savings account that would drain quickly if I weren't careful. I couldn't afford to waste a drop. I planned on using bars of soap as face wash after the cleanser ran out.

I had trained my body to stop eating when I was full. I'd always been hungry from exercising daily in the home gym of my parents' basement, but I cut my workouts in half to curb my appetite. My new habits were part of my plan to save calories and money on food.

I dried my face and hands with the pastel-blue towel. I contemplated the destination of my toothbrush. I was reluctant to leave it in the bathroom with Bob the Slob. I was afraid he might spit on the travel bristles, brush his own teeth with it, or rub it on his pubes and put it back in the case. I did not trust anyone I did not know. I seized it and put it back in my purse.

I crashed on the air mattress. It was wrapped in my queen-size fitted sheet, flat sheet, and matching dual-sided comforter, which I'd ripped off my bed in Indy. One side was lilac and the other was mulberry-colored and lilac-striped. Some air had escaped from the mattress, making it wobbly to sleep on. I stared straight up at the ceiling in the abrupt darkness until I became distracted by the light in the bathroom. I heard the toilet flush and the sound of a faucet. Then I heard the ripping of a paper towel from its perforation.

CHAPTER 3

I watched Chad stir in the maroon recliner. His rough tippy toes scarified the carpet as he propped his feet. He wore a white T-shirt with "Purdue Alumni" in gold letters. My T-shirt was white also but read "Indiana" in crimson letters.

"That's an ugly shirt," Chad said jokingly about the rivalry. "You can't wear that in my house."

I laughed. I thought of my sisters, the Purdue Boilermakers in the family. They'd tease me about being an Indiana Hoosier, with the IU jokes always on hand, and refer to my mishaps as a result of my IU education.

"We need to put that futon in your room." Chad sat up while lifting the TV remotes off the arm of the chair to prevent them from falling.

I couldn't figure out how to use all the remotes, and when I tried, there was always a roommate watching TV with me.

He slouched back down into the engorged fabric of the recliner.

The futon leaned against the wall in the living room, its edge landing about two inches from the eggshell, drip-painted front door frame. It had arrived the night before, my third night in Houston. I'd abandoned the wobbly air mattress for the solidity of the floor and used my dual-sided comforter as a faux sleeping bag. I hadn't acknowledged the futon. I verbalized no enthusiasm or eagerness for trading in a deflated mass and a carpeted surface for upgraded sleeping grounds.

I lost sleep at night yearning for my own space and worrying about the doors that were unlocked day and night in the fourth-largest city in the U.S. My roommates did not carry house keys. I couldn't bring myself to sleep on the couch near the unlocked back door, fearful that the serial killer would attack me first when he breezed right in and was entertained by the lack of effort in breaking and entering. I slumbered in my locked bedroom instead, feeling safer with backaches.

"I think I might move out." I didn't know why I said "think" and "might." I was confident in my decision even though I had already signed Chad's one-page lease, pointing out grammatical errors in the process. He had left the white-page document on the kitchen table for me to sign and had mentioned it several times, with the intent of being passive-aggressive.

Chad forced an uncomfortable laugh.

I found him to be an amateur at fake laughing.

His eyes flickered and flashed. He glanced at me, blinking expeditiously. "Moving out?" He pretended to concentrate on his TiVo programs. "Where are you moving?"

"The west side."

I had explored Uptown Houston and the surrounding area when I interviewed at The Wire, the appointment I had scheduled before moving. I used Williams Tower as a directional focal point. I was certain the area was where I wanted to be in the moment, with its upscale restaurants and trendy boutiques, midrises and high-rises, a blending of businesses in savvy glass buildings, luxury hotels, halo street signs of stainless steel, the 610 Loop, the Water Wall, and the 2 million square feet of shopping at the Galleria Mall. The area hammered the tarnished routes of my hometown. It was the drastic change I had envisioned, an illustration of fate, a result of shattered circumstances.

I drove around Houston aimlessly for days, blindly discovering frontage roads and observing insignificant details such as horizontal stoplights. I accidentally got trapped in an HOV lane, a type of single-lane roadway that I had never seen nor heard of. 103.7 was my favorite rock station and I jammed to it every day in the Vigor. The Texas flag fluttered in the wind from poles everywhere I looked. I felt as if I were in a different country. I tried to visualize the Indiana flag each time but could not quite sketch the exact design in my mind.

After going on my first interview in my new city, I treated myself to a turkey sandwich on orange rosemary bread at eatZi's Market & Bakery and splurged on an overpriced wedge of red velvet cake for dessert. Houston was supposed to be the fattest city, but as I looked around at all the ethnically diverse Houstonians, I effortlessly concluded that more fatties resided in my hometown. I found it abnormal that some Houstonians wore jackets and long sleeves in 90-degree weather. I noticed that Houstonians seemed friendlier than the residents of my hometown. They were quick to make eye contact, smile at strangers, and start conversations about nothing.

Indian people were all over Houston—pushing strollers in saris along the sidewalks of Westheimer, in the cars next to me on I-10, at the grocery store, in restaurants. I noticed a lot of blue-collar Indians in Houston—a rare sight in my hometown.

I drove under the stainless-steel arches on Post Oak Boulevard facing the three AON buildings and, while turning right onto San Felipe, received a honk and wave from a dark-complected man in a red '90s Pontiac Firebird convertible. As the sports car completely passed, I saw the yellow-green Indiana license plates.

I went on a second-round interview with the senior news editor from The Wire and was waiting to hear back. I had interviewed with the same company for a position in its Chicago office while living in Indianapolis, making it through two rounds but losing to another candidate. They referred me for an opening in their New York office. I made it through two rounds of phone interviews but failed to be their top choice.

The roommates constantly asked me about the interviews.

"Any news on the job front?"

"Why don't you have a job yet?"

"What do you want to do?"

"Dude, I heard back from NASA the day after my interview and it was a Saturday," said Jordan.

"I had my job lined up at NASA right after college," said Matt.

"*NASA* was the first job that I applied to," Bob said.

"I had about four job offers," said Carl. "But I wanted to get out of Lafayette."

"So do you have *any* news on the job front?" Chad asked. "I've asked you for your résumé every day."

The roommates were baffled by my unemployment, and it had only been a few days.

I told the roommates that my field was different and competitive. It was the only response I was willing to give. I didn't need to explain myself.

They always stared through me as if they were looking down into a well with no net. I could tell what they were thinking—she must not be trying, she's lazy, there's something very wrong with her.

"So you're moving out? You're liking the west side of town, huh?" Chad didn't look at me. "Have you found a place yet?"

I hesitated, fumbling with the pockets on my navy blue cargo pants, the Velcro grating my taut-skinned knuckles. "No. I'm going to stay in a hotel first."

Chad exhaled a laugh. "A *hotel*?" He rubbed the back of his neck, his pinky pointing upward into his grungy blond hair.

The scene reminded me of when I told my father a few weeks earlier that I was packing up and renovating my life down South. Chad had just met me through abbreviated, detached days sprinkled in passing. He would never react the way my family and friends did to my moving notice. He would never know that I shed my curly locks everywhere— disorderly bundles on the carpet, more apparent on tile floors of bathrooms and kitchens. Chad would never know that I like to microwave Rally's leftovers, hate the fleshy texture of cantaloupe, and own a Heart greatest-hits CD with 37 songs. He would not feel the deep, echoing void as my favorite people did when I packed up the Vigor and left. He'd advertise his vacancy instead, recruit a NASA techie as a tenant, and learn his lesson about outsiders.

"I just like the area better."

"A hotel will be expensive."

The hotel room was $1,600 for a three-week stay. It would be available in two days—not soon enough for me. Chad's house was only $350 per month, government-subsidized for the college-educated, and an ideal rent for an unemployed character new in town. The logical and responsible decision was to live at Chad's while finding a job, making friends, and salvaging my life savings.

Jency advised me to stay at Chad's during our chat on the phone earlier in the day. "You don't know anyone and you don't have a job," she said. But I didn't drive all the way down to Houston to settle for something I didn't want.

*

The air mattress was deflated in the corner of the room, an irregular mass and a representation of a worn-out welcome. My black luggage was lined up in a row in front of the window I had looked out of only once—the day I arrived. I viewed the contents of my first Texas bedroom without turning my head.

The zipper compartments on the outside of the large suitcases bulged like an overstuffed wallet. I had hardly unpacked. I opened the suitcases, my arm tracing three-fourths of a rectangle as the zipper moved over, down, and under.

I began sorting my belongings for the next location. I separated daily-wear purses from evening bags. In one of the large suitcases, I added a few pieces of business attire for possible interviews, three weeks' worth of short-sleeve tops and tank tops, four pairs of jeans, blue-green capri pants, my favorite mini jean skirt—frayed and ripped throughout the denim—bras and panties, a fitted white terry-cloth zip-up sweatshirt, my favorite house shorts—light gray, thigh-hugging with two dark gray stripes up the sides—pajama shorts and tanks, gym shorts, and T-shirts.

In the carry-on suitcase, I kept shampoo, conditioner, mousse, gel, a hair dryer, a diffuser, toothpaste, toothbrush, face and body lotion, deodorant, floss, and a makeup bag containing honey-colored foundation, matching powder, cherry-chocolate lip gloss, waterproof mascara, nutmeg-colored blush, and an eyelash curler with fringes of black lashes jammed into the clamp. The two suitcases and the laptop were for my hotel stay. The other suitcases were to stay in the car. I would live gypsy-like, with the Vigor as my storage unit.

Chad peeked in while knocking on the open door. "Packing up for tomorrow?" He looked freshly showered, with damp hair and a cleansed face.

"Yeah." Thoughts of my own space made me smile.

"We're all going to a little get-together if you want to go." He stepped backward out of the room and pressed his hands against the crown molding of the doorway. He leaned back on his right leg as if he were stretching his calf muscle. "Some friends from NASA. They're vegans." He smirked. "We'll probably get Taco Cabana afterwards."

I laughed. I had noticed a lot of Taco Cabana restaurants while exploring. "Is that place good?"

"I eat it a lot. I always get their Super Mexican meal."

"I'll have to try it sometime."

"You're going to be eating a lot of good food. Houston has the best restaurants."

I had noticed the multitude of restaurants. I had never seen so many in one place before. I declined on the party but thanked him for the invite. I had eaten bagged frozen chicken breast for dinner that I had purchased while grocery shopping at Food Town. I had convinced myself that I was satisfied, ignoring my rumbling stomach and howling taste buds. I wouldn't survive a veggie party anyway. I was a meat-eater. I had been labeled a vegetarian before simply because I'm Indian.

It was a Saturday around lunchtime during my junior year of high school. I worked as a grocery bagger at Marsh Supermarkets. I planned on a 12-hour shift, offering to take the hours of a co-worker who went to a nearby public school and was depressed about a breakup with a boy who'd rarely taken her out in daylight. I didn't mind working extra hours. I wanted more money, and it got me out of the house and away from my parents.

I drove down 135 in my father's Vigor at lunchtime. My Marsh apron was in the passenger seat, with the name tag pinned around the strap. My salami cravings were strong. I ached for an intense, chaotic sandwich with tiers of salami and every topping, excluding jalapeños. I should've been capable of handling the peppers as an Indian but couldn't manage the feeling of wanting to tear up or gag when one grazed my tongue.

A bell erratically chimed as I pushed open the door of the sandwich shop. I caught a reflection of the wind blowing through my untucked white, short-sleeve dress shirt.

An employee behind the sandwich counter wore a flesh-tone uniform top. A coordinating visor was suctioned around her head, with straggly, auburn chunks of hair calculated to hang to the base of her chin line.

Three customers were eating in the place. A woman was with her young son, whose hair was the color of a school bus. There was a diaper bag on their table but no baby or high chair or other signs of an infant. An older man was alone at a corner table, his thick, vanilla-colored suspenders observable against a black shirt.

"Let me guess." She put her hand on her hip and slanted her head. "*You* want a veggie sub, don't *you*?"

A teenage boy with atrocious posture hovered over the cash register. His puny frame of insecurities presented a silent fear. He avoided eye contact with me and then punctured me with curiosity, looked away, then back at me again through the corner of his eye.

"*No.*" I furrowed my eyebrows. "I want some meat on *my* sandwich." I assumed the sandwich artisan thought of me as a health-conscious priss who hit the gym at 4 a.m. every morning, counted the calories in bubble gum, and didn't consume carbs. I analyzed the fixings to see if there was brown lettuce, slimy tomato slices, moldy American cheese, or spicy-mustard bottles with crusty tops.

"You *do*?" She walked over to the bread.

"I'll have salami on wheat with American cheese and everything on it," I said. "No jalapeños."

She sliced the wheat bread horizontally on wax paper, reluctantly sliding it in front of the meats. She picked up the salami, hesitated, then layered the meat as it soaked into the tiny craters of the bread. "I thought Indian people don't eat meat. Aren't you Indian?"

"Yeah. Hindus are Indians that don't eat meat."

She piled on the veggies. Heaping stacks of black olives, crisp lettuce, tomatoes, red onions, yellow-green banana peppers, green peppers, and pickles hid the salami. "So it's only a certain *religion* that doesn't eat meat?"

"Yeah. It's a religious thing." I was pleased that she grasped the concept and also recognized me as Indian—not Mexican, Iranian, Bangladeshi, Algerian, Colombian, Pakistani, Moroccan, Italian, or Native American.

"I didn't know that." She brightened. Her voice escalated in the thrilling stir of learning something new. "What are you?"

"Catholic."

"The people who own this restaurant are Indian." She firmly rolled the sub in logo paper, a small tear resulting as she tucked in the right corner and then the left to enclose the sandwich. "The wife is *real* skinny. She can't lift anything. I'm always tellin' her to eat some meat so she can be stronger."

I hoped she would not repeat that statement to her boss or anyone else ever again after the day's culture lesson. I paid the cashier with a 10-dollar bill, suddenly recalling his presence after he'd remained mute throughout the whole discussion.

"They eat a lot of beans, a lot of beans," he said while looking down at the money. "They eat *a lot* of beans."

I stared at him, expecting more vocal contribution.

He handed me the change and a customer-appreciation card with five stamps.

*

Word of the move spread like fire during the remaining days of my stay at Chad's house. The roommates' cell phones rang nonstop.

"There *is* an opening. You heard right."

"The new roommate is moving out."

Three prospects were competing for the open room about six hours after I had told Chad I was leaving. It was *the* place to be but not the place for me. I followed my gut. It became my best decision-maker.

I moved out of Chad's house around 11 a.m. while the roommates were on NASA Road 1. I dropped a $10 Taco Cabana gift card and thank-you note on Chad's dark, galaxy-patterned bedspread. I hoped he was not insulted by my preference for a hotel over his festive home with palm trees by the pool and a circle of friends via NASA.

I subtly left a report on Houston's crime rate on the kitchen counter. I hoped it would persuade them to lock the door at night and during the workday. I left the back door unlocked, but the cognac-colored car-door locks shot down in place as I buckled my seatbelt. The Vigor was packed in the exact way I had packed it before leaving Indianapolis.

The stereo slurped my Whitesnake CD. I pressed forward to track four.

*

A contemporary square rug of irregular olive-green and azure stripes, framed with excessive, ropy gold lines, gripped the floor of the hotel lobby. The front desk was an inviting, systematic box with a shiny black counter, maps, Houston guides, and two smiling faces. A distressed-wood side table with three swirled legs led up to a circular stand brandishing hotel brochures and pens. Silk trails of gold flowers flourished in a shimmery, blackish-gray vase. Above the table was a wheat-colored oval mirror with subtle yellow carvings.

The staff of my new home, an extended-living hotel, chatted with guests who filtered through. Jency suggested living in one while learning the particulars of my new city. A front-desk employee told me she was from Chicago while looking over my Indiana driver's license. "I don't miss the wind and cold," she said as she swept her sleek, dark brown bangs away from almond-shaped eyes. She smiled at me while handing over the keys. "But it *does* get too hot in Houston."

I deposited the key downward into the slot and removed it quickly. To the right was a white, small-scale kitchen with a tan countertop around the sink, a plugged-in black coffee maker, a black, silver-accented toaster, a microwave, and a two-burner stove. I opened the cabinets above the sink and found plates—dinner and dessert—simple bowls, and Teflon pots and pans with deep scratches. The drawer cradled metal dinner forks, butter knives, stacks of spoons, a wok spatula, a soup ladle, and an 11-inch cooking spoon. I envisioned my meals—microwavable single-portion sausage pizzas, Lean Pockets, and frozen mixed vegetables in Pasta Roni for nutritional value.

The carpet, composed of beige nylon yarns, was checkered with bars of dark browns and mauve loops. The bed was centered against the wall. The plastic headboard was brown with tactical blemishes of soft black contours. A magenta comforter tucked under and over the pillows, starchy to the touch, had connected diamond shapes of stitching throughout the surface. Next to the bed was an intimate office area with a pencil-legged desk garnished with a brass mini-lamp and shade, a framed panoramic photo of the downtown Houston skyline, a Texas-flag paperweight, and a hotel-logo legal pad. The dresser held a spider plant in a petite, violet-blue pot of dark, chunky soil and a television with bed view. I disliked the channel changes in different cities but realized the Houston channels might be my permanent channels. A plump red chair with microscopic off-white dots posed window-side with a matching, slightly lighter footrest. A soft-blue ironing board was upright in the corner.

I heard back from The Wire as I settled into my temporary digs. I would not be disseminating news releases over the Web. I was dispirited for a moment but told myself to suck it up and get over it. I was in a new city. Things were going to happen.

I crashed on the bed. My legs dangled over the end and I kicked them up and down. I was relieved to be out of Chad's house, comfortable, and finally in my own space. Then anxiety suddenly surged through me. I realized that I *was* all alone. I knew no one, not a single person in the large city of humidity, refineries, cowboy hats, crawfish, guns, and constant "y'alls." The few people I did know, I disowned after a few days.

I snapped out of it, as I was happy to be in a tank top with no bra and eyewear dating back from high school, with the TV turned up so loud—via one remote—that

I was guaranteed to never miss a syllable. I set the Sleep, placed my pink glasses on the nightstand, and turned out the light. I said my usual prayers for friends, family, Krupa, employment, and my new Houston life and prayed that my family and friends wouldn't die any time soon.

I rolled onto my side. I needed to get some rest. I had an interview in the morning.

CHAPTER 4

"Congratulations. I thought you'd end up getting a job in oil and gas, though."

"I don't even know what that means, Sara." I hung up with my sister.

Lopez Finance & Accounting offered me the job 20 minutes after I had left the interview. I would be creating its brochures, marketing materials, and newsletters and proofreading reports, writing news releases, and using my skills for anything else necessary.

The job offer left me speechless as I pressed the phone against my ear, ring fingernail clawing my chin. I had just parked the Vigor at the hotel and turned it off. They said they were impressed with my go-getter story—packing up and leaving and looking to a bigger city to fuel my ambition. I accepted the offer right away. It had never been that easy.

I had interviewed incessantly for gigs in my field in my hometown and spent my workday at Midwest Bank on the computer selecting "all locations" when searching Monster, JournalismJobs, CareerBuilder, Talent Zoo, and Mediabistro. I had studiously applied for jobs from my desolate cubicle among supervisors, rap music, misspelled mass e-mail communications, and blather of spending minimum-wage paychecks on Louis Vuitton purses. I had refused to settle for a job I despised.

I had driven to interviews in Cincinnati, Louisville, Detroit, and St. Louis and to six interviews in Chicago. Not a single company had reimbursed me for my mileage, and some neglected to validate my parking. I had become desperate and was willing to labor anywhere to get the tiniest crumb of experience. I had gone through several rounds of interviews with the same company, usually making it to the top two but never landing the job.

My parents called as I picked up one of the wrapped mini-rectangular soaps the hotel maid had left in the bathroom while I was out. There were also new white, flimsy towels and matching washcloths. I usually avoided the phone when the number was a mystery, but the digits stretching through the screen and the +91 country code in the caller ID was an indication that it was my parents calling from across the miles.

My father was on the line. I could hear my mother sobbing in the background. Before I could tell him about my employment news, he said my grandmother had passed away. I didn't cry, but a sense of grief rushed through me because I couldn't be there for my mother. I briefly spent time with my grandmother on my few trips to India. We did not have a close relationship, because of distance. I didn't tear up about her death. I felt only a spell of sadness, though I cried often about my deceased sister I could not remember. The mystery of our sibling bond made me forever sad and lonely.

Lopez Finance & Accounting faxed an offer letter to the hotel for proof of employment. I requested this confirmation as evidence to prevent the same kind of mess that happened at Midwest Bank.

It had been a sunny May morning, and crisp, square shopping bags with white, twisty handles roped my brown arms as I headed back to my cubicle to apply for more jobs online and catch up on Zane and Goines novels passed on to me by co-workers. I was on my first lunch break of the day.

I shopped at Circle Centre in downtown Indianapolis during my Midwest Bank workdays, meandering through the Arts Garden and pausing at Cinnabon for a free sample from the server, who knew me by name. I always exited through Parisian after slowly browsing the Juniors department, Shoes, and Jewelry.

I crossed at Meridian and Washington, passing a homeless woman claiming three starving children when none were in sight. I considered a Qdoba queso burrito or a leisurely walk next to the cobbled-brick road of Monument Circle, where people ate lunch on the steps of the monument and shared stories of work troubles, family drama, and Indiana sports. I thought about stopping at South Bend Chocolate Co. Chocolate Cafe for Death by Chocolate ice cream in a chocolate-dipped waffle cone. I decided to saunter back into Midwest Bank instead.

I did not want to go back to work, disturbed by the standard office jargon:

"Oh *hell* nah."

"Ok*aaaa*y."

"I'm tryin' ta have a baby by Jermaine O'Neal."

"Oh no he did*n't.*"

"Ma man, he locked up."

"Ma baby daddy got three other baby mamas."

Shoddy weaves and tacky airbrushed fingernails with fake diamonds and lightning strikes were very different from my boy-cut, velvety curls and medium, naturally rounded nails with soft cream tips.

I smirked as I passed the bald fortysomething janitor with a coarse rat tail at the nape of his neck. He sagged in Dickies held up by a brown belt and wore a navy blue Indiana Pacers sweatband around his head. There was a rumor going around that I had slept with him.

"We don't do that here!" shouted Rakisha, addressing a customer through the phone. Rakisha was an attractive black woman with lovely flower-petal eyes with authentic lashes and a modest application of color on bursting lips at all times. She appeared to be about 29 years of age but was only 22. "You ain't listenin' to me!" She hung up on the caller. "These folk get on ma damn nerves."

I put my purchases in my cubicle. Rakisha's attitude and tone were nothing new to my ears but shocking when I'd first begun as the office coordinator. My co-workers disrespected customers regularly, with no repercussions.

"Whatch you got there, Mala?" Rakisha glided out of a fully decorated cubicle. Tacked on a board were funnies from the newspaper, a faded Eminem-concert ticket stub, Steak 'n Shake coupons, a Sybaris gift certificate, and a memo dated four years prior with "waive" spelled "wave." A photo collage of friends, pets, and family wallpapered the interior of the cube. A set of high school senior photos displaying Rakisha in various graduate poses and wardrobe changes was secured in a long, double-decker graduation-themed picture frame.

My name was spelled "Mula" on the outside of my cube. I had asked a few times for a new nameplate, but no one ever bothered to mount a replacement. I blew it off because I had planned on being there for no more than three months. I was the only employee on staff lacking cubicle décor. I believed that cube celebration was for lifers who committed their existence to losing their sparkle in office squalor. If ever fired, I could simply throw my purse over my right shoulder and walk right out. Boxes would not be necessary for packing up *my* belongings—lip balm and a 3.5-ounce bottle of lotion.

"Girl, that is *real* cute." Rakisha yanked open the handles of one of the shopping bags, pulling out a soft, flushed-yellow, striped scoop-neck tee. Her Midwest Bank photo badge with employee number and name hooked crookedly on the strap of her throwback jersey dress.

I refused to distastefully adorn myself with the badge. Management had threatened, in six separate incidents, to write me up if I continued to disregard policy. I was never in distress over the warnings. I was too bitter to take management seriously. "I like the brown and light blue stripes against the yellow. They had it in pink and green, but I liked this one the best."

"That's real cute," she said. "Um hmm, I like that." She pulled out the jeans. The legs naturally unfolded out of the bag. The bronze embellishments on the back pockets clashed with the seven gold, clunky rings on Rakisha's semi-ashy hands. "Them are cute too." The denim was a light color with strategically placed, fine-spun rips on the front thighs. It was a pale fabric unsuitable during menstrual cycles or on rainy days where mud could be splattered on backs of pant legs.

I discovered the top and jeans on a mannequin together, an inspiration for a complete outfit. I was buying everything in sight—earrings, gaudy bracelets, purses, sunglasses, kitten heels, casual tennis shoes, jeans, capri pants, mini-skirts, socks with creative prints, bras, panties, perfume, scented lotions, mocha coffees from Borders, Starbucks, and the Nordstrom espresso bar, Giorgio's Pizza slices, and other food from the restaurants around the Circle. It was a daily show-and-tell for my co-workers. I was convinced that

I was shopping because I needed things and not because I was depressed.

"I like this belt." The price tag got caught between the twisty twine handles of the shopping bag as Rakisha pulled the belt out. Five sections of silver-lined holes perforated the white leather. Eight miniature holes sandwiched each section. An oversize silver buckle fetched the white color like fluorescent pink marker on recycled loose-leaf paper.

"I never wear belts, though." As I put the clothes back in the bag, my six rigid, sparkly, maroon bangles glimmered in movement. A musical sound emerged.

"Ooh. I like those." Rakisha forcefully touched my bangles, causing them to swivel around my wrist. The bangles were vibrant in color, with leveled strokes of design and squinting spheres that looked cutting.

I had a frenzied shoe box of assorted Indian bangles. Some were broken and some no longer fit, but I kept them anyway, along with jingle-bell anklets from my childhood and empty circular Indian jeweler boxes with felt interiors.

"Where'd ya get 'em?"

"India."

"You *Indian*?" Rakisha leaned to the side and out of her chair. She looked me up and down with crumpled eyebrows. Her jaw dropped as her lips tilted in disgust.

"*Yeah*," I replied in one swift, harsh syllable.

"You don't *look* Indian." She rolled away from me, back into her cubicle, until her chair hit the desk. She sustained her head with her fist. "You ain't be lookin' like those other Indian people I see."

"I'm Indian."

"And you ain't be smellin' like rice and curry." Rakisha whirled in her own world. "And you ain't got one of them dots on your head." She tapped her forehead as if a bindi were suctioned to her skin. "I knew you was mixed. I just didn't know what."

"What?"

"I knew you was mixed. I just didn't know what you were."

"I'm *not* mixed. Both of my parents are Indian."

"Oh, I know," said Rakisha. "I knew that you was mixed. I just didn't know that you was Indian."

I turned away and went into my cube, unable to handle any more of Rakisha's ignorant comments. I locked up my purchases and purse in the middle drawer of my filing cabinet. Theft was a common occurrence around the office. My hand sanitizer had been stolen on my first day.

There was a letter on my desk in a Midwest Bank standard envelope. I immediately knew what it was—a job offer for the upgraded dead-end job that I had applied for. A promotion. I ripped it open with my fingers, the torn sections resembling a skyline of different-sized buildings. The letter said I didn't meet the qualifications. It then referred me to the job bank for many more wonderful opportunities at Midwest Bank.

I was stunned. Mr. Brown, the head of the department, had been discussing the position with me on a daily basis. He said that I would definitely get the job but that management had to follow HR guidelines and was required to interview a certain number of people. I walked over to Mr. Brown's office, confident that it was a misunderstanding. I handed him the letter.

"Well, it looks like you didn't get the job." Mr. Brown wrapped his hands of discolored knuckles around the base of a stainless-steel Ivy Tech coffee mug. He lifted it effortlessly as if it were empty and, before bringing it to his thick, equal-sized upper and lower lips, looked me straight in the eyes.

"Well, what are we supposed to do? You said I got the job."

He leaned forward, his gold-rimmed glasses accentuating his look of playing dumb. "I don't know what you are talking about. I never said that you got the job." Mr. Brown leaned back in his chair.

"Yes, you *did*," I snapped. I couldn't believe what I was hearing. It had been almost four months since my direct supervisor was promoted, and Mr. Brown assured me that in due time the office problems would no longer be my responsibility. I would be taking over a manager cubicle with a leather swivel chair with head and neck support, 20-inch computer screen, and waiting chair for visitors. I wasn't thrilled or motivated by the promotion promise, but it offered a salary increase and required a college degree. It would be worth it while I continued to look for a *real* job.

Mr. Brown leaned forward. "I don't appreciate you disrespecting me."

I was fuming, exhaling a frustrated rage, as I stormed out while he was in midsentence. I threw my purse over my right shoulder and walked out of Midwest Bank. I sat on the steps of Monument Circle and cried myself into another mini-nervous breakdown. I had lost count of my frustrations. I had lost count of how many times I had cried on Monument Circle. I couldn't get out of my dead-end job, not even for an upgraded dead-end job. Some of my lifer co-workers had even moved up to different positions.

I thought finding a job as a fresh college graduate would be a breeze. Reality was brutal. I had moved back into my parents' house after graduation and worked in downtown Indianapolis as an office coordinator at a call center. I was the head of the office-supply catalog, the girl to complain to about phone problems, leaking ceilings, and toilet-paper shortages in the restrooms. My salary was $16,000 per year.

Midwest Bank, near Monument Circle, was a hellhole of daily degradation. It was a dead-end job that I had accepted a few months out of college. It was for the paycheck, a job to perform only until I found careerworthy opportunities—as a copywriter for an ad agency, a magazine editor at a fast-paced weekly, a proofreader who pinpointed typos that no one else could, or maybe a columnist for *The Indianapolis Star.*

I put a timeline on Midwest Bank. I didn't see myself working there for more than three months. It turned into a one-year nightmare, a depressing, hard-to-wake-up-for job. And when friends and family asked how work was, I always replied, "I *hate* my job."

I dragged my feet to Borders on the corner of Meridian and Washington, blowing off greetings from co-workers on the street, sleazy smiles from men in ties and dress shirts with bulky laptop bags, and hollers from men with their names embroidered into their work uniforms.

I read the back covers of the hardback best sellers on the front tables downstairs and sipped on a steaming mocha au lait with whipped cream while relaxing on the upper level in an easy chair with solid oak legs and a deep back cushion. Paperbacks and fashion, women's, news, and music magazines were stacked against the right side of the chair where I could reach down and pull one up. I placed the flipped-through materials on the other side. I cooled off after three hours. When I returned to my cubicle, I stabbed the computer keys with my fingers, maliciously composing a complaint e-mail to HR. I sectioned it in paragraphs to empower each point. HR responded about 45 minutes later, misspelling my last name. There were two fonts, an indication that a template letter had been cut and pasted. The e-mail referred me to the job bank for more wonderful opportunities at Midwest Bank.

*

"I've never heard of a Vigor," yelled the tow-truck driver as he hooked the car to the truck. His black hair was matted down with rainwater. He bent to tie his shoe in the drizzle.

The storm poured the biggest drops I had ever seen, submerging me in the infamous Houston rainfall and floods while the sun was still shining. It had only been sprinkling when I called AAA from my hotel room. It was Jency's idea to become a member for emergency situations. I shielded my head with my hand even though I knew it would not suffice as an umbrella. "They only made them for a few years, '92 to '94." My curls were suctioned to the sides of my face. My light-gray Indiana T-shirt looked dark gray. "It's a rare car. I don't know why it won't start. I've never had this problem."

He opened the driver's-side door of the truck. "Get in." He got behind the wheel as he shut the door.

I considered taking a cab to the Acura dealer. I was apprehensive about getting into a vehicle with a stranger, especially when it was pouring down rain and no one would be able to hear me scream or see me clearly through the window. No one would know if I returned safely. There was no one to account for me.

Jency had given me pepper spray for my drive down to Houston. I kept my hand near it and leaned into the passenger-side door in case I needed to leap out to safety. I looked back at the shamrock-green bordered windows of the hotel as we towed the Vigor behind on a platform trailer.

"I'm in school for engineering," he announced proudly, cracking a smile that emerged into a spirited beam. "Petroleum engineering." He smelled like sweat to a degree, perspiring from attaching the car to the tow truck in the Houston humidity. "I'm an Aggie."

"What's an Aggie?"

He laughed. "Texas A&M."

I had never heard of the college. I had no idea where it was located or the prestige behind its name. I didn't know about petroleum engineering either. I had never heard anyone say the words before. I was used to hearing about electrical, mechanical, or agricultural engineering.

"It's a good engineering school. I love drilling and well operations."

"Oh." I was silent as we drove west on Westheimer. I was able to take a closer look at the throngs of restaurants, retail stores, panhandlers, gas stations, buses, and people on the busy road because I was not driving. I told him that I had a sister who was an engineer and graduated from Purdue. I lightened up a bit, naturally plunging into the conversation. It was the most in-person conversation I'd had in a while. I had been eating at restaurants by myself, secure in sitting at my own table instead of the bar, going to the movies alone, and even going to lounges alone to have a drink.

"Oh, Purdue is a *great* engineering school!"

"My other sister went there, too, but she's a pediatrician."

The tow-truck driver was from Bahrain but moved to Houston when he was 16 years old. His three older brothers were engineers who graduated from Texas A&M. His father owned an import/export business, and his mother threaded eyebrows at a salon on Hillcroft. He told me my Indian features were obvious to the eye.

"Do you take credit cards?" I realized that I only had my Discover Card.

"No, just cash."

I made a run for the bank in the downpour, failing to completely shut the truck door, splashing through two large, rounded-diamond-shaped puddles in front of the entrance. The tow truck was not fit for an ATM drive-through. There were no customers inside but one bank teller behind the counter.

"Indiana?"

I glimpsed down at my soaked T-shirt, which sent more water trickling down my face from my hair.

"What's with the shirt?" The teller was stocky, solidly built, with light brown hair in a crew cut and unnoticeable brown eyes. The back of his starchy blue collar was flipped up sloppily, revealing his necktie.

I told him I had graduated from Indiana University and was born and raised in Indianapolis.

"No kidding," he said dryly. "I lived there for a couple of years. I played football for Butler."

"That is so crazy!" I was thrilled by the Indy connection.

He didn't share the same enthusiasm. "You have a northern accent. So how do you like it down here?"

"Oh, I love it down here! The people are so nice."

He smirked in disagreement as he looked at the computer screen. "My aunt and uncle are from Indy. People up there think we are so country." He kept his eyes on the computer screen. "Yup, an Indianapolis account." He handed me cash and a receipt. "Enjoy Houston." He rolled his eyes.

*

I sat on my hotel-room bed in my damp clothes and looked at the battery receipt from the Acura dealership. I survived my first dramatic situation of my new, big-city life for the price of $190.67. I was positive I'd been overcharged but not surprised.

The porter had told me I had good taste in music as he handed me the keys and checked his hair in my side mirror. "Kix has some good songs."

The service guy hypothesized that the battery was dead because I had never used my AC before. "You're from up North and it's cold year-round," he said. "Your car couldn't handle the Houston heat."

I looked at him as if he were a moron while briefly spelling out the four different seasons of my hometown.

Then there was the "up North" reference again. I realized that I would be labeled as a Northerner in my new life. Northerners and southerners were two distinct identities in the South.

I pulled out undergarments from my suitcase. I didn't unpack them into the drawers of the dresser. I took off my shirt, dropped it on the floor inside out, groped my bra-clad breasts in one abrupt jiggle, and noticed, out of the corner of my eye, a black darting movement through the partially open window. I gasped and let out a lone scream as I cringed at the cockroach charging up the wall to the ceiling.

The last time I encountered a cockroach of that stature was in Alwaye in my grandparents' home. There was never just one roach but a mass of murkiness marching through the living room while I watched Malayalam serials with my cousins, aunties, and uncles. Even worse was when the roaches would congregate near the squat toilet outside. I refused to pee unless one of my relatives killed the pests. "Cockroach" was one of the few words I could speak in Malayalam and be understood. I screamed "*paatta*" one night as I knocked a cockroach off my chest while sleeping in my grandparents' house.

The cockroach in my hotel room was unreachable. I didn't have relatives or friends to annihilate it, and I didn't have anything to kill it with. I cringed again as I imagined the roach frenziedly crawling all over me in the sheets or terrorizing me while lathering, shaving my legs, or conditioning my hair in the shower. I frantically zipped up the suitcases, roughing my hands up in the process. I did not want to transport large insects through my deviating course in Houston.

I pulled my shirt over my head, wearing it inside out, and picked up the phone. The clerk at the front desk laughed at my request but assured me that someone would be up soon to kill the cockroach.

The room attendant was dressed in an all-white uniform and laughed when he saw my horrified expression. "It's just a roach."

"Kill it!" I yelled. "Please, just kill it!" I huddled in the corner of the mini-kitchen as he beat the roach with a stiff broom. He laughed, scooping the carcass into a trash bag and taking it with him. The door leisurely closed behind him. I never opened the window again.

*

Lopez Finance & Accounting was located near the Telemundo building. It was a building that would likely never exist in my hometown. Amy Jenkins, my direct supervisor, embraced my presence at the door, happening to race by as my hand was turning the knob. "Mala! Good morning." Her eyelids were like powder-pink hoods. Amy's hair was an unoriginal brown, slicked back into a chic ponytail spilling from the back center of her head. She wore a coal-black polyester pencil skirt emphasizing her lean physique, with an indigo-striped liquid-like blouse and dwindling, snappy heels. She smiled brightly, exposing crystal-white, organized teeth, which drew a smile from my own face.

We shook hands with an unprofessional, unfirm jerk.

I couldn't remember the last time I had smiled in the workplace, was eager to show up at my job, and didn't arrive late with plans for leaving early.

"I'll show you to your office," Amy said, walking. "We interviewed 27 people. You were the only one who stood out. I told Miss Lopez that we needed to hire this girl right away before someone else does."

The expression of compliments boosted my ego. I was finally the No. 1 selection. I never had an office before and was pleased to have a personal distance from my colleagues, shut the door when desired, and chat on the phone to Jackie and Audrey without censoring my language. It was unlike the tragic cubicle I was trapped in at Midwest Bank, overhearing details of child-support court dates and the tales of having babies to write them off on taxes.

The door to my office was completely open, presenting a desk with a dark walnut finish and octagonal patterns smoothed into the front enclosed base. A smaller replica sat behind the desk, against the wall under the tall windows, holding a pen-doodled desk calendar, a junior box of antibacterial tissues, envelopes—10"x13", 9"x12", and No. 10—and unopened narrow packages of 2" x 4" labels. The executive-style carpet was green. The painting on the wall was a forest-green passage of fluidity centered between paths of uneven concrete over mirrorlike water. Tall trees lined the walkway, with only the trunks visible. There were smeared homes with blue and rust-colored roofs in the background on yellow-green, overgrown grass. The painting was set in a baroque 48" x 36" frame.

I imagined myself whirling between the two desks, multitasking and working hard at my new job in my new city. A flat-screen computer was angled on the corner of the larger desk. An inflexible black, six-slot file sorter was in the opposite corner, and a pop-up dispenser filled with hot-pink sticky notes was positioned crookedly next to it. Pens, pencils, and highlighters were packed like sardines in a pencil cup. I set my purse on the extended-width tabletop that was large enough for me to make imaginary snow angels or take a nap on at lunchtime with the door shut.

Two chairs, for visitors or co-workers, leaned into each other in front of the large desk. Its stain matched the other furniture. Gold beaded balls lined the armrests. An enormous gold pot with a soaring plant of dripping green leaves towered near the window. I thought it was potted silk until I pinched a leaf.

I looked out the window. Pinnacles of striking red wove within the light blue clouds sliced by downtown buildings. A small plane flew by with an ad for the Houston Shoe Hospital flapping behind it.

"We'll get some paperwork taken care of and some training stuff." Amy placed a stuffed manila top-tab folder in front of me. "Let me know when you're done filling all that out." She pointed at some empty open boxes in the corner. "Oh, those are trash. Just write 'basura' on them when you get a chance."

"Write what?"

" 'Basura.' "

I looked at her blankly.

" 'Basura.' It means 'trash' in Spanish."

I took the folder to Amy's office about 20 minutes later. Her desk was neatly piled with red, orange, and yellow top-tab folders and papers fastened with small and medium-sized black binder clips. Business cards were upright in a plaquelike holder with her name and title inscribed on it, and on the corner of the desk was a burgundy letter tray next to a gold-plated work lamp with an adjustable arm.

Photos in a coordinating frame set were strategically placed on a bookshelf, along with thickly bound white binders with papers peeking out, a porcelain scorpion, and a vintage ceramic ballerina in a violet tutu. Amy's face was down in work. "Oh, wonderful." She politely accepted the completed paperwork and energetically ejected herself out of the chair and her office.

I instinctively followed.

"Let me introduce you to the staff."

I heard my co-workers as we entered the bullpen.

"Yes, I'm calling from Lopez Finance & Accounting."

"Thank you and have a great day."

"Thanks for returning my call."

Amy turned halfway to me as she spoke. "Miss Lopez doesn't usually get in till about noon."

I'd briefly met Miss Lopez at the interview. I overheard her claiming to be very busy when Amy insisted that she meet me. Miss Lopez *did* sacrifice three minutes of her time, looking courteously at me over two lipstick-tormented grande cups of Starbucks and a relentless stream of signatures on a heap of documents stapled in the center instead of in the corners. The sun gleamed optimistically through the considerable office windows as she spoke. "You seem very qualified for the job and a good fit for my company."

CHAPTER 5

The newsletter, a four-page monthly highlight of Lopez Finance & Accounting, looked fantastic. Included on the second page was a message from Miss Lopez ghostwritten by me. The portrait-style photo next to it was not a current image of Miss Lopez. Her hair was blond. She was not smiling. A triple-strand pearl necklace was intertwined around her neck.

The topics included small-business tax tips, private mortgage insurance information, a list of charities that were sponsored by the firm, and the importance of reviewing life insurance coverage. I designed the newsletter with contrasting fonts, a mixture of greens and absolutely no reds, and precise lines and boundaries in a range of widths. I adjusted well to my new work environment on my second day. I had a new job in a big city. It was exactly what I had wanted.

I came to a stop in the middle of a sentence on a marketing letter, hungry for lunch. I threw my purse over my right shoulder. Taking multiple lunch breaks at my new job was not possible, and I had no desire to partake in the slacking that had ushered me through the day at Midwest Bank, anyway. I was too motivated for the opportunity that I had been relentlessly pursuing for the past year.

Theresa was already up front waiting on me, talking to the receptionist about the hazards of paying less than $100 for a haircut. She was an accountant who had been with the company for about a year. She bitched about having a job, not the tasks of the job but actually having to hold a job, left work early every Tuesday to get a massage, and left work early every Wednesday to get a facial. She had a reputation around the office for being a snob. My other co-workers seemed more down to earth. It was the most diverse staff I had worked with: whites, blacks, Hispanics, and Asians.

Theresa didn't really acknowledge me until she found out that I went to IU. She'd attended Indiana State on a golf scholarship.

I put my hand on the knob as a young man popped up on the other side of the door. I smiled, tight-lipped, at him through the glass.

He opened the door fully as my hand was still on the doorknob. I jolted forward.

"Oh, I'm, uh, I'm sorry." He placed his right hand on his chest as if he didn't know what to do with it. "I'm Cyril. Cyril T. James." He was dumpy, and his hair was dark brown, nearly black. He had see-through, pale-brown eyes.

Theresa was already down the hall, speaking animatedly on the phone with a diva-demanding look on her face.

"Mala."

He looked me up and down, holding a prolonged stare at my breasts before shifting back to my eyes. "I work a few suites down. For EnergyForce. I'm a senior account executive. I'm friends with some guys that work here." The white, French-cuff collar of his herringbone-weave, sunset-colored dress shirt looked uncomfortably tight even though it was unbuttoned. "I heard there was a new person."

"Yup, I'm the new girl." I didn't hear the office door click shut as I caught up with Theresa. It was an indication that Cyril watched me walk away.

*

"Well, I quit the golf team because I didn't like it, but I stayed because I really liked the school." Theresa took a bite of her veggie burger.

I imagined Theresa's parents regarding the out-of-state tuition like a penny they were throwing into a fountain.

"After graduation, I told my parents that I didn't want to work. I mean, who actually wants a job, right?"

I swept three fries in ketchup while narrowing my eyebrows.

"I went to L.A. after graduation and lived like a bum." Theresa took a sip of wine. "My parents paid for it." She spoke as if the phrase were a regular part of her vocabulary. "I didn't want to deal with the real world yet. I'm living with my boyfriend now." She pressed her fork into her couscous. "Do you have SocialYou?"

"No. There are too many weirdos on that site."

"Well, it's a good place to learn about the parties in Houston," Theresa said in soft defense.

"I have an account on an Indian dating Web site to meet Indian guys. I haven't started filling it out yet."

"Well, SocialYou is a good place to meet people, too, and keep in touch with friends or find friends that you've lost touch with."

"I don't want anyone to find me." I laughed. "My social circle *did* quickly diminish over the past year."

"I know what you mean." Theresa fiddled with the cuff of her long-sleeve shirt. "I've been out of school for three years and I only talk to a few of my college friends regularly. I spend most of my time with my boyfriend."

I reached for my black and white snake-print cloth wallet after the waiter brought the check.

"Oh, I'll get it. I'm rich." Theresa flipped her hair off her shoulder. "I hope you liked the food. Houston's is one of my favorite restaurants."

*

Cyril was still in the office after lunch. He knocked on my door as I checked my e-mail. "Here you go." He handed me a zipper sandwich bag with a ball-like, breaded substance inside. "I just wanted to bring you something. A congratulations on your new job." Cyril smiled, lips looking pink and stained against white teeth.

"Thanks," I said wearily. It was a little unusual, since we had just met about an hour ago, but cute in a way. I held the clear bag directly in front of my face, the grease from the food pressing against it like a kid's face to a window. "What is it?"

He looked concerned and baffled by my question. "Well, it's a boudin ball." He stuck his hands in his pockets as if he would be in my office for a while.

"A what?"

"A boudin ball."

"I don't know what that is."

Cyril was silent.

"I'm not from here. Is this some Southern thing?"

"Some *Southern* thing?" He laughed. "Yeah, I *guess* it is. I never really thought of it that way. Where are you from?"

"Indianapolis, Indiana."

His eyes surged with curiosity. "What are you doing all the way down *here*?"

I swiveled back and forth in my chair, indicating that there was a story to tell. "I just packed up and drove down."

Cyril's eyebrows soared as his chin fell. "Okay, fan*tast*ic!" He turned around as if he was going to walk out and then faced me again. "*What*? You just decided you wanted to leave and left right away?"

"Not right away but about two weeks later."

"Okay, fan*tast*ic!"

I laughed hard. I had a feeling that "Okay, fantastic" was Cyril's signature saying.

"So you didn't even have a *job* lined up?"

"No. I just wanted a bigger city with more options."

"Okay, fan*tast*ic!"

We both laughed, amusement fading at the same time. I watched him stare at me. I could tell he was into me. I planned on only being into Indian guys.

"Are you Indian?" Cyril picked up the bagged boudin ball from the corner of my desk and protectively lowered it back down.

"Yes." I was impressed that he knew.

"And what about you?"

Cyril's smile took its own sweet time. "What do you think I am?"

"I don't really like to guess." I thought he could've been Hispanic. There was such a large population in Houston. I had been mistaken for Hispanic many times.

One time, it was a wintry, Bloomington, Indiana, weekend night in October that breathed the usual agenda. College parties were defined by inebriation and, quite often, the depreciation of dignity.

As it was a cold, party night, skin needed to be protected by fitted turtlenecks with plush collars, sweaters, fleece pants, corduroys, knitted scarves, thermal underwear beneath jeans, or puffy coats with fur-lined hoods and angled pockets with room for wool gloves.

College party girls didn't worry about their chattering teeth, protruding nipples through tube tops, or freezing legs from mini-skirt exposure. They exaggeratedly stepped around in 12-degree weather without thinking twice just as long as their appearance conveyed a balance between sluttish and pleasingly pretty.

My thin, curvaceous legs steered tight, black party pants cautiously to my waist. Every girl I knew owned a pair. They were the take-me-home pants, the booty pants, the sorority-girl-at-a-frat-party pants. I'd told myself I would never buy a pair. I made fun of girls who wore them.

The pants flared at the bottom and accentuated parts that were not accentuated while I stared at the controversial Benton mural during lecture at Woodburn Hall 100 or killed time on Showalter Fountain—the mist a refresher on a hot August day before class. I always felt sexy in my party pants. A thong with adequate fabric was in place to prevent evil lines caused by packaged underwear or panties from the clearance rack at L.S. Ayres.

I looked at myself in the full-length mirror that was attached to the back of the door with peeling adhesive. The electric-blue framing was chipped in areas as a result of the mirror's bungee-jumping off the door too many times. I stood in my bra and party pants. My stomach bulged slightly, and I sucked it in to approximate the abdomen I desired. I shifted to the side, remembering that I was satisfied with my breast size. I had a belly that fluctuated in dimension but preferred it to boylike A-cups.

Up all Night played thunderously in my room while I dressed, carelessly stinging my ears at times. I had never met a single person my age who knew of Slaughter except for a drunk white guy in an AC/DC T-shirt who asked if I worshiped cows. He sang *Fly to the Angels* with me over six cups of beer at an early-morning Little 500 pre-party before sticking his tongue down my throat. It was my first kiss.

A taut, cream-colored sleeveless V-neck shirt brushed my eyelashes on the way down. Small slits crept up each side, revealing an insignificant yet sizable amount of fair brown skin.

I positioned a Y-shaped piece of jewelry around my neck, fingers merging under my hair to secure the clasp. The necklace consisted of gray links with tiny, transparent rose and blue-gray beads. It dangled down the V-neckline of my shirt and landed fearlessly at the peak of my cleavage. I could feel the coldness of the beads between my breasts when I shifted in a certain way.

Fully clothed, I checked out my ass in the mirror and the shirt length in relation to the pants. I liked the way I looked. I thought about Krupa and wondered if we would've looked alike as adults, if our body shapes would be the same or if we'd both have hairy upper lips and faces. I freed myself from the single Willkie room on the eighth floor of the North building. The balls of my bare feet touched the cold bathroom floor—right, left, right—which connected to Audrey's room. I could hear Audrey singing at the top of her lungs, the sound of her voice rising and falling as if she were moving around the room. I didn't listen to rap or hip-hop but knew some songs because of Audrey.

I pounded my fist against the door, the fleshy part of my hand acting as more of a cushion than I had expected. Audrey flung the door open. We hollered face-to-face, constructing huge, rapid air circles with our arms.

Audrey wore a slithery fitted black mini-skirt that illuminated her ghostly white legs. Her top was cream also but had a sparkly sequin catfish with calligraphic whiskers across the chest. The sleeves gripped the edges of her shoulders.

Audrey's Turbie Twist hung on the headboard of a rumpled bed covered with jersey-knit sheets and clean, unfolded laundry that had been there for more than two days, even while she slept. T-shirt bras and days-of-the-week underwear lay scattered across the floor like a ring toss gone bad.

"Tom and Jackie are here." Audrey took a bite of her Dagwood's sandwich. It was her usual: the Vegetarian Sub with Havarti cheese and Dagwood's Special Sauce. "They're coming up."

We applied our makeup in the bathroom together over two sinks and in front of one large mirror with school-cafeteria lighting. We only wore makeup on party nights.

My hair dryer and the removed diffuser were on my side of the sink surrounded by contact solution, pump hair spray with a missing cap, spilled nutmeg-colored blush that left a trail in the basin, mousse for perfect curls, an economy-size bottle of gel for smooth curls, a flattened tube of cavity-protection toothpaste, a pick with curvy strays of short black hair, and a set of retainers even though the bottom piece no longer enclosed my teeth.

I traced my lips with a shadowy chocolate pencil and filled them in with hurried yet concise strokes, creating a smooth, dark finish. As I pressed them together, my teeth felt as if they were attempting to break free from captivity.

I curled my eyelashes, counting to 28 before releasing the curler. I applied three coats of ink-black mascara, moving the wand vertically against the tiniest lashes at the inner corner of my eye.

Audrey's lids were powdered with green eye shadow. The creases were a shimmery light purple. Brown mascara rippled through her lashes, as opposed to black, for a more realistic

71

look. Her pet peeve was jet-black mascara on blondes. Two high, vivacious buns encircled her head with an engraved zigzag part. "I cut my bangs too short again." She leaned into the mirror as close as she could, pulling down certain pieces as far as the hair could stretch, hoping it wouldn't spring back up.

"This professor has no idea what she's talking about," said Jackie as she walked in with Tom. "And I hate when people start asking questions right when class is about to end. I'm ready to go, you know?"

Tom nodded, saying "right" and "uh huh" a few times. His heavy sweater was a blend of orange and golds and looked bold against his dark-wash jeans and casual treaded brown shoes.

Jackie plopped onto the bed, flashing the inner back of her knee-length hooded cardigan, shouting over the music while turning down the volume. "The guy that's throwing the party is in my bowling class."

I returned to my room, looped my forearm through my white leather purse embellished with multicolor rhinestones, and knocked the light switch down. "Is he cute?" I yelled. I turned the bathroom light off as I walked back through in black, chunky heels.

"No, not really." Jackie rose off the bed. "Every time he talks to me, I'm like please don't ask me out, please don't ask me out."

The door automatically locked behind us.

"You should give him a chance," said Tom.

The three of us ignored him as we waited for the elevator. The down button brightened. We descended immediately to the first floor.

"He'll probably ask you out." I looked over at the two male students working the front desk. They were both in more weather-appropriate attire: weighty hooded sweatshirts, fleece pants, and corduroys. "He's in love and he'll be drunk. He must've heard that your cookies won the 4-H contest in grade school."

Our laughter was unrestrained.

Jackie walked around the rear of her red Blazer, dinging the door as she missed the keyhole on the driver's side.

"I'm not drinking." Tom turned to Audrey and me in the backseat, his long, reddish-brown hair illuminating his face in the soft blackness of the car.

I knew Tom would be parading around the party, holding two beers at all times, and we'd be the final few people left at the end of the night.

"We probably won't drink that much either," I said sarcastically.

We all broke out in laughter.

Audrey and I were lightweights. My voice blew up to three times its normal amplitude, and Audrey practiced lessons from her sign-language class with an exaggerated, animated face and overemphasized hand movements that could bring on arthritis.

Jackie could hold her liquor, but the indicators of her drunken state were a red face and hiccups.

It was 18 degrees. The cold hit me fiercely. The winds blew across my cheeks, over my lips, in my eyes, and pulled my curls away from my head. "I need to move somewhere warm after graduation. I really hate winter." I crossed my arms over my chest. I inevitably breathed in the wind through my nose, the wintry blasts tearing through my body, as I huddled with my friends and walked the few blocks to the party.

The street was dim yet lighted up with unsystematic house parties of people on porches wearing tech vests with long-sleeve T-shirts, zip-up fleece hoodies, frayed jeans, or unzipped winter coats with tank tops underneath exposing cleavage. There was shouting over booming music, unstable plastic cups of alcohol, and couples making out on the chilled concrete.

The party was at a small, apple-colored brick dwelling that seemed quiet and quaint like Grandma's house. It was as if she were waiting inside with a tender, flavorful pot roast, buttery mashed potatoes and, for dessert, a homemade apple pie with strips of crust crisscrossed over the top on a table set with monogrammed doily linens and an antique clock ticking away against the wall.

Or, instead, deep-fried vadas served before a pot of chicken biryani with cashews and raisins, greasy pappadums with cumin flavor, and stacks of plates in the sink stained with turmeric powder and yellow onion remnants. Trimmed curry plants would sit in the corner of the room maintaining a supply of aromatic leaves for cooking.

It looked as if no one were home. Soft lighting appeared through the curtains, and not even the slightest sound leaked from the house. Tom opened the door to relieve us from the cold. The scent of alcohol threw itself at us like a drunk, horny freshman girl who never got any when she was sober. The room we entered was dark, lighted by cigarettes and the cracked chandelier in the next room, and packed with intoxicated, predominately white college students grinding on each other to Nelly. It was impressive that the party seemed nonexistent to the outside world, a shindig that law enforcement would pass up in a heartbeat. I felt safe at the party as an underage drinker.

"Let's see what's going on in the other room!" Tom shouted over the bass. He led the way as we all squeezed through the crowded dance floor in a single, weaving line. Beer spilled onto Jackie's sleeve.

"Omigod. I'm like slo sorry," slurred a stocky brunette in yellow-orange flip-flops, a transparent sarong, and a triangular bikini top with an origami-structured lei showcased around her neck. "Like omigod. I'm so sorry."

Jackie rolled her eyes.

The girl staggered and then involuntarily balanced herself by grabbing Jackie's elbow. "I just came from this Hawaiian party and ... " She slurred some more, her voice fading as we continued on.

A long wooden table dominated the room, surrounded by people playing Cups. The table was trashed with bottle caps, beer bottles, beer cans, red and blue plastic cups, alcohol-soaked paper towels, cigarette butts, and a freezer zipper bag filled with marijuana.

A girl with sweat circles under her eyes, smeared lipstick, and hair that was mysteriously drenched, slammed her beer and repeatedly attempted to flip the cup face down while her teammates hounded her to get the job done. The team across from her was already two people ahead. She finally flipped the blue plastic cup and the next guy in line on her team chugged his cup of beer.

"I'm going to play!" Jackie rushed to the table. "I love this game!"

A tall young man in brown corduroys and a plain, dark blue T-shirt approached Jackie, screaming her name at the top of his lungs. Twisted, sienna-colored hair fidgeted on his head as if he had tossed and turned all night. His cheeks blushed pink on pale skin. He was clearly delighted by Jackie's presence. He held a short stack of red cups at an angle as he gazed into Jackie's eyes, trapped in a dreamlike state. "You all can drink for free." He handed each of us a cup and walked us to the kitchen. "I'm Dylan, by the way."

Jackie flinched, realizing that she hadn't introduced him to the group. "Yeah, this is Dylan," she yelled, turning sideways. "I was spacing out. We're in the same bowling class."

An irregular line of students extended throughout the kitchen, originating from the keg in the corner. "Do you wanna go home with me or do you wanna go home with your roommate?" asked a drunk who was too wasted to try to get laid the conventional way. "Do you wanna go home with me or do you wanna go home with your roommate? What will it be, ladies?"

"Let me get a picture of you guys." Dylan rewound a disposable camera covered in green packaging with a rip near the flash.

"Mala and Jackie, get on the sides, since you're shorter," directed Audrey. She threw her long arms around Tom and me. We smiled big and fake, but it looked genuine in the actual photo.

"He'll probably cut us out so he can masturbate to it," Tom whispered to me as the four of us joined the keg line.

"I'll be back," said Dylan as he attentively looked around the party, indicating that he had to tend to host duties that were imperative to a successful soiree.

The line was barely moving. Two guys pumped the hell out of the keg.

"This keg better not go dry."

"No shit, man!"

"I gotta get fucked up tonight."

We entered the even more packed dance floor after 20 minutes of waiting in line.

"I need to play Cups before we get out of here!" Jackie held her beer cup high and danced to the music.

"Anyone need another?" Tom tipped his empty cup forward to show everyone.

Audrey rolled her eyes. "We *just* got beer, Tom."

"I'll go with you," I said. The line was like a maze through the kitchen, funneling into the next room. "Looks like we won't be getting drunk tonight."

"I'm getting two this time," said Tom.

"The keg is dry!" It was every college student's party nightmare.

"The keg is dry!"

"The keg is dry!"

"The keg is dry!"

"Is there another keg?"

"Someone get another keg!"

"Let's leave."

"I have a party ball!" Dylan was distraught. His fly was open and the neck of his dark blue T-shirt was stretched out. He scurried through the rooms of the house. "Wait, don't leave! There *is* more alcohol!"

No one was listening to him.

"What's a party ball?" I asked.

Audrey signed "party," shaking "Y" shapes on both hands. Then she signed "ball," fingertips of both hands touching, forming a circle. Her head jerked with an open-mouthed smile.

Jackie and I followed Dylan as he bolted up the stairs.

One of Dylan's roommates was in the bathtub with the party ball. "I can't figure out how to tap this thing!" He slapped the party ball over and over and then transitioned to punching. "This fucking thing won't open!"

Jackie and I looked at each other, alarmed and amazed at the level of misery caused by the party ball. We headed back down to Audrey and Tom, stopping in the middle of the staircase to find the once-roaring party, with people shoulder to shoulder, mostly cleared out because of a dry keg. I fell forward as a girl with pastel skin and unbending mahogany curls ran through us like a game of Red Rover. I saved myself by clutching the railing.

"Omigod! I made out with this guy but I came to this party to see Jeremy." The whites of her eyes were bloodshot red. She was dressed in loose-fitting boot-cut jeans and a white cardigan. Her plastic cup was empty, and it seemed as if she had been toting its bareness around for a while. "Jeremy saw me make out with him!" Her hands flailed in every direction. The left side of her neck was covered in hickeys, with the start of one on her collarbone. She explained the dilemma to Jackie and me as if we were all old friends who used to play in the sprinkler and watch Saturday-morning cartoons together.

The girl's drunken regrets amused me because she was still in a drunken state of mind.

"Don't worry about it," Jackie said.

"Yeah, it happens." I laughed.

She let out a sigh so deep that she almost toppled over. "I'm Julianna," she said in a deafening breath.

I cringed at the loudness of her voice. I told Julianna our names and pointed to the couch. "And that's Audrey and Tom." I realized that introductions were useless, since Julianna would probably not recall our names in five minutes.

"Could you give me a ride home?" she asked comfortably, tucking her hair behind her ears. She raised her cup as if it had liquid in it. "I live in Willkie-North."

I told Julianna that Willkie-North was my home, too. The five of us headed toward the car. Jackie and I held Julianna up while she staggered through the streets. There had been a large temperature drop since the beginning of the night. I tried not to think about the shivery weather as I crossed my arms and scrunched my shoulders up to my ears. My teeth chattered. My nipples were as hard as rocks. Goose bumps hoisted the skin off my arms.

"It's so cold," complained Julianna. "It's so cold. It's so cold. It's so cold. It's so cold. Jeremy saw me!" Julianna banged her face into her palms five times, causing her to stumble around even more. "Jeremy saw me!"

I slid over in Jackie's Blazer behind the passenger seat. Julianna followed my lead. Audrey sat behind the driver's seat.

The streets were practically vacant at night. It was an intense contrast with the daytime life of the campus, with students on the way to class through the paths of the Arboretum, where some stopped to nap by the pond. Masses exited the Indiana Memorial Union through the revolving doors. Piles of students waited for the Stadium Express with their ID cards out or walked through the Sample Gates to Kirkwood Avenue to shop at Greetings, Steve and Barry's, Cha Cha, or Urban Outfitters or get happy-hour stuffed breadsticks at Kilroy's. And there was that student who sat by the music school between classes and listened to the violin.

We were on 10th street, turning right onto Jordan Avenue in front of the library. An Indian man wearing a white puffy coat and overloaded backpack pedaled quickly on his bike. He was about to cross Jordan as Jackie entered the street. He slammed on his brakes as he noticed the Blazer.

We all gasped.

"Whoa," I said as I pulled the seat belt off my chest and let it fall back with the inside of my thumb.

Julianna looked at me. "The Indian people on this campus are stupid."

My eyes grew as my mouth dropped. "What?"

"Mala's Indian, you douche bag!" Tom laughed with barely a sound. His face descended into the console as he let it out.

"No. *No* she's not!" Julianna looked horrified. She scrutinized my facial features. "Omigod, you *are*? I didn't think. You don't look like. I thought you were Hispanic."

"My stomach hurts," said Audrey, her words difficult to decipher through the laughter. "My stomach hurts." She leaned over, clutching her abdomen. "I can't stop. I can't stop laughing."

"Mala *is* Indian," Jackie said sternly.

"I'm sorry," she said, looking deeply into my eyes. "I'm sorry. I'm so sorry."

Julianna stopped talking. Her silence grounded the laughter as we pulled up in front of Willkie.

"I can't be racist!" she burst out in strong revelation. "I'm Jewish!"

The laughter re-erupted. Audrey signed "Jew."

I unhooked my seat belt. "Okay, *Jew*-lianna."

*

"I'm black," said Cyril.

I laughed.

"Seriously. I'm black." He opened his wallet. "See, here is my birth certificate."

I glided forward, leaning into my desk, finding it strange that he was carrying around his birth certificate.

"Look, it says 'Negroid.' "

"*Negroid*?" I looked at him, then at the word on the birth certificate, and found it odd that it was in print on a record.

"I carry it around with me. No one ever believes that I'm black. I'm a Creole. My family is from Louisiana."

I did not know what a Creole was. "You carry around your *birth* certificate? Do you break it out at parties?" I joked.

"I have quite a few times actually. No one ever knows what I am."

"I know what you mean."

"People think I'm Hispanic. Oh hold on." He lifted his phone off a black belt clip. "This is Cyril. How may I assist you?" He bustled out of my office.

I didn't see him again until the next day when he brought me another boudin ball and asked me out. I declined.

Cyril brought me a boudin ball the following day and asked me out again. I said no. And on Friday he brought me a gallon-size zipper freezer bag full of boudin balls.

I laughed at the sight, blushing at the gesture, and agreed to go out with him. I told myself it was just for fun.

"I saw one in the trash," he said.

I was embarrassed he knew of the disposal. I didn't deny it. I was curious about the boudin balls but apprehensive about eating food from strangers.

"So I thought I'd bring you a *whole* bag." He laughed. "That and my office is moving to another location and I needed something big for my last chance." Cyril's southern accent grew bolder and richer as if he were being himself, as if it were a sign of confidence. He was eager, asking me out for dinner right after work or for the weekend. I told him I wasn't available until the following week because I was moving out of the hotel and into an apartment.

CHAPTER 6

I put two suitcases on the floor. I looked at the Vigor through the balcony view of my new studio apartment. The regal plum-pearl paint looked glossy as it shone in the sun. The headlights looked thin and mean. I read, "Burglars will be shot. No exceptions," in the window of the apartment across from me.

My new place was off Westheimer. It was the perfect street for a newcomer, packed with everything I needed, even though there always seemed to be a lane blocked or a stoplight out, creating a halt of traffic dissatisfaction, an array of lives scattered on an eight-lane road.

The apartment complex was full of Indian people, mostly young families who were acclimating to U.S. culture. When I toured the complex, I noticed Indian men on treadmills working out in their professional attire and Indian women in churidars riding exercise bikes.

A queen-size bed came out of the wall. When in the wall, the bottom of the bed was a massive mirror. Built-in shelves rose to the ceiling on both sides of the bed. I envisioned my belongings in my new place. My shoes would take up the shelves on the left side of the bed. The other side would store towels, sheets, and pillowcases.

The kitchen was a few feet from the edge of the bed. It was slightly bigger than my hotel-room kitchen. The six tall cabinets were dingy and manila-colored. There was no dishwasher. The counter was about 15 inches in width, L-shaped, and presented the opportunity for bar stools.

The bathroom counter was spacious. After the furnished mattress, it was the major selling point. I liked to have my hair dryer, mousse, gel, hair spray, hair pick, deodorant, contact solution, moisturizers, retainers, face wash, toothpaste, floss, eyelash curler, and makeup brushes together on one platform. I used the cabinets under the sink only for pads, tampons, bars of soap, unopened items, and other products that were not used daily.

The closet was in the bathroom next to the sink. It had bypass doors and a top shelf that I'd have to stand on a chair to reach. It wasn't my dream closet but had plenty of space for two suitcases of clothes.

I looked in the mirror. "My own place," I said. "My own place." I didn't look like someone who had just gone through a moving day. I only had to make three trips to the car. My first Texas apartment and third place of residence in Houston was perfect for me and my Vigor full of stuff.

The apartment did not have windows, only a screen door leading to the balcony that overlooked the courtyard and parking lot. The courtyard consisted of uneven, flattened stones circling a dainty fountain. Pink roses and trees with authoritative branches cast shadows onto the plain stones. A wrought-iron mesh table was to the side of the fountain, with one of the two chairs pulled far from the center.

A squirrel sprinted through the yard. I hoped to see a rabbit instead. They were a sign to me. A rabbit would hop through the backyard sometimes while my family ate dinner together. I would watch it wander through the grass knowing that it was Krupa. I had heard stories of people's faith in their deceased loved ones—feeling a breeze on completely still days, seeing them in a stranger's smile, thanking them for an unexpected parking spot in a crowded lot.

I was almost 4 years old when my sister died. Krupa was riding her bike between the driveways in the neighborhood. The teenage driver did not see her.

I had always wished I'd suddenly remember a time I played with Krupa or fought or laughed with her. Photos from my mother's albums of sticky back pages were all I had. I was obsessed with them as a little girl, one in particular. With rounded corners, it was a 3.5" x 5" print of Krupa and me. I had carefully peeled it from the sticky page, as it did not want to break loose from the album. I took it with me to Houston. A dull brown and ointment-colored plaid-tweed couch leaned against a banister in the background. The middle back cushion fell forward, trapped in a tilt because of the support of the other two stiff cushions. The carpet was burnt orange. A fraudulent leather, pea-green chair reclined parallel to the couch as if someone had jumped out of it without pushing down the handle to lower the footrest.

The top and left side of the front door frame was visible. A round, opal ceiling light dangled in front of it. An end table held a tall Indian brass lamp with an abrupt round salmon-colored base, deep carvings, and an unoriginal off-white shade. Next to it was an elephant in motion, a hand-carved wooden statue with threatening white tusks. Pasty curtains were pulled open at the top right corner of the photo, and through the window was the red brick of the house across the street, its roof washed out in the sunlight.

I played on my stomach on the kitchen table in a carnation-pink onesie with food stains on my chest. Head up, my cheeks puffed out as if I had just spit up. My thick black hair curled above both my ears. A playpen was behind me like a safety net for a fall from the table.

An Indian cloth draped the table. It was a saturated, sheltered pink of laced fibers with embroidered circular spats of amethyst flowers. Crowded tropical-green cloud shapes hovered around the flowers. Turmeric-colored united teardrops outlined the cloud shapes. And peppercorn-sized dots circled the teardrops.

Half of the backrest of one of the six table chairs found its way into the picture, sliced by the edge of the Kodak paper. The light through the kitchen window separated the chair into light brown and dark brown.

Krupa's Eli Lilly T-shirt was mostly faded in the sleeves. Straight bangs seared across her forehead. Her black locks were wavy, as if they'd been let loose from pigtail braids. Krupa's left arm twisted outward as her left cheek rested on her left shoulder. Her palm was up with my little fingers in it. Krupa's right arm rested on the table, hand under her left arm and discolored elbow dangling off the side as she smiled playfully. I reached with my left hand for a stacking toy with blue, red, yellow, and green rings on a rocking base. In front of me was Krupa's white rabbit in a cage.

*

Derrick, a tax supervisor, brought in a rectangular pan of cheese grits on Monday for his birthday. He wore his fluffy yellow Lopez Finance & Accounting button-down shirt proudly. There was a plastic spoon, knife, and fork in his left breast pocket. His belt was brown leather with a silver buckle and cattle horns along the strap, looped through jeans with a small ink stain on his left kneecap. His muscular chest, forearms, and biceps blazed through clothing. Derrick's skin was darker than mine. His hair was also blacker and gelled, with the front sculpted upward into a delicate point.

I wondered what cheese grits were as I scooped about five bites' worth onto a Texas-shaped plate. "Did you get any good presents?"

"Oh yeah!" His face lighted up. "I got a gift certificate to the gun store!" He reached for a napkin.

"The *gun* store?"

"Yeah, I haven't been to the range in a while! I need to go, practice my skills." Derrick pulled a fake trigger with his hands and made a firing sound.

"I'll go with you, man," said Jerry, an auditor.

"I also made shrimp po'boys and drank some beers with my buddies. My mom's making me a traditional Mexican home-cooked meal tonight."

"What's a po'boy?"

Derrick stopped in midchew, his head making a sharp turn as if he had reacted to a loud crashing noise.

I smiled, embarrassed, realizing in my short time in Texas that it really is its own country. The South is a completely different world. I decided not to ask about the cheese grits or the traditional Mexican meal.

He continued to chomp on the cheese grits. "It's basically a shrimp sandwich," he said, talking with his mouth full.

"Oh." I had never tasted such a thing. Shrimp between two slices of bread did not sound appetizing.

He laughed at me. "You'll start saying 'y'all' soon."

"No I won't."

"Trust me. You will. We all do."

Theresa entered the kitchen in a navy suit consisting of a skirt that stopped below the knee and a conservative jacket. A simple white dress shirt peeped through, buttoned to the neck. Basic pumps hugged her feet about an inch off the ground.

Theresa's Internet profile told a different story. I had investigated SocialYou, curious about Theresa's defense and promotion of the Web site. Theresa squatted provocatively in her main profile photo. Her legs were spread open in white, skin-tight shorts that were practically panties and electric blue fishnets that descended into clear 6-inch stilettos. She wore a white, skin-tight shirt ending above the belly button that read, "I love pussy," in black bubbly letters.

I couldn't look at Theresa's other photos, since I didn't have an account, but noticed the photo slide show on the main page. Close-up snapshots of Theresa's ass and pushed-up cleavage flashed before my eyes as well as a group kiss including two other girls and her boyfriend, Todd. I couldn't pull myself away from the computer, stunned by the double life of my co-worker. I wished I hadn't investigated. I couldn't seem to get the trashy Internet photos out of my head every time I talked to Theresa.

"Like omigod did you hear that they fired Cynthia?" Theresa bent down at the cheese grits. She picked up a plate and then put it back on the table. "I don't want to go over my carb limit."

"*Fired*?" I scooped half a plate full of cheese grits for seconds. "What did Cynthia do?"

"Well, they let her *go*. We are losing money and Lopez doesn't even care about her own company. She's always in France visiting her boy toy." She tossed her hair off her shoulder, hand remaining in the air to overemphasize her attitude. She followed me into my office. "You know what I hate?"

I stared at Theresa's conservative apparel. "What?"

"I hate when I'm like shopping at Saks in my sweats and like the salespeople give me dirty looks. You know, just because I have my sweats on and I'm like omigod *you* are the ones *working* at Saks."

I avoided eye contact as I sat down in my swivel chair. I took a sip of water, finding the cherry-colored lip mark on the inside of the red plastic cup more interesting than Theresa.

"What are you doing after work? You want to get a drink at Belvedere?" Theresa occupied one of the visitors' chairs cautiously as if it were contaminated.

"No. I have a date." I leaned back in my chair.

"Oh you do? With Cyril?"

"No, this guy that I met on that Indian dating Web site."

I was hesitant about posting my information online but wanted to be open-minded in my new, big city and actually meet some Indians, preferably Christians, preferably Catholics. When I checked my account the day after creating a profile, my inbox was flooded with messages from interested Indians and one white guy in mountain-biking gear who claimed to love Indian women. I didn't need the Internet to meet white men. I could pick them up anywhere.

I sorted through each prospect, noticing several posed with Mercedes, BMWs, and Lexuses but mostly Infiniti G35 coupes. I was amused by one guy in particular who modeled his Honda Accord with a caption that read, "My new pride and joy, 1998 Honda Accord." Some showed variety in their photos, with head shots, partying scenes, and group wedding photos of Indians in cultural garb. I did not know enough Indian people outside of my family to pose for a group photo. I was disturbed by some of the profiles of men who had weight and fair-skin requirements when they were not attractive themselves. I laughed out loud at a restaurant server's request for doctors or women in medical school. I deleted those fresh off the boat and men in obvious need of a green card.

My uploaded online photo closed in on a makeup-immersed face, eyes bold and pronounced thanks to freshly threaded eyebrows and a tube of chunky, expired black mascara. My lips were stained burgundy on a smile, revealing molars and a perfect alignment between the tip of my lip and the line created by my two front teeth. My forehead, cheeks, chin, and nose were touched up with foundation and set with too much powder. The curls on my head smacked into each other, creating a thick, moon-shaped line on the right side and a smaller version on the left. Four wiry strings of minuscule silver squares clung to my neck and chest like magnets. I showed a sensible, classy amount of cleavage.

I filled in the profile info. Age: 23. Religion: Catholic. Location: Houston. I chose "Non-Veg" for Food Preference. I left Skin Tone and Body Type blank, feeling it was contributing to unnecessary vanity.

I agreed to go out with a petrophysical engineer named Dinesh Gupta who worked for Shell. The petrophysical part was a mystery to me.

Dinesh was from Oklahoma, and had been in Houston for three years. He posed by his Infiniti G35 coupe in his main profile photo, an image I found cheesy and arrogant. Dinesh did not look the same in some of the other photos, but his eyes were consistently hazel green with each click. I had come across only one Indian person with light eyes, and that was at a restaurant in Trivandrum while ordering parotas to go with my cousin. The man was very dark and wore a greenish-brown lungi and a big gold cross around his neck.

The last set of pictures were of Dinesh's moss-green Infiniti, set against the downtown skyline, near Williams Tower, and in a driveway of a monstrous home with rounded balconies, double-front glass doors, overbearing white-coated pillars, and a driveway that curved from the front yard to the back of the house.

Dinesh contacted me with a grammatically correct message of inquiries and a brief synopsis of his story. He recently bought a house in the Galleria and was taking two-step dance lessons. His profile listed him as a meat eater and 5 foot 10 with an athletic build. I couldn't see his body in the pictures. He concluded his message by making a suggestion to check out his profile. He inserted several exclamation points and a smiley face.

I convinced myself it wouldn't hurt to go out with him. I rarely found myself lustfully attracted to an Indian guy but had not come across many in my lifetime. I decided to go out with the ugly ones just in case.

It would be only my third date ever. I had never kissed anyone on New Year's, received flowers or gifts from a man, celebrated Valentine's Day, or walked around the mall hand in hand with a significant other. I had a boyfriend for three and a half months whom I met drunk at a party in my first semester of college. We never went on any real dates, just parties. The most recent date was in Indy, a blind meeting in which I didn't approve of his shirt. It read, "This is America Speak English." I uncomfortably introduced myself and, before sitting down, decided I didn't have to waste my time when I already knew, by an article of clothing, that I would not be interested in the guy and I didn't have to be polite. I walked out of Broad Ripple Tavern satisfied with my decision, grateful that I didn't foolishly fritter away my time.

The other date was in college with a frat boy I had picked up in the loud group-work area in the entrance to the library. We sat diagonally from each other, books and study materials useless in front of us. I jiggled my Indiana Hoosiers pen between my fingers, holding it like a cigarette, as we exchanged smiles and stares, one after another. I couldn't concentrate, finding him attractive and tempting, which was not an everyday thing for me.

His hair was maintained with perfect, subtle brown spikes that matched tender, toasty brown eyes. He introduced himself as Matt and invited me to a frat party at his house. I told him I wouldn't be caught dead at one of those. I didn't attend them anymore and hadn't trekked down North Jordan since freshman year.

He still asked me out, suggesting dinner the next evening at Malibu Grill. "I have a couple of acquaintances in town, but it's not mandatory that I hang out with them."

I found it odd that he used the word "mandatory" to describe socializing. I played it cool, saying I wasn't free, following my friends' examples and always taking their bad advice about men.

We met up the following Wednesday. I checked my curls, powdered face, black mascara, and chocolate lip liner in the bathroom of Ernie Pyle Hall after leaving magazine-editing class, one of the few courses left to earn my certificate in journalism. I had never applied makeup for class before. I bought a new shirt for the occasion, my first meal date.

Matt was already sitting at the table in khaki cargo pants and the same brown sweater he wore when he asked me out at the library. There were crumbs in front of him, as if he'd eaten pre-meal bread or sat at a table that had not been wiped. He smiled beyond measure, folding the newspaper, sweeping it off the table and into his backpack as soon as he noticed me.

I was instantly displeased with his carelessness in selecting an outfit for our date but quickly dismissed it as insignificant. I ordered barbecue chicken and garlic mashed potatoes, pretending to view the menu meticulously when I had actually looked it up online the night before.

"It comes with a regular side," said the waitress.

"Broccoli." I ordered food that could be eaten with utensils, following my friends' instructions. It was food that my parents would have eaten with their hands in the privacy of their home, licking their palms afterward and possibly the plate, claiming that the food had more flavor when eaten with their fingers.

"It'll be out shortly." She smiled, taking our menus without having written down our order.

"You're Indian, right?" asked Matt.

"Yeah." I had a bad feeling, caught off guard by his racial abruptness.

"There's an Indian restaurant that I like to go to on the west side of Indy. That's where I'm from. The chicken that I get is really hot. It says it's DC hot."

"DC hot?"

"Yeah, it says that it's DC hot. I'm not sure what that means."

I frowned, contemplating the term. "Do you mean desi hot? Is it spelled d-e-s-i?"

"Uh, yeah. It is."

"It's desi," I said. "It basically means 'Indian person.' "

"Hmmm," he grunted.

"So Matt," I began.

"It's Mike."

"What?"

"My name's Mike."

"Oh, I'm sorry." I was quietly embarrassed, wordless. I could've sworn his name was Matt. It was an easy white-boy name I should've had down. I glanced at the three girls in university apparel with no makeup, hair in disheveled, floppy ponytails, chatting and laughing boisterously at the table to the left of us. It was a scene I was more accustomed to.

"My name's Mike Miller," he said in a tone indicating that he didn't like his name.

I laughed, locking eyes with him as I leaned forward, then back.

"I know. I know. It's a really plain name."

"What's your middle name?" I asked.

He leaned back in his chair, hesitating. "Sam."

I laughed harder. "No it's not!"

"Yup."

"That's so funny," I said, feeling more relaxed after the laughter. "I was afraid you would say 'Bob.' "

"What's your full name?" He squeezed mustard onto the top bun of his burger and flipped it back on top of the meat.

"Mala Mary Thomas."

"That's pretty easy," he said, covering his mouth while chewing. He pushed his sweater sleeves up, but the right one tumbled back past his elbow.

"My dad's name is Jose. But people always screw it up and pronounce it 'Ho-ZAY.' " I laughed and shook my head.

"Well, how does he spell it?"

I looked up at him, realizing he wouldn't find it amusing. He would pronounce it 'Ho-ZAY' also. I pressed my fork into the mashed potatoes. "J-o-s-e." The food was too hot, burning my tongue and the roof of my mouth, but I pretended it didn't bother me as the potatoes heated my throat and chest.

"Oh. Well, that's the Spanish pronunciation of it."

"I know, but … " I didn't explain. He wouldn't understand why it was so amusing. Uncomfortable silences lingered while we ate, filled with unnatural talk of school, family, friends, and, worst of all, the weather.

"You know what, Mala?" He pushed his sleeves up again and took a hefty bite of his oozy Malibu cheeseburger. "I have an Indian friend. A girl I went to high school with. Sometimes she wears one of those dots on her head." His index finger landed between his eyebrows. "She's Hindu."

"Oh, really." I was happy to almost be finished with my meal.

He started to speak but put the burger down first as if he needed full concentration. He furrowed his eyebrows at me while he finished chewing. He pushed his sleeves up again. "Why did you go to Catholic school?"

"I'm Catholic." People assumed I was either Hindu or Muslim, among other things. "There's not very many like me. Just a small percentage of the population."

He looked puzzled with a waffle fry pinched between his fingers, an inch from his mouth. "So, do you become Hindu when you visit India?"

*

Dinesh called to tell me he was at the museum and would wait right outside the parking garage in the entryway of the gift shop. He said during our initial phone conversation that the Houston Museum of Natural Science was one of his favorite places in Houston. I was relieved to hear no heavy breathing, high-pitched tone, or annoying laugh during our conversation.

It was my first date with an Indian, the wrong kind of Indian but an Indian. The Vigor failed to start on the first try. My left calf muscle rubbed against the frame as I got out of the car and left the door wide open. I turned the gas cap until it opened and then I closed it—a trick I learned from Fred. It fired up right away.

I parked the Vigor, making note of the creature that represented the second level of the parking garage so I would remember where I parked. I put my cell phone charger in the glove box along with the empty CD case for Stryper's *To Hell With The Devil*. I fixed my hair without a mirror while walking into the elevator and adjusted my top, which had risen during the drive.

The photos had not depicted the real Dinesh. I knew it was him by his body language and the look he gave me—as if we had met before. He was the only Indian guy standing in the center of the brightly lighted gift shop and the only person who was not shopping. I did not smile as I approached. He was about 5 foot 4 and thin as a rod. I could tell he felt my displeasure. After a long, deadening stare and mean thoughts, I forced a smile to make the situation more comfortable as introductions took place.

"Have you been to any of the museums here?"

I stared at him, unable to blink. "I wanted to check out the Museum of Fine Arts," I said slowly. As we entered the permanent exhibit halls, I couldn't remember standing in line to purchase tickets. I was still in shock. Dinesh looked nothing like his pictures except for his hazel-green eyes.

We walked into the Hall of Paleontology. I looked up at the large dinosaur fossils as Dinesh did not stop to look at the exhibit. I followed him even though we were walking side by side. We stopped in front of the Weiss Energy Hall. "Energy" was lighted up in bright orange. I looked up at the Foucault pendulum as it knocked over pins and was surrounded by people.

"I like your shirt," he said as we entered the exhibit.

"Thanks." It was a rounded V-neck that I bought at Parisian while shopping on the clock at Midwest Bank. The shirt was striped green and light green with a thick waistband. The armpits were stained from excessive wear. I paired it with dark jean capri pants that had sand-colored beads dangling from the hips. I noticed that his shirt color-matched mine.

"It's my favorite shade of green. It matches my car."

"Oh really." I browsed the exhibit. I had no idea what I was looking at. I pressed the button on the pipeline-pig demo and read the description. I learned that the pig removes debris from the pipeline. "I don't really know much about this stuff. So oil is big here in Houston."

Dinesh was silent as he looked at me. "Yeah, it is. But what was I saying? Oh yeah. I love my car. I had a premier paint job done on it because I *love* green."

"I love my car, too." I looked at the enclosed, neon-lighted refinery display against the wall, yearning to put my hands on the glass like a little kid.

"What do you drive?"

"A Vigor."

"A what?"

"It's an Acura Vigor," I said. "It's my Vigster."

He had no reaction to my car pet name.

"They're not very common. They only made them for a few years."

"Oh. I drive an Infiniti G35."

I fell into a zone, losing focus on the content of his low-quality words as he went on about his car. I looked at the five crude-oil samples against the wall as people turned the hand pumps to observe the viscosities. One of the samples was labeled "North Sea gas condensate."

"So you just kind of randomly moved here? I've never been to Indiana."

"You'll know you're there when you see all of the basketball hoops," I said. "I couldn't find a job back in Indy."

"I had a hard time also," said Dinesh. "It took me over a year."

I was surprised about his luck, since he was an engineer. I was relieved that he didn't judge me. He understood what it was like. "What did you do then?"

He rolled his eyes. "I had to work in sales."

"I almost had to do that, too." I looked at a display labeled "Christmas tree," only it wasn't holiday-related. It had several valves, and Dinesh explained that it controls the flow of liquids from an oil well. Next to it was the Geovator, but it was temporarily closed.

"That takes you to the bottom of an oil well," explained Dinesh.

"No one would hire me. It was interview after interview."

He nodded in agreement. "I grew up in a small town, so my options were limited there and I started looking everywhere." He seemed engrossed with the fishtail drill bit as we moved on to the drill-bit collection. "We were the only Indian family. My dad was sort of the town doctor. I didn't really know any Indian people until I went to college. I was one of the founders of my Indian fraternity. We were so cool. I really take pride in my frat days. All that brotherhood. There was an Indian sorority, but they were annoying."

I frowned at the thought of being in an Indian sorority. I frowned at the thought of hanging out with Indian frat boys. I frowned at the thought of hanging out with frat boys in general. My Indian sorority "sisters" would tell me to straighten my hair and grow it long and wear Indian clothes and date Indian boys. I looked at the Hughes Simplex dual cone bit, and then at the drilling video on the vertical screen. "That must've been a really good way to meet some Indian people."

"Yeah, it was."

"Indianapolis isn't really a small town, but it is predominantly white. I was the only Indian girl in my grade school and high school. I went to Catholic school. I've never met any Indian Christians besides my parents' friends, and none of them are Catholic. I met a few Indians in college, but I was never close with any of them. There was always so much drama. I couldn't handle it. I had a Pakistani friend once, though."

"You're really light for a South Indian."

"I know. People think I'm North Indian."

"All of my friends back home are white," said Dinesh. "I figured that since I have to marry an Indian, though, I should try to meet one." His phone beeped twice. He opened it and read a text message.

"My sisters are married to white guys."

Dinesh stopped in mid-read. "Your sisters are married to *white* guys?" He looked at me disapprovingly while snapping his phone shut with one hand.

His attitude change bothered me. I pursed my lips.

"Did they get disowned? Do you still talk to them? Doesn't it bother you that they married white guys?"

"Of course I still *talk* to them. We're really close. I'm really close with my brother-in-laws, too. My parents were upset at first, but they got over it." I was stunned that Dinesh was acting like he was fresh off the boat. "They fell in love. They couldn't help it. Indian parents would never understand this concept. They just get married."

"How many brothers and sisters do you have?"

"I have two older sisters."

"How old are they?"

"Thirty-three and 36."

"You're far apart in age with them."

I was quiet.

"I'm not that close with my brother," said Dinesh. "I probably talk to him or e-mail him every few months."

I talked to Sara and Jency once a week and e-mailed them almost every day.

"Would *you* marry a white guy?" He looked disgusted, as if he already knew the answer, almost glaring at me with judgmental dark thoughts.

"You were born in the states, right?"

He nodded.

"Yeah, I would. I don't have a problem with that. I grew up with all white people. I'm also Christian, and not very many Indians are." It suddenly bothered me that I was justifying my answer. I sometimes felt like a white girl trapped in an Indian girl's body. I didn't even own Indian clothes.

"I grew up with all white people, too, but I think we should stick with our own. I dated a Latin girl before for fun. Her family was kind of trashy. She had a sister that was pregnant and wasn't married. The girl's family *has* to be perfect."

"Good luck with that," I said sarcastically.

"I went and visited a bunch of girls in Texas from the Web site to see if I liked them. They were in Dallas, Austin, and San Antonio."

I looked at him skeptically. "It's like a real Indian arranged marriage." I laughed alone at my own joke.

"Yes, it is," he said seriously. "I have a great job, great house, and an awesome car. All I really need now is a wife."

"You must melt the hearts of Indian parents everywhere." I laughed alone at my own joke again. I was confused about why he'd asked me out in the first place. I wasn't his Hindu dream.

"So you want to marry a Hindu?"

"Of course," he said. He looked at me as if I were a moron.

"So why did you ask me out?"

"Well, I'm always up for making new friends and, well, I liked your photo. You're really hot. A Hindu and a Catholic would not work. And I like women with long hair."

I thanked him for the museum trip and lied, saying I would call him sometime as we exited through the gift shop together.

Dinesh sent me a text message on the drive home that read, "I had a great time at HMNS."

I was confused, wondering what he thought was so great about it. I dismantled my profile.

CHAPTER 7

I had been dating Cyril T. James for four months. I could be comfortably silent around him or go into a monologue about Mick Mars' *Piece of your Action* guitar solo in front of him. I could let my stomach hang out of my white tank pajama top in front of him after eating the Big Texas Cinnamon Roll he purchased for me from the vending machine at his office. I could be myself around Cyril in a way I couldn't with other men I had met, feeling as if the dates were job interviews or interrogations with upscale southern cuisine, bottomless glasses of cabernet sauvignon, and one-way discussions of dreams and aspirations in which I was protectively private.

Cyril always had my bedtime glass of water ready on the nightstand even though I never drank it and in the mornings turned the air conditioner off before we walked out the door—two of my essential routines that he had memorized. We did everything together from going tax-free shopping at the Galleria (a designated weekend in which I did not know existed) to evacuating for Hurricane Rita.

On our first date, under the sombrero-shaped ceiling-light fixture at Lupe Tortilla, he touched my hand with a single caress and ran his fingers up my arm in a swift movement. It was a simple gesture that sent a tingle through a place where usually more than a simple hand movement was needed to reach. He told me he liked my hair and asked if he could touch it. I giggled a lot on the date, realizing I was giggling a lot with a guy I had planned on not getting serious with.

I was in denial, spending every free moment with Cyril but telling myself and him that it was just for fun. "I just want to be upfront," I would say often. "I just moved here and don't want a relationship."

Houston gave birth to my dating life, making up for the nonexistent one I had become accustomed to my whole life. I squeezed a lifetime of dating into my short time in Houston, even going on three dates in one day: a lunch, afternoon coffee, and dinner, all in the company of Indian men. Cyril understood, but I perceived the disappointment in his reaction when I mentioned dates with other men.

The "T" in his name stood for "Tracy." He had two older brothers and one younger brother, all residing in Houston. The crew of siblings appeared to be professionally successful. The oldest brother was a tax lawyer for ExxonMobil, the second-born a director of underground gas storage for Kinder Morgan, and the baby of the family a marketing intern at Aker Kvaerner.

Cyril was 13 when his mother died of breast cancer. He told me about her death with his head down, providing no details. His father was a mortgage broker and lived in north Houston. His grandparents on his father's side were French-speaking Louisiana Creoles. His parents met at the New Orleans Museum of Art, marrying only six months later. He found my parents' arranged-marriage story incomprehensible. "What if they don't get along?" he asked.

"Mine don't."

"Your parents won't like me, will they?"

"No."

He cooked sausage gumbo for me with the greenest okra served over white rice, salty pork jambalaya with celery and tomatoes that were incompletely diced, shrimp Creole with sautéed red, green, and yellow bell peppers, and chicken breast drenched in Tony Chachere's Creole seasoning. He pronounced it "seasonin'" instead of "seasoning" and could not believe I did not own a shaker of Chachere's.

I wanted to cook South Indian food for Cyril but did not know how. I did not even know the recipes, but they did not seem like recipes when I was growing up. I was embarrassed that I was so uncultured compared with him, with my freezer full of processed meals and a pantry stocked with boxed dinners containing the canned meat, mix, and pasta in a variety of flavors.

We dined out mostly. Cyril was highly educated about Houston dining, citing a distinguished dish from each restaurant—fast food or fine—along the congested streets we drove down. It was evident in his fluctuating mound of a belly, cheeks that bulged like safety nets for his eyes when he smiled, and the extra line below his chin. He ate out for almost every meal, repulsing me when mentioning his visits in one day to Whataburger, Luby's, and Jack in the Box.

I realized I was in love with him one Sunday evening over the #17—the Pupster Corn Dogs combo meal with tots and a coke—at James Coney Island. I sat to the side of him and had an epiphany, finding him gorgeous from a side view, unable to keep my eyes off him.

I met up with Cyril at Pappadeaux on our sixth date. It was one of my favorites, one of the many restaurants he introduced me to. I had never experienced such delicious seafood in my life, Cajun and Creole style creating the amazing taste. I vowed to never go to Red Lobster again.

Cyril was sitting at the bar watching sports when I arrived. He carried his glass, ice to the rim, of Grey Goose and Sprite to the table. His other hand was confidently placed on the small of my back. It was a first, a bold move, as if he believed I was finally his. He wore, on a 97-degree day, a striped long-sleeve Sean John shirt with confetti-like embroidery down the right side, untucked over Sean John jeans. Casual black-leather Kenneth Cole loafers were on his feet.

The waiter brought a plate of fried alligator, an appetizer that I did not know existed. I wasn't reluctant to try it but didn't expect to like it as much as I did.

"Aren't you glad you met me?" Cyril joked. "You're getting all these free dinners." He closed his eyes over his plate of gator.

"What are you doing?"

"I'm praying over my food."

"Oh yeah. I always forget you do that."

Waiters and waitresses breezed by, hands held high under trays of crawfish platters, po'boys, gumbos, dirty rice, and other specialties. Without looking at the menu, Cyril ordered the Louisiana seafood gumbo. I ordered the Cajun Combo: blackened catfish fillet served with dirty rice and shrimp Creole over white rice.

I missed catfish. It was a favorite that my mother would fry up in turmeric powder and other spices, tiny bones present, and serve with basmati rice and vegetables. I had no idea how to prepare it even though I had been in the kitchen with my mother while she cooked or had smelled the spices while hurrying to the garage to get in the car and escape to my friends.

"I miss my family." I looked down and swiftly back up at him. Krupa's death anniversary was in two days. I always thought about my family and what they were doing in the days before and how they didn't know their lives were going to suddenly change. Cyril was always comforting in the short time we had known each other, like an old friend's voice, shots of Everclear on a bad day, or a pan of chocolate fudge brownies after a breakup. Dinner was always an element of our time together. Conversation over food made me feel at home and more settled into my new surroundings.

I'd gone to dinner with my parents quite often in my hometown. I was drained one summer evening after a lingering and mind-numbing day of squashing bugs and hurling packages at Aviation Plus. I had worked extra hours in the hot sun. A day of overtime typically resulted in a Don Pablo's dinner on U.S. 31 with Jackie, Audrey, and Tom over margaritas and queso, but Audrey and Tom had to go to his nephew's third birthday/Euchre party and Jackie had to crochet a blanket for a newborn cousin. I went home to my parents.

"We're going to Fujiyama!" My father lighted up as he mentioned food. I assumed coupons were motivation behind the choice, an unspoken understanding. He folded up a thin flyer with ripped perforations and motioned for my mother to put it in her purse.

"Okay," I said unenthusiastically. I took off my sunglasses, the left ear frame scratching the deepest innerness of my right palm as I closed them. I shut the front door, unconsciously locking it, and ran my fingers over the indentation left on the bridge of my nose. I could feel the sweat between my bra and inside-out T-shirt. "I need to take a shower first." A Japanese beetle flew out of my hair as soon as the warm water bombarded me.

After scrunching my curls while drying them with a diffuser, I picked out a beaming yellow boat-neck top and dark jeans with brownish-yellow stitching—more prevalent on the back pockets—and laid the clothes on my bed.

I thumbed through the hangers of trampy tank tops, skirts of insufficient length, shirts with necklines that dived into my stomach, and pants that were drawn to my legs and behind. Mostly purchases from 3rd Street and on Kirkwood, the wardrobe appeared in college almost magically, as I did not realize I was changing. I wasn't consumed with the clothes around my parents but did not keep them a secret either, as they were all hanging side by side in my closet in their own section.

I was looking forward to the end of the month when I could return to IU and not be under surveillance. I could come home at 4 a.m., plastered, devour Mad Mushroom Cheesestix, and pass out in bed or on the bathroom floor. I wouldn't have to recite my agenda for the day or list off the people I was hanging out with.

I listened to my parents argue as I got dressed.

The yellow top made my heat-darkened skin look like the sunrise above the ocean. I colored my lips with a chocolaty-red lipstick and assaulted my hair with aerosol hair spray. Yellow flip-flops haphazardly supported my feet.

*

The hostess was short. A black pantsuit blasted against her pale Asian features. My parents and I gathered around the large hibachi grill. I sat between them. Two middle-aged Caucasian couples were already seated around the grill. They all appeared to be equal in size, buffet-style consumers with immense stomachs immersed in miserably tight shirts. I knew they would not need to-go boxes.

"I haven't had Chinese food in a long time."

"It's Jap food, Wanda."

I cringed at their redneck singsong conversation and the deep-purple stretch marks and butt crack Wanda flashed while bending over to retrieve something from her purse.

Flushed skin outlined Wanda's nose. Her hair was a squirrel-brown color with sporadic sprigs of blond and cut like a boy's. She wore rose-colored sweatpants with roomy hems and a light blue sweatshirt.

The performing chef cruised toward us with a cart of salmon, shrimp, beef, bean sprouts, tuna, asparagus, mushrooms, zucchini, mixed vegetables, noodles, spatulas, and glistening knives. His complexion was unlighted. Black hair seeped out of a tall white chef's hat. He wasn't Japanese. The chef made flirtatious eye contact with me. I looked away in embarrassment.

"Hello." His accent breathed a hint of familiarity, sending my parents and me into an attempted subtle discussion.

"I think he could be Indian," my mother said loudly.

He read through our order before firing up the grill. "What's *your* name, pretty girl?" he asked as flames rose. He looked at me, then back at the ingredients in front of him, gazing sleazily at me while chopping and slicing.

It was awkward being hit on in front of my parents. I glanced at them before answering, finding my mother and father oblivious to the chef's flirtatiousness. "Mala."

"Mala Mala," he sang, chopping more intensely on each "la." "How old are you?" He served beef on all plates.

"Twenty." I wondered why I was being so obedient to his requests. I dipped a piece of beef into sauce.

He winked at me as if he approved of my age. "What school do you go to?"

"IU."

Wanda and her friends had devoured the meat, practically panting like dogs, waiting for more.

"What's *your* name?" I leaned back with my arms crossed, left fingers tapping my right bicep.

"Jack."

I laughed at his "American" name. "What's your *real* name?"

"Amit. But I go by Jack." He perused me and my parents, hands moving inventively across the cuts of meat and fish. "Are you Indian?"

"Yes, we are Indian," my father said. "And you?"

"I'm from Indonesia. I always watch Indian movies though. Bollywood!" He cuddled the uncooked shrimp with one hand and flicked his fingers out four times on the hibachi, the shrimp landing side by side. He executed the tails, throwing them behind his back. He caught most of them in his hat but one nailed a young man in the head. "She did it!" He aggressively pointed at me.

The young man picked up the tail, stood, and flung it at me. He looked like the stereotypical high school football player who was prom king, dated every cheerleader, and gave math and science nerds wedgies. His white skin was tan, and his biceps were contained by a red Ball State T-shirt.

I ducked, the tail landing on the floor. "You actually thought that *I* threw it?"

He shrugged and sat back down in his chair.

"Throw one of the tails in my hat, pretty girl," teased Jack. "If you miss, then I want you to do an Indian dance for me." He rocked his hips back and forth.

I laughed in his face. "I don't know any." I aimed for his tall, hollow hat.

Jack jumped out of the way so I would miss the hat. "Ha!" he screamed. "You have to do an Indian dance for me!"

I refused to dance.

"Come on, pretty girl." He jerked his hips back and forth slowly behind the hibachi and shot his arms to the side, looking at them with each hip movement. "Come on, pretty girl." He gave up, bowing instead for completing his job.

Everyone clapped for him. I joined in late, half-clapping, taking in the weirdness of the experience.

"Thank you." He bowed again and walked away, pushing the culinary cart. Then he turned back and smiled flirtatiously at me.

"This food is really salty," said my father. He noticed the waitress walk by. "Oh, excuse me, excuse me. I have a coupon."

"The cook seemed to really like you," said Wanda. "He gave you a lot of food."

I smiled at her with my lips closed tightly.

"So, are you guys visiting America?" asked her companion. His round eyeglasses were crooked across his face, throwing his bald head off center. His belly sloped over a brown leather belt in a position that would not have changed if he stood up. Plumpish arms oozed out of a short-sleeve red, black, and tan plaid shirt. "How do you like it here? It must be so different."

My father chuckled a little. "No, I've been in the U.S. for over *30* years."

He squinted at my father, eyebrows furrowed in confusion. "But I thought you said you were Indian? How could you have been in *this* country for over 30 years?"

Wanda suddenly turned to us. "There's a guy that works at the gas station by my house and he's Indian. Do you know him? He wears one of those turbans. He might be Muslin."

I stared at them, speechless.

"Muslim, you mean," corrected my father. "No, we don't know him."

"*Really*? But he's *Indian*," said Wanda. "Are you Muslim?"

"Catholic."

*

I had heard of bread pudding but had never tasted it before. I burped it up along with the Cajun Combo as Cyril drove to Midtown. "I'm taking you to a surprise place. You are going to love it."

My Pappadeaux to-go box was in the backseat of his Ford F-350 King Ranch, a truck that seemed as common as the word "y'all" in Houston. 100 Club membership decals were on the back windshield. It was the first time that I was a passenger in his vehicle.

"Wow, you actually got in the truck with me," he joked.

I said a prayer to myself that Cyril was not a serial killer. I threw out guesses about our destination, pressuring him to budge.

Cyril grinned instead, guarding the surprise.

We entered a building with no sign. "What is this place?" I asked.

"They play your … your music," said Cyril, "'80s rock."

"Omigod! No way!" I stopped to listen to the music. *Sister Christian* was blaring as we entered.

"You know this one," I said to Cyril as if he would sing along. I belted it out, waiting for him to join in.

"I've never heard this song before." He shrugged.

"It's Night Ranger!" I rolled my eyes. I held his hand as we walked through the bar. It was a mixed-age crowd. I was surprised, expecting to see only people in their late thirties and forties.

We kissed a little throughout the night on the zebra-print couches, against the multicolored walls and poster-

110

size photos of '80s rock heroes, on the roof under the lights overlooking downtown, and on the winding staircase.

"I like how you don't wear makeup."

I didn't tell him I was wearing lipstick, foundation, eye shadow, powder, and mascara.

"I know another bar that you will like," he said. "It's on Westheimer."

"What *isn't* on Westheimer?" I slurred.

"We have to come here every weekend," I said. "I love this place."

"Okay, fan*tast*ic."

I talked about the '80s rock bar during the entire drive to Westheimer and Fountain View. The valets slid into Bentleys and expensive Mercedes in the parking lot of the next bar as if they owned them. It was the first time I had seen a Bentley. The parking lot was filled with couples, groups, singles, men entering the bar alone, and two Hummerzine limos parked in front.

"Indiana?" The bouncer gave back my ID and opened the door for us. He was huge with a purposely bald head. Muscles busted out of black short sleeves. There was a tattoo on his left bicep that I did not have time to study but caught an outline of the Texas Panhandle. "Did you live on a farm?"

The bar was an eclectic place, mostly brown people in an enforced code of dress shirts, flawless hair, perfectly pushed up breasts, and open-toe stilettos. Indian- and Arabic-inspired music and different languages were heard throughout. I penetrated a lighted bar of darkness that was suddenly lined with a spark of lighted cigarettes. It was an intimate setting, a coffee lounge as well with black bar stools at eloquent, sharp, shiny tables. No cultural bar existed in my hometown, and I viewed such a lounge in a simple strip center as another advantage of my big move.

A table of Indian men stared at us as we sat down at the bar. I ordered a Bud Light. Cyril found it amusing that I ordered beer when we went out instead of fruity martinis and margaritas. He carried a glass of Grey Goose and Sprite, his arm around my waist, as we entered the cozy dance floor in the next room. The back wall was outlined in couches in the seclusion of the room. Along the sides were small tables with plush red chairs. Contemporary impressions circled into the center of the floor, leaving the outsides encased in stylish lines. Bhangra beats blasted. Indians were on the dance floor. I sneakily checked out a couple of Indian guys, wishing Cyril wasn't there so I could approach the men I envisioned myself to be with. There was a surplus of Malayalees in Houston, and I was convinced that one of them was my future husband.

Cyril squeezed his arms around my waist and kissed my face and neck. "You are so gorgeous. I really like you. I've never met anyone like you."

I felt guilty. I sat on a bar stool with my beer.

Cyril slowly rubbed my back as he stood to my side. "Your legs are thick."

"What?" I scowled.

"You're thick."

I looked away from Cyril, watching the bartender make a mocha, offended that he'd called me fat.

"What did I say?" Cyril asked. "You know, you're little but you still got some meat on you."

"I'm not thick."

"That's sexy to us."

"Oh."

"I didn't mean to offend you. I was complimenting you."

*

Cyril had no furniture in his two-bedroom condo, creating a space beyond the actual square footage. Two beige patio chairs were in front of a big-screen television. Next to the TV, on the floor, was an organized stack of DVDs and Lil Wayne, Slim Thug, Mike Jones, Bun B, Paul Wall, and Al Green CDs.

I slipped off burnt chestnut-colored kitten heels, bringing me to my honest height. I looked down at the three thin strands of leather that crisscrossed over the top and remembered when I bought them on clearance at Parisian while on the clock at Midwest Bank. They were a $6^{1/2}$ because Parisian was out of my size, 6. It was one of my many depression purchases that I *had* to have. I felt another surge of happiness that Midwest Bank was a thing of the past.

I was a little nervous to be with him in his place during what would be a night of expectations in most dating lives. It was a night that, for me, would illustrate my lack of experience with men. I said another quick prayer that Cyril wasn't a serial killer. The thought never would've crossed my mind if he were Indian.

He brought in a matching chair from the patio and put it in front of the TV. "I just rented *Ocean's Twelve*. Wanna watch that?"

I told him I had seen the first one and liked it. I was certain we would not make it to the end of the film. I sat down in one of the chairs.

"What's your favorite movie?" he asked as he rounded the bar into the pristine kitchen. His untucked shirt looked somewhat sloppy.

"*Wayne's World*."

He thrust his lips to the side in uncertainty. "Never heard of it."

"Mike Myers. Dana Carvey. They're these too rock junkies and they have this cable access show."

"Hmm. Don't think I know it." Cyril poured two glasses of red wine. A drop trickled down the side of the bottle. He didn't wipe it off.

"You have a really clean kitchen."

"I have a maid."

I couldn't imagine hiring a maid, as I regarded housecleaning as exercise. "Why do you have a maid?"

"I have allergies," he said defensively. "I need my place to be really clean."

He lay on his side and beamed up at me with a smile that concealed his teeth.

I clanked my teeth on the glass as I looked down at Cyril. I was thoroughly intoxicated from the night but diligently sipped the wine. I finished off the glass, tilting my head completely back until the glass looked empty. I put it down, watching remnants trickle to the center in a small puddle.

He rose from the floor and joined me in the beige outdoor chairs. He leaned in and kissed me.

I didn't let it continue, as I pretended to focus on the movie.

Cyril farted. He glanced at me in mortification through the corner of his pale-brown eye.

I didn't acknowledge the bodily function that was so normal yet such a societal taboo. I ignored it for him and pretended to watch the movie. "Is that a *gun*?" I stood up to look at the shotgun on the shelf above the bar.

"Yeah," he said nonchalantly.

"Why do you have that?" I sat slowly with my eyes fixated on the gun. "Do you go hunting?"

"No." He laughed. "So guns aren't popular in Indiana, huh? Y'all aren't armed? This is Texas. Everybody's got a gun." Cyril kissed my lips again, more expressively.

I gave in.

He pulled me slowly out of the chair.

I felt a flash of unstableness as he lowered me to the carpeted floor, his lips still on mine. I realized that my bra hooks had been undone but couldn't recall when it had happened.

Cyril slid the strapless bra off under my red off-the-shoulder top.

I took my shirt off. I wrapped my jean-covered legs around him. It had been years since I'd been half-naked with anyone.

He swirled his tongue around and into my nipples, concretizing them.

I called out softly in fulfillment by such minor stimulation. "Oh Cyril. Oh Cyril."

His fingers fumbled with the buttons on my jeans.

"No," I said softly.

He lifted me up and took my hands in his, causing them to look smaller. Cyril faced me as he led me into the bedroom, smiling. He laid me down on a makeshift bed, crisp white sheets on the floor with two tough pillows in mismatched cases and a thin bedspread with ruptured stitching.

"Kiss my neck." I held his head in my arms. "There's something under my pillow." I lifted it up. "Omigod! There's a gun under my head!"

"It's okay." Cyril pushed the gun away onto the beige carpet. "There's no clip in it."

I frowned. I had no idea what that meant.

"Tell me what you like."

I didn't know what to tell him.

Cyril went for my jeans again. His hands gently probed my hips. He stopped and looked up at me for approval.

I pushed a curly hair-spray-deprived sprig of hair off my forehead and scooted my jeans slightly off my hips to give him permission. The inside of the button was surprisingly cold against the small roll of my lower stomach.

He pulled the jeans completely off, along with my white microfiber panties, his nail beds swabbing the outermost slices of my calves.

I wished I'd worn sexier underwear but had convinced myself while getting dressed that I wasn't going home with him and chose a plain white pair instead. I didn't want to waste a pair of lacies on a night alone, especially since I had to clean my clothes in a group laundry room in my apartment complex and it cost $1 to wash and $1.50 to dry.

I was completely natural. I had never been completely naked with a man before. I was self-conscious, all nerves aroused. I noticed that his shirt and jeans were off. I acknowledged his velvety-rough, light skin against mine and his hairless chest. His stomach made mine look small.

"You're body's so smooth," he hummed.

I caught a matchless scent of his scalp, a natural aroma unlike hair products. It was dispersed across his pillows and scattered vigorously throughout my body. I thought Cyril was inside me but wasn't sure. "Is it *in* me?" I panicked. I didn't plan on losing my virginity that night or to him. I got lucky. Cyril had a Texas-size penis that wouldn't go in.

"I'm trying," he whispered. "Put it in."

I looked him straight in the eyes. "I've … never … had sex before."

Cyril let out a laugh of shock, not ridicule, as he rolled onto his back. "Really? You are so hot. You are so beautiful. I really can't believe it." He rolled onto his side. Cyril looked at me, eyes latching onto my eyes, descending to my lips, breasts and below my abdomen, then back up to my face. "I just can't believe it." He kissed the light hairs between my breasts that I usually waxed. "Why?"

"I don't know." And I didn't know. I was not waiting for marriage. I assumed I'd have sex in high school but never did. Then I thought for sure I'd have sex in college but never did. I wasn't a happy virgin. Virginity was an inconvenience, a pain, a hassle. "I guess I just haven't gotten around to doing it yet."

Cyril put his arm over my stomach.

I looked across his forearm. Thin dark hairs cluttered his mass of skin.

He laid back and took me in his arms as we shared a tough pillow, his southern accent bulky like an overstuffed bag of groceries. "I can't believe it."

"I'm a 23-year-old virgin," I said. "I'm a rare find. Like an Acura Vigor."

CHAPTER 8

I hung up the phone. Miss Lopez wanted to see me. I suspected it was about the great proofreading I did on the company's new promotional piece. I'd been unaware of Miss Lopez's presence in the office and wondered why she was even there.

I stared at Theresa, failing to get her attention, while sauntering past a group of accountants on the way to Miss Lopez's office. Theresa's eyes were glued to the screen, mouth moving as she probably read about the latest restaurant food poisoning, produce scare, heiress/celeb wannabe sex tape, celebrity divorce, or hottest arrivals at Louis Vuitton.

I knew I would have an inbox of e-mails from Theresa, threatening me with bad luck for life if I forwarded them to 0 people, bad luck for 50 years if I sent them to 1-10 people, bad luck for 25 years if I sent them to 11-15 people, and good luck for life if I contacted 20 or more.

Amy was sitting across from Miss Lopez in one of the guest chairs. She drilled the floor with eyes that seemed to pop more when her hair was down instead of half-up. She offered one uncomfortable smile.

Miss Lopez motioned for me to sit down. I landed in the chair, hand sloping down the armrest, incapable of keeping my eyes off Miss Lopez. She was seldom in the office, frequently partaking in trips out of the country that never seemed to be work-related. If in the office, she arrived late and ended the day early. On these days, Miss Lopez's voice rippled in monotone throughout the office, seeping into my and Amy's open doors. I kept my head down in proofreader's marks or other projects, eyes cunningly up, pretending not to watch Miss Lopez pass my open door while the FedEx guy slipped me his phone number or Post-it notes fell off my computer screen. I did not know how to converse with someone so disconnected, closed, and removed.

Miss Lopez's nostrils looked like collided eggs centered on colored cheekbones of blushing tea roses. Her hair was dripping red as if it were right off the cover of a hair-dye package. It was slicked back into a ponytail, with a few wisps biting the back of her neck. Brown roots were revealed. Her eyes were like pools of creamed spinach, enhanced by crispy lashes coated in black mascara, olive-colored eye shadow, proficiently smudged black eye liner, and rimless glasses. Stenciled eyebrows arched like rainbows above the lenses.

I sensed that Miss Lopez had aged well, sustaining her attractiveness with heavy makeup and Pilates.

"We're going to have to let you go," Miss Lopez uttered rapidly in a humdrum tone. Her hand loosely grasped a Starbucks cup with a lid that was smacked with maple syrup-colored lip imprints. A pinky with dusky fingernail polish wavered from the base.

I heard the rushed words, a verbal slap across the face, an unexpected, devastating blow to my newfound ego. "What?" I clenched my jaw. My cheeks burned up into my eyes. I had moved to Houston to *find* a job. I watched Miss Lopez casually continue on, barely noticing her lips moving and hearing no words from her mouth. Then I caught the words "bad" and "financial" as Miss Lopez talked with her hands in structured calculations.

Miss Lopez handed me a check for my unused vacation days and a check for the current week and one extra pay period. "Your insurance will continue for one more month."

I looked to Amy for answers, but she failed to raise her head and remained mute. "But … ," I stammered.

"We'll have to cut back on your department to save money," said Miss Lopez as if she were saving me from finishing what could've been an embarrassing remark. "Business is bad. I'll have to take over your job."

I snickered at the idea of Miss Lopez in the office regularly. I looked at the calendar on her desk. The date displayed was from two months ago. I stood insecurely, my arms awkward as if they were from another body, catching the pristine purity of Miss Lopez's desk. The computer keyboard still had its protective covering, the mouse was unplugged, and the pump of a bottle of hand sanitizer was unreleased.

"We hope to hire you back once business is good again." Miss Lopez handed me unemployment info. "Call them right away so you can start receiving your checks."

"What?"

"Your unemployment checks. They'll send me a form and I sign it as proof of unemployment. You can do it now if you want, but I'm sure you don't feel like sticking around here." Miss Lopez took a sip from her coffee cup. She put her hand on her keys, singling out the BMW key as if she were getting ready to leave and had come in for the sole task of letting me go from her failing company.

Amy followed me back to my office. "I need to get your passwords before you leave."

I didn't look at Theresa this time. I couldn't talk for fear of tears.

Amy stood inside my office near the door as I put my lip balm and 3.5-ounce bottle of lotion in my purse. The bottle had been refilled upon becoming empty, contents mismatched with the faded label.

"You don't have much stuff," Amy remarked lightheartedly.

I ignored her, wishing she would leave. I wanted to be alone to register the news.

Amy continued chatting, in contrast with her ghostlike presence in Miss Lopez's office. "It really sucks when we find good people like you and we have to let them go."

I rolled my eyes as I wrote my passwords on a sticky note. I wished Amy would shut up. I felt dramatic as I turned over papers on my desk and glanced around when I knew that one tube of lip balm and a 3.5-ounce bottle of lotion were my only belongings.

Amy, holding the sticky note with my password, presented a barrier between me and the door.

"Move," I demanded, naturally. I accidentally rammed Amy's shoulder as I exited, noting two stacks of computer paper on the receptionist's desk. She had been let go a few weeks before.

"If you ever need a recommendation ... "

My first Texas job was history. I didn't hear the rest of Amy's parting words. I was out the door with my purse over my right shoulder.

*

"It's okay, Mala. It's just a job. You'll find something else. Things aren't that bad. This is Houston. This is a big city." I gave myself a pep talk on the drive home. It was a chameleon-like version of the pep talk that I'd given myself in my hometown after each job rejection. I was calm. I was not looking forward to the realization that would hit me later.

I heard a gun-store ad and turned it up as soon as the man's deep southern drawl kicked in. "Don't let that robber get away. You don't need to call the cops."

The sky poured down sluggish, saggy raindrops that spread on the windshield like pyrotechnics. A heavy shower developed, but I did not reduce the speed of the Vigor. I pulled into the median to turn left, waited for the few cars to pass, and entered the lane. I heard screeching tires and a loud crash as a silver car flashed before my eyes and swerved. "Oh shit! Shit! Shit!" We both pulled into the turn lane. I scrutinized the car, trying to figure out what I hit. "Oh fuck!" I screamed as I realized it was an Aston Martin convertible. "Fuck!"

A blond woman gingerly surfaced from the car, an umbrella expanding precisely with the opening of the door. She bent to inspect the damage and then walked toward me. Big breasts bounced out of a low-cut top. Her waist was small but would've looked smaller if she wore a looser top. Jeans were skintight, with slender pockets on the thighs.

"I'm sorry," I said as I stepped out of the Vigor with no umbrella in hand. "I just did *not* see the car." I looked at the left side of the bumper. It was slightly pushed in, but the headlight was still intact. The regal plum-pearl paint was chipped, creating fragments of white in areas. My precious Vigor had never been wrecked before.

I had been in only one other car accident. It was in Indianapolis on the 4th of July. I was 16 and leaving Hardee's, my first job, in my mother's Lexus. My favorite Hardee's breakfast item was Cinnamon N' Raisin Biscuits with smooth icing topping. I would eat two each morning shift I worked and boxed some extras to bring home for the family. I turned right on Stop 11 and passed Meridian Middle

School with a box of biscuits in the passenger seat. I shot forward. The seat belt pressed me back. The box of biscuits smashed into the floor mat along with my *Metal Health* CD. I gasped as I heard the crashing sound. The man in the blue Ford Ltd. walked up to my side. He wore a Hawaiian shirt that sloped over his belly and khaki shorts, with tall black socks and black sneakers. The hair on his legs weaved a quilt on faint skin. "Are you okay? Sorry about that."

I looked down on the smiling Hardee's star on the left breast of my shirt. My uniform top carried a grease stain in the bottom corner. My hair felt free, as if the impact of the accident had loosened my stubby ponytail.

He stepped back as I opened the door. "I'm so sorry."

The rear of the Lexus was completely smashed in.

"I'm more concerned that you're okay. It's more important than the vehicle."

"I'm fine," I said, feeling more and more annoyed that the car was wrecked. I looked back at the holdup of white people in their cars created by the accident.

"Are you Indian? India?"

"Yeah." I was caught off guard by the subject change and the correctness of his ethnic guess.

"That's okay," he said reassuringly, sticking his hands in his pockets. "There's nothing wrong with that."

"Wrong with *what*?"

"With being Indian."

"I didn't say there *was*," I snapped.

"Indians in Indiana," he joked as if I hadn't heard that one before. "Indians in Indiana."

"You know how I can tell?" He looked down at me through bifocals. His index finger landed at the cartilage in the tip of his nose and met the glasses as they slid down.

"Tell *what*?"

"That you're Indian."

"By *looking* at me," I said sarcastically.

"By that cross around your neck."

My fingers rushed to the gold crucifix. It was 22K gold, purchased at Bhima Jewelers in Ernakulam, with feminine corners and inner loops of gold that looked like grids of lace.

Cars drove around the accident. Passengers gawked at us.

I was hushed, confused by the comment. The cross typically baffled people, as they believed that Indians could be only Hindu or Muslim, unaware of the small percentage of Indian Christians. "This cross has nothing to do with me being Indian." My pinky nail cut into the grooves of the necklace. "I wear this cross because I am a Christian."

"Oh." He shrugged enthusiastically. "I can also tell because of the Lexus. You Indians are always rich. Your dad's probably a doctor. Or an engineer. Or owns a business."

I looked away.

"You know, I'm going to be speaking in India soon, and I've been trying to get things together for my trip. I'm having some real problems with the Indian consulate in Chicago. They don't seem to want to help me or answer my questions. Do you happen to know anyone that works there?"

I was silent, narrowing my eyes. "No."

"Oh, okay. Well there's a lady that I work with who is from Sri Lanka."

*

The Aston Martin driver was, to my amazement, nice and suggested that we get into her car to exchange insurance information. "It is raining too hard out here," she said. "It's easy to get in a car accident. It will probably flood."

I couldn't help but stick my head into the backseat of the Aston Martin. I had never seen one before. Red leather interior accentuated the flawless seat stitching. I subtly skimmed the console, stereo, steering wheel, and air vents with my eyes only, keeping my head still. A Gucci charm hung from the rearview mirror. Gucci shades with smudged lenses peered out of the console.

"I need to call my husband," she said through unnatural-looking, collagen-stuffed lips. "My husband bought me an Aston Martin for my birthday. I didn't like the color, so I exchanged it for this one."

I could hear a loud man through the line on the verge of yelling.

"I'll call the cops. I'm sorry, honey," she mumbled. "It's a young girl." She closed her cell phone. "I need to call the cops to file a police report."

I had heard that no one calls the cops in Houston for car accidents and that tickets were written. I really couldn't afford it. "Do you *have* to call the cops?" I begged.

"I'm sorry, girl. I have to. My husband wants me to get a police report. And we just got in a fight this morning. I want to get a breast reduction but he won't let me. I have implants right now."

"The cops don't come," I said, ignoring her last statement. I had heard from Houstonians that police officers were sometimes a no-show. "I'll get a ticket."

"You might get a ticket, but I won't have a home and I live in *River* Oaks." She dialed up the Aston Martin and explained the situation. She opened a large, sand-colored signature Gucci tote with double straps. She pulled open the straps and then stopped, holding up her hands. "I'm still shaking."

"Yeah, me too," I lied. I ogled her wedding ring. It was blinding, emerald-cut, set in platinum.

She pulled out a white pen with a Gucci-engraved clip and copied my insurance information.

"Uh, just to let you know, your insurance card is expired," I said. "They send you the new one in the mail. You may have thought that it was junk mail." Her name was Whitney Saunders and her husband's name was Austin. I stopped in midwriting when I noticed that the cars listed were three Dodge trucks ranging from 1998 to 2001 and the Aston Martin, the only high-end vehicle. Twenty minutes had passed. There was no sign of the police. "I guess they're not coming."

"I have a girlfriend that lives on this street," she said as she continued copying my insurance information. "You live right by my friend." Whitney dialed again and the operator said the cops would be there shortly. "We're in an Aston Martin," she said as if it would speed the cops up.

"I'm going back to my car."

Whitney seemed apprehensive, as if I would drive away from the scene.

I looked back at the Aston Martin as I walked to the Vigor. I called my insurance agent to report the accident. I felt the agent flinch through the phone.

"Oooh," she said. "Wow. Holy … "

I sighed.

"Car accidents happen as often as crawfish boils around here," said the agent.

A cop car pulled up within five minutes of Whitney's second call. I didn't particularly care for blue-collar types in uniform, but the side mirror revealed that he was attractive. I wondered if what I heard was true—could I cry to get out of a ticket? Would he ask me for oral sex? I rolled my window down at the exact moment he bent down at the door.

"Hello, ma'am. Are you all right?"

I nodded innocently as I scanned his features. I thought he could be Indian, but law enforcement was never Indian. He was the best-looking cop I had ever seen. His hair was black, long and gelled messily back over his head as if it had no destination. He was flawlessly bulky, with a faint mustache and goatee. Dimples emerged without a smile. Dark globular eyes took the focus away from a sea of four cocoa-colored, dotted birthmarks curving from his temple. He bent to assess the damage and then walked over to Whitney. He returned with a completed accident-information form. Whitney's address and phone number were on the form, along with the vehicle make and model and insurance company. The blank for place of employment had a line drawn through it. I skipped down to the name of the officer: J. Patel. I wondered how his parents reacted when he decided to go into law enforcement. I was curious about *their* occupations.

"I'll have to give you a ticket."

"How much is it?" I asked, somewhat performing the worry in my voice, collapsing my shoulders.

He opened his mouth and then shut it as he filled out the report. "And where do you work?"

"I just got laid off about 30 minutes ago." I felt the tears in my eyes as his face looked blurry for a split-second.

He looked up sharply, dropping his pen. "Oh, I'm sorry." He paused. "I won't give you a ticket. Phone number?"

"317—"

"317?" He interrupted. "Do you mean 713?"

"No, 317."

"And where's that?"

"Indianapolis. Indiana. I just moved here."

He looked at me sympathetically. "Well, welcome to Houston."

I parked the Vigor in the usual covered spot at my apartment complex. I was relieved to be home. Simply standing in the parking lot put me at ease. I shut the car door, noticing what I thought at first to be a squirrel a few feet in front of me. Then I spotted its white cottontail. I stopped dead in my tracks and stared at the brown rabbit in the grass. It seemed to be staring back—strong eye contact, a connection. It ran at me, passing my feet. I turned to watch it run away.

CHAPTER 9

"Hi, Jim. This is Mala Thomas and I wanted to follow up with you in regards to the editorial position." I left my information, voicing the 317 phone number twice for a more thorough message. "Thanks, Jim."

I closed my cell phone with one hand, grasping it tightly in frustration, the skin under my nails pink and pinched. I rolled over on Cyril's couch, elbow jutting over the edge of the cushion and eyelashes brushing against the shamrock-green accent pillow. I faced the big-screen TV. I reached into an open box of chocolates on the coffee table from Cyril, but there was no candy left in the tray, just brown wrappers. Things were rocky between us, but there I was—on *his* new couch, watching *his* TV, and eating *his* food. And I'd been wearing the same pajamas—a white tank with a turmeric powder stain above my right breast and white drawstring shorts covered in mini-shapes of Texas—for five days. I yelled, "It's a couch," before sitting on it every time. I was wound up about a conventional piece of furniture that I did not have in my studio.

It had been three months since my layoff and no one was calling me with a job offer. I was picky, applying only for job openings I was truly interested in. I didn't drive all the way to Houston to work a dead-end job.

I wasn't too concerned about money when I received my first unemployment check for lounging around on the couch. It was $896.80. "Holy shit!" I shouted when I saw the amount, as if there were people in the room who would respond to my joy. The checks were a stress reliever. I also had the stash I put away for emergencies. I could take my time finding the job I really wanted.

I dreaded the job-searching and interviewing. The thought of spending hours on the Internet and preparing my résumé made me want to apply for a mail-order dark-skin doctor husband from Kerala to pay my bills so I never had to work again. The thought of having to respond articulately to the classic interview questions made me want to apply for welfare.

"Tell me about yourself."

"If you were a tree, what tree would you be?"

"Tell me about your proudest accomplishment."

"What are your strengths?"

"What are your weaknesses?"

"How do you deal with difficult people?"

"How would your last boss describe you?"

"Do you prefer to work alone or in groups?"

"How do you handle stress?"

"Describe your ideal working environment?"

"Do you like working in a team or independently?"

"Where do you see yourself five years from now? Ten years from now?"

I had been on a couple of interviews since the layoff. The most recent was conducted by a newspaper editor who'd attended the Indy 500 every year with his buddies when he was a college boy at Texas Tech. He didn't believe my story of packing up and leaving for better job opportunities. "No one just packs up and leaves their life," he said. "Tell me why you really moved to Houston."

I volunteered at a few places to pass the time. I helped unemployed people use the Internet to find jobs—without telling them I was unemployed myself, served food in a kitchen for a support group for kids who'd lost siblings or parents, and assisted with an arts and crafts class at a women's shelter. I watched *Wayne's World*, online '80s rock videos, and memorized daytime television schedules. I also caught up on my favorite soap opera, *The Young and the Restless*. Victor Newman was up to his old tricks, and Phyllis Abbott and Nick Newman were having an affair. I hoped Sheila would come back from the dead before I had to go back to the 9-to-5 grind.

I looked through old cards, envelopes discarded, from friends and family. The latest were goodbye cards, but I went all the way back to birthday cards dated on my seventh birthday from Audrey and Jackie and my parents. I had thrown away cards from friends I had fazed out over the years but never tossed any cards from my family and Audrey and Jackie.

I kept my soft drinks cold in an Indianapolis Colts coozie and drank water from a Hoosiers travel mug while snacking out of Cyril's fridge and pantry. I preferred his deli cheese slices to my value cheese that didn't melt and his Mrs. Baird's Honey 7 Grain Recipe bread to my perfectly square slices of value bread.

I abandoned my studio apartment for days, preferring Cyril's big screen over my black, 13-inch TV/DVD combo. I used its packaging as a TV stand and covered the box with a purple sheet, creating the illusion that the TV was on a small table. I loved the Texas-themed commercials: Dairy Queen—"That's what I like about Texas"; Luby's—"Tastes like Texas, feels like home"; Ford—"Ford is the Best in Texas." I also looked forward to Marvin Zindler's investigative reporting on Houston restaurants.

I favored Cyril's new king-size pillow-top mattress over my used bed that was comforted by a mattress pad and drenched with disinfectant. I did miss using my EZ-TAG, referring to it as the pass to the VIP lanes on the toll roads, while I lived like a hermit in Cyril's home and saved money on gas.

Even though I was financially making it without a job, I was depressed about being unemployed. I hoped my money would not run out, forcing me to work a dead-end job. My biggest fear was making money at a place like Midwest Bank again. I wondered what employment opportunity could possibly be out there for me next.

I called Audrey, Jackie, and Sara every day to vent about my unemployment situation, an injustice to my big move and pursuit of adventure and opportunity. I kept my unemployment a secret from my parents, lying to them every week when they asked about work and new things happening in my life. "Not much is going on," I would reply. It wasn't entirely untrue.

And to top off my unemployment predicament, Austin Saunders called me every day threatening to sue. "This is Austin Saunders, the owner of the Aston Martin that you *ran* into. You need to call me immediately." According to the insurance company, Saunders was trying to collect his deductible from me. I saved each message just in case. His tone became nastier and nastier with each voice mail. "We don't want to take this to court. I get free litigation." He cackled. "You don't want to do that. You don't want to go downtown. The insurance company laughed at me. Well, you know what? I always get the *last* laugh."

I found each message amusing. I didn't understand why Saunders would think I would return the phone calls when he left such obnoxious, cocky messages. I could tell I was overtaking his life, consuming him, hoarding his cell-phone minutes, and distracting him during his work commute. It was pathetic. I felt sorry for his Gucci-toting, plastic surgery-infested wife. He was definitely a wife-beater. All the Gucci in the world would not be enough for me to settle for a man like Austin Saunders. He finally gave up after 16 rude voice-mail messages.

*

"Did you apply to *any* jobs today?" Cyril was supportive and positive when I had crying fits about the layoff or was disappointed by a job interview, but he became more and more agitated when he came home for lunch and found me pajama-clad on his couch. "Churrascos is hiring waitresses."

I was appalled. "I didn't drive *all* the way down to Houston to work a dead-end job, Cyril." I rolled my eyes at him. "I am way too sexy to be working as a waitress. I'll pretend that you did not just say that to me."

"Okay, fan*tas*tic." He undid his $70 tie. I had seen the receipt on his kitchen counter. The stripes were of silver grids outlined in taupe. It lay like a horseshoe unevenly around his neck, the left end side touching his stomach. All of Cyril's ties were from Bachrach.

When we first started dating, I looked through his closet and other places, usually when he was in the shower but sometimes when he was in another room. His closet was lined with white hangers only of Sean John and Bachrach suits, dress shirts with white French cuffs, Sean John casual wear, and Bachrach ties and belts. Also in the closet were Kenneth Cole dress and casual shoes, bags of dry-cleaned clothes, and white-on-white low and mid Nike Air Force 1's. There was also a cowboy hat on the top shelf and a brown leather belt with a buckle in the shape of Texas. He said the hat and belt were part of his attire for networking events at the rodeo.

Cyril worked until the sun had been down for hours. Loosening his tie for an hour and half was a form of relaxation, akin to getting a full eight hours of sleep or watching an entire Texans game in shorts and a T-shirt. He had a motivated, career-driven quality to which I was attracted yet indifferent. He started his own consulting firm while staying on at EnergyForce full time.

I hated that his phone rang during our time together. I'd get frustrated or hurt when he canceled our dates or brought me along to last-minute business-dinner meetings with southern-accented men in conformist suits with wives or girlfriends who filed their fingernails with their eyes.

I had ended our relationship several times, deleting his number from my phone each time we got into an argument but later realizing I did want him after he convinced me that we were meant to be. I caved each time, lacking the energy to stand my ground against his quick defense and persuasive arguments. I'd psych myself up to end the relationship but wuss out in the moment.

"We need to talk," I began.

"This is Cyril. How may I assist you?" He looked up at me and gestured with his index finger to wait a minute. "I'm open on the weekend by appointment only."

I peeled myself off the couch to go home, with no desire to have lunch with him or wait on him. "I have an interview tomorrow."

*

After college graduation, I was strict about my appearance for interviews. I always wore my Ann Taylor suit. The fabric was an unspoiled gray with light blue pins of color that only

134

I noticed. I brought out the color by wearing a crisp, light blue, collared shirt under the jacket. The skirt was past my knees and coordinated with low, black, chunky closed-toe heels.

My mother purchased the suit for me during junior year for a summer media internship. I loved the suit. It was the first time I had ever felt business-like and physically professional. Over the years, my opinion changed into a strong conviction that the suit was overrated. It also no longer fit.

Petroleum Insight had an opening for a writer. I applied for the job, positive I wouldn't get it. I knew nothing about oil and gas except that my new city was recognized around the world for its energy industry.

I had interviewed at about 30 publications after graduation. No one wanted me. One of them was a health magazine in Indianapolis located in The Pyramids. It was about five months after graduation. I put on sheer, tan, irritating pantyhose, the Ann Taylor suit, the collared shirt, and the closed-toe heels. I curled my lashes, counting to a specific predetermined number before releasing the curler, and applied only two strokes of deep black mascara. I rolled lip balm from border to border of my mouth. I checked my curls three times before leaving the bathroom.

Every job-interview pamphlet from career centers, occupational books from stores, and online job sources advised to keep appearances simple to guarantee success in securing a job.

Daniel Behr was president of the publishing company. It owned a quarterly health magazine focusing on topics such as diabetes, health care, medication, and fitness. I arrived 15 minutes early for the interview, as I did for every interview, following the advice from the career sources. I read over the five staff names as I waited in his office and found a typo in the table of contents. It was a trendy work space, with magazine covers framed on the walls in wooden display boxes. Two identical floor lamps were in opposite corners of the room with cream shades that carried a pattern with no pattern and squiggly-shaped bases. An ivory sofa against the wall appeared to be brand new and uncomfortable, with steel legs and inflexible cushions with gold zippers.

I decided, as Daniel walked in, that he was a good-looking older gentleman. He was physically fit, tall with dark hair, dark eyes, and a plush white complexion of clarity.

He explained that he'd broken all the records at Martinsville High School and attended IU on a swimming scholarship. "I graduated from the Kelley School of Business. I had a lot of good times there."

"Yes, me too," I said in a professional tone, my back as straight as a paddleboard, wondering when he was going to start the interview.

"Are you Indian?" He touched a plaque on his desk as if he were trying to get me to look or ask about it.

"Yes." I found it odd that he was asking illegal questions and not discussing the position.

"My sister-in-law is Pocahontas," he said lightheartedly. "She has Cherokee in her blood." He smiled. "Ravi over there is Indian, too. I think he's Cherokee, too."

I leaned back and turned my head to the side, frozen in position as I looked at Ravi in his office. He had his right foot propped on his left knee, with about an inch of light brown skin exposed above a tan dress sock. There were six Starbucks cups on his desk, lids abandoned, that appeared to be empty, probably consumed in the first four hours of the workday. He zoned into the computer screen, his right hand clicking away at the mouse. His nameplate read "Ravi Khan" in black letters on white.

"Sometimes I hear him talking on the phone in another language." Daniel laughed. "And I wonder if he's talking about me."

"Indian as in India," I said.

"What?"

"We're Indian," I replied, speaking up for a guy I didn't even know. "As in India."

He smiled inelegantly.

"And Pocahontas was Algonquian, not Cherokee," I corrected.

A disruptive silence emerged.

"You know, you always think you're talking to some customer-service rep in Iowa or somewhere in the U.S.," said Daniel. "But it always ends up being someone in India named Habeeb or Abdul."

I frowned, stunned as usual by routine racial comments, unable to adapt to them or anticipate them. "I found a typo in your table of contents." I pointed out the misspelling of "coronary."

"Well. It was nice meeting you Mala." He stood up. "We have a few more people to interview and we'll contact you sometime next week."

I wanted to tell him not to bother with communicating the rejection "sometime next week." I knew he would not offer me the job. I would've accepted though. That's how desperate I had become.

*

According to the Web site, *Petroleum Insight* was located in the Energy Corridor near BP. I arrived at 9:59 a.m., one minute before the scheduled interview time. I wore gray polyester pants with two hooks above the zipper. My stomach slightly toppled around the waistband of tightness.

The pants were a piece of an irregular suit from Value City. I could no longer button the jacket but kept it hanging in my closet anyway. My shirt was a black scoop-neck, infested with fuzzies, a result of excessive wear. It was ready for donation, held together by iron-on hem and the persistent trimming of loose threads.

I sported jeans almost every day at Lopez Finance & Accounting and never updated my professional attire. My curls were smooth like lapping ocean waves. I developed techniques to oppress frizz in Houston's treacherous humidity.

"We're a great place to work," said the receptionist. She was a young woman, about my age, with deep-set, ocean-colored eyes that looked faked with blue contacts. Her hair was head-hugging, highlighted in chunks of caramel with short layers and black roots. She stood halfway out of her chair, placing one hand on her skirt, leaning forward, flashing cleavage. "Here's a pamphlet on our publication."

Two men in their late 50s walked through the lobby wearing suits and eyeglasses. Press passes dangled from their necks. "I told him to have some respect. This is Shell," said one of the men. He was bald, with a section of light brown hair mixed with gray, shaped like a slice of watermelon, across the back of his head. He held a thick catalog-style book against his side with car keys between his fingers. Over his shoulder was a double-strap bag that read "Blohm + Voss Repair GmbH." His voice trailed off as he walked into the office with the other man.

It was 10:18 a.m. and I was still waiting. I listened to the receptionist answer phones. I looked around at the oil-and-gas-related décor signs, framed paintings, and displays in the lobby.

"Reese Beveridge," a man said in a southern accent, sounding like an anchor on the local evening news.

I turned around, then shook his hand firmly and stated my name while standing up.

Reese appeared to be about 50 years old. Gray hairs spiraled through his original hair color on the sides of his head, while a full mass of brown hair thickened down the middle. "I'm sorry I'm late. I had a doctor's appointment." His suit was gray and pinstriped. He wore a yellow tie with blue stripes and between each stripe were four carrot-colored stripes. The corners of a matching handkerchief in the breast pocket flowed outward like flower petals. He looked like a supermodel compared with me. Change jingled in his pocket as he led me into a small conference room.

My low black heels from a $10 shoe store squeaked as I walked through a freakishly quiet work environment. I looked into the cubicles on the way, finding only men ages 50 to 60 facing computer screens and wearing glasses and polyester pants. I heard mouse clicks and someone cough once. They were the loudest sounds in the room. Then I heard the sound of junk mail or scrap paper being trashed in exactly two rips.

"Have a seat." Reese cleared his throat twice and then unbuttoned his jacket while sitting down across from me.

I smiled, expanding my face to full capacity, the tip of my lip touching my gums. I tugged my shirt down a little, an unhinged section of iron-on hem scratching my finger as I sat in the interviewee spot. My stomach pushed against the waist of the pants. I'd worn them unbuttoned during the car ride for comfort.

"We're waiting on editors Max Foss and Harold Kidder."

Max Foss looked to be in his mid-40s. His face opened up like a flared vase. His eyelids were invisible. There was a permanent indent above his left nostril and two identical creases in his earlobes. His beard looked like it had been drip-painted with stale chocolate sprinkles. He introduced himself, smiled meekly, and put his business card in front of me and on top of Reese's as he held on to his armadillo-patterned tie. He sat next to Reese.

A black business phone with a tangled cord and fingerprint-smeared screen was centered on the oval conference table. The first few sheets of a yellow legal pad were flipped over its cardboard, resembling a snail. The pad, in front of the head chair, was covered with writing I could not read because of distance.

Harold Kidder pulled out a chair next to Max. He was tall and wore glasses that appeared to be used for only meetings and driving at night. His hair was completely gray, but he was quick and light in his steps.

I made a mental list of the typical questions to ask the interviewer. Advancement, daily tasks of the position, travel, staff size, challenges, short-term and long-term goals of the company, and working environment were filed in my mind. I was ready for *them* to proceed with the bullshit interview questions. I re-memorized my standard template answers and revised them to include my experience at Lopez Finance & Accounting.

Reese leaned back, then forward, in his chair, folding his hands on the table. The skin on his knuckles looked like an accordion folder. Two sets of veins on the back of his hands popped, towering above the skin. He wore a yellow-gold wedding band and a gold watch with a dark blue face on his left wrist. He welcomed me to *Petroleum Insight* and introduced Max Foss and Harold Kidder. "*PI* started as a quarterly report 20 years ago and is now a monthly publication and the most famous."

I listened to Reese continue on about downstream and upstream, crude oil, catalytic hydrocracking, FEED, contractors, operators, gas processing, and other terms and acronyms I did not understand.

Reese raised his eyebrows. "*Petroleum Insight* is the most famous publication in the industry." He sounded brainwashed, the boasting rehearsed or part of the mandatory daily duties of working at *PI*.

I was impressed, though. The small publications in my hometown could not compete. I felt at my best, interviewing at such a respected news source. I put on an act of confidence, as I truly believed I would not become part of a staff that wrote and edited a topic so foreign to me. Then, all of a sudden, I felt guilty, thinking of Krupa and how she never had the chance for a career.

Reese put an issue of *Petroleum Insight* in front of me. Each issue cost $15. On the cover was a photo of a refinery under construction, taken at sunset.

I turned each page, reading the words but not understanding the meaning. There were ads in the back. One was for a refinery for sale. I did a double take on a Red Wing Shoe ad marketed as oil-and-gas footwear to rig workers. It was the closet thing to fashion in the magazine.

Reese continued on about the writer position, moving his hands around, clearing his throat, and leaning back and forth in his chair as he described the tasks of the position.

I did not jot anything down, unlike in previous interviews where I recorded the details offered by the interviewers, scribbling, noting, and formulating follow-up questions. I sat back, listening to Reese go on in breezy animation about the publication's focus and audience. I wondered how I would ever be able to write about the energy industry.

Reese pushed forward a white binder, then pulled it away as if it had secrets. "This is our manual of style. We follow this obediently."

I nodded.

"Do you have any questions for us?" he asked.

I went to my mind-filed inquiries. "Are there any opportunities for advancement?" It was the first question that came out.

"Well, yes." Reese beamed proudly. "I've worked for *Petroleum Insight* for about 18 years in two different positions and then became the editor in chief of *Petroleum Insight*. He looked over at Max as if he expected him to contribute. "Max Foss has moved up with *PI*."

Max smiled meekly to verify the fact. "I started out as *PI*'s editorial assistant right out of college, then continued to move up. I've worked here for almost 12 years."

"Did you have oil-and-gas experience?" I asked.

"No." He looked down for a split-second, flashing his eyelids. "But I picked up a lot when I was the editorial assistant."

I considered them to be lifers but not in a negative way.

"I've worked here for seven months," said Harold. He seemed to be mentioning his employment duration for the sake of not being a mute during the entire interview. "The position is open now, Mala, because our latest employee's personality did not work out here. We are looking for someone who cares about their work."

"Why are you not working now?" asked Reese.

"I was laid off."

"Working here will open doors for you," said Reese. "We are a prestigious publication. People rely on us for information. We are the best in the industry. We are the only publication with a paid subscription. Other publications. Our competitors. They are free. I noticed most of your experience is in Indiana. What brought you to Houston?"

"I wanted a bigger city with more options and more career opportunities. I needed a change." I was stunned that

142

they hadn't dropped a single typical interview question. I had re-memorized the template answers for nothing.

Reese ran a capped *PI* pen down the length of my crammed résumé. "I'm impressed that you are such a go-getter. Since your experience is primarily based in Indiana, my main concern is that you will return there."

"I'm not going back."

Chapter 10

I arrived at *Petroleum Insight* at 6 a.m. the next day. It was Krupa's birthday. I always called my mother on Krupa's birthday and death anniversary, but we never discussed Krupa during our conversations.

I set my VCR to record *The Young and the Restless* on a daily recurrence. I wore a new pair of black dress pants and a purple-striped, buttoned-up collared shirt with a white thin-strap tank underneath. The clothes were my best finds after hours of cringing in front of fitting-room mirrors at the Galleria.

Reese asked me to be there early to fill out paperwork and get situated. He also sent an e-mail instructing me, in a passive-aggressive manner, to get plenty of sleep because I was going to need it.

Max showed me where the coffee was first.

"I don't drink coffee," I said. "Except for those Starbucks Doubleshot drinks when I'm really tired."

He laughed. "Oh. Well, you'll start." He introduced me to a realm of gray-haired people, mostly men, during a tour of the office. "A lot of people are out today." He tilted his head to the side with a gentle smile. "They're at OTC."

"What's OTC?"

Max stopped, his curly brown hair halting in midbounce and eyebrows shooting upward. "The Offshore Technology Conference." His smile turned into cold stones. "It's one of the biggest conferences in the United States. It's at Reliant Center."

"Oh." I had never heard of OTC. I felt as if I were being punished for not scheduling the conference on my calendar, creating a countdown, or observing it as a holiday.

"You're going this week. We'll get you a press pass."

"Oh," I said with uncertainty. "Okay."

"And wear comfortable shoes."

I wasn't going to take shoe advice seriously from a man.

"You can take the light rail if you can't find a parking spot. People from all over the world come to OTC," said Max. "They can even pick up their badges at the airport. Also, I should tell you that a publisher was fired yesterday, so the mood around here is a little ... " He shook his hand back and forth. "He was from up North and didn't really fit in around here."

*

My office was between Reese's and Max's. I had an L-shaped desk with six unwieldy stacks of papers facing the window, a struggling plant in the sill, four *PI*-logo coffee mugs filled with highlighters, red thin-point pens, and *PI*-logo retractable black-ink pens. A flat-screen computer was covered in dust and atop stacked phone books for height. I looked out the window. The clouds moved freely like sheets of tissue over the sky.

"These are all press releases. Oh, and you have to find photos, too. Don't include anything that is not approved. No feasibility studies. Make sure you have all the information before discussing it. If you don't know what stage it is in, don't report it. If there is no projected completion date, make sure you mention that. Try to be as specific and accurate as possible. For pipelines, make sure to say if it is crude, gas, or products. We want to list capacities for LNG in million tonnes per year. Consult our manual of style. You'll have to do some conversions. Coking—fluid or delayed? EPC— engineering, procurement, construction. FEED—front-end engineering design. You'll see that a lot. We want to provide the best information for our readers. They look to us as the most reliable source of information. Let me know if you have any questions." He smiled and walked away.

"Wait," I pleaded.

Max stuck his head in my office.

I didn't know what to ask.

"Here are some examples to look at." Max pulled a few *PR*'s off my shelf. "Let me know if you have any questions. Oh, and here is our manual of style." He dropped a thick stack of white paper, held together with a large binder clip, onto my desk. "Always remember." He picked up the manual of style. "This is very important." He came back with a binder marked "PETEX." "This is a correspondence course. Fundamentals of Petroleum. You can work on this on the weekends and at lunch."

I stared at the screen while my computer booted up. I took a deep breath, but it did nothing. I lifted a press release from the first stack. A pipeline expansion was in engineering stages and would be completed at the end of the third quarter. It was 130 miles and 14/16 inches in diameter.

I knocked on Max's open door. "Could you explain this?" I looked at the assortment of armadillo figurines on the cherry-wood-finish shelves to the left of his desk. One in particular stood out. It was silver-plated, with detailed dents to show the bands of its shell. It sat upright and held two drumsticks in front of a silver-plated drum.

Max looked at me as if I were an idiot. "It's 130 miles of 14-inch and 16-inch pipe."

"Oh." I furrowed my eyebrows.

"Don't forget to consult the manual of style."

I went back to my office, questions unanswered, baffled by Max's up-and-down attitude. I Googled "pipeline construction," but the search results lead to *PI*. I realized my new job would be a challenge, a responsibility like no other, but worth it when I read my name in print in an international publication.

I went back to Max's office. "What is Claus?"

"It's pronounced 'clowss.' Rhymes with 'mouse.' We're not talking about Santa here. It's all about the sulfur."

"Oh." I was quiet but had another question. "This company here." I pointed at the press release. "Total."

"It's pronounced 'toe-tal,' not 'total.' "

"Oh."

"By the way, we're having a staff meeting at 2 to discuss shale gas."

I attempted to furrow my eyebrows again, but they were already in position. "Shale gas," I said aloud as if verbalizing it would provide a clear meaning or whip me into an expert.

A bubbly young woman knocked on my door. "I'm Alyssa." Her hair was medium length and light brown with blond highlights and a sharp widow's peak. She wore gray gaucho pants that revealed black stiletto pumps, and her tight cotton top was pastel pink. "I work for *Petroleum Insight*. It's like the *Vogue* of the industry. I heard there was a young person, so I wanted to come over and introduce myself."

I smiled. "Alyssa," I repeated as we shook hands. "I'm Mala."

"Mala," repeated Alyssa.

"It's so good to see a young face. We should do lunch sometime."

"We should," I said. I found it amusing that Alyssa wanted to have lunch simply because I was in her age group.

"I've worked at *Petroleum Insight* for about a year and a half. I've lived in Houston for about two years. Are you from Houston?"

"Indianapolis."

"Omigod!" She hopped up and down in little movements.

I laughed. "What?"

"I'm from Ohio!"

"Omigod!" I screamed. I couldn't help being thrilled about the Midwestern connection. "Where?"

"Ashland."

"Ashland?"

"It's a small town. An hour south of Cleveland and an hour north of Columbus. Houston is so big. I moved here to be with my boyfriend, but we're not together anymore." She looked down, then up again. "I hate him. I have *Petroleum Insight* sent to his e-mail every week so he is reminded of me. We met at Ohio State. Go Buckeyes!"

"Go Hoosiers!" I said cheerily to deter Alyssa from bitter breakup talk.

"Omigod, you went to IU? I have a friend of a friend that went there. Kayla Stevens. Do you know her? Probably not."

"Nope."

"Yeah, it's a big campus, but you never know. Do you want to have lunch *today*?"

"I'm having lunch with Reese."

"Ah, lunch with the old guys." She laughed.

"With the old guys?"

"Everyone here is … older."

"I noticed that."

She prolonged her focus on my face. "You have really nice eyebrows. Do you get them threaded?"

"Yes."

"I did that once and I really liked it, but the lady was mean."

I laughed.

"She kept telling me that I had a mustache and that it looked horrible. Then she said that I have way too much facial hair. So basically, she threaded my entire face."

I held my stomach while laughing. "Yeah, that's how they do it. They have no tact." I zoned in on Alyssa's eyebrows but was distracted by her eyelashes, which looked like clusters of spiky twigs.

"I really liked the way they looked, but I couldn't bring myself to go back there." Alyssa sighed. "Okay, well, we'll have to get lunch sometime soon. Y'all have fun."

I found it amusing that an Ohioan said "y'all." I had started to say the word, naturally breathing it twice in the past month. "Definitely."

Reese sent an e-mail saying he was receiving foot injections and allergy shots and would work from home in the morning. He arrived in the office around 11. By then I had gone through three press releases and answered a couple of phone calls from readers, unable to comprehend the jargon they tossed around so fluently. I couldn't even put on a performance and bullshit my way through it. I was stumped, replying with long "uh's" or just silence. I told most of them I would return their calls. Then I asked Max about their questions. He would get annoyed, give me dirty looks, or kindly help.

"Lunch at 11:30," Reese said as he knocked on my door. He was dressed in a dark suit with a subtle-designed black handkerchief pressed against yet flowing out of his breast pocket. His tie matched the handkerchief.

"Okay."

"Lunch at 11:30, Max."

"Yes, sir."

I was unaware of Max's attendance.

"So how is everything?" asked Reese.

"Oh fine."

"Good. Well, let me know if you have any questions." He handed me two copies of the manual of style. "I was fixin' to give you these."

"I already have one," I said, holding up my copy.

"Well, you can keep one copy for home and the other copy for the car."

*

I gave the Vigor a long look in the parking lot as we drove by it in Reese's Infiniti. It needed to be coasted through a car wash. I had washed it only once since I had moved to Houston, at Lone Star Car Wash. A friend of Cyril's owned a body shop and repaired the damage from the Aston Martin crash for free. I noticed the mismatched paints in the damaged section every time I got behind the wheel.

Reese was born and raised in Waco. His uncle took care of him because his mother suffered from depression and his father sporadically entered and exited his life. I was envious of his openness over Caesar salads, mushroom ravioli, fettuccine with Italian sausage meatballs, and a bottle of merlot at La Strada. He used words like "delicatessen" instead of "deli" and folded his napkin on his lap until the edges touched evenly. He had a journalism degree from the University of Alabama and his master's from the University of Arkansas. Reese worked at various newspapers in Alabama and Arkansas. His first job out of college was writing the obituaries for *The Birmingham News*. He didn't discuss much about petroleum other than saying that oil and gas is an easy industry to learn.

Max said he was from San Antonio when I asked. It was the only piece of information he dispensed.

I never went to lunch with Midwest Bank employees. I was usually gone for hours for the purpose of getting away from my co-workers. I sometimes brought my lunch, which was typically a chicken fajita, chicken parmesan, or meatballs and mozzarella Lean Pocket. When I changed it up, it was a turkey sandwich on wheat made with love by my mother with mayonnaise on the top piece of bread, a half-slice of cheese, mustard on the meat, and tomatoes and pickles in a separate bag to prevent sogginess.

Midwest Bank's break room was set up cafeteria-style, with long folding tables and mismatched, wobbly chairs. I ate my lunch there and then left in order to people-watch from the monument, shop at Circle Centre, stroll around the Circle, or pursue other downtown ventures.

There were two large refrigerators, one beige, one white. The beige fridge quit working from time to time and was repaired only after several weeks of paperwork processing. The white fridge had a foot-size dent at the bottom and a brown drip trail originating near the handle that ended at the bottom of the door. My lunch had been stolen a few times. I could not believe that grown people would swipe my food.

I always searched for a vacant table in the break room. It was a quest to avoid engagement in rotting and offensive conversations with the Midwest Bank employees I had quietly nicknamed "The Scaries."

One Thursday, I was eager for the weekend not because I had big plans but because I cherished my short getaway from my dead-end job. I wore a red Indiana University Basketball baby tee with letters in white embroidery. It also had a white IU emblem in the center of the chest. My gray sweatpants were low-waisted capris, with the IU emblem on my left hip in red. The drawstring dangled to midthigh. I purchased the outfit my sophomore year at T.I.S. bookstore to wear for class during my hangover days. Mr. Brown wrote me up for violating dress code because sweatpants were not permitted. I was ecstatic about receiving the write-up instead of the usual warning.

There was no makeup on my face, but my eyelashes were curled. Two dull silver sets of Indian bangles looked like Slinky coils on my arms. An empty table, fairly excluded, awaited me in the break room. I claimed my territory with an O'Malia's plastic bag containing my lunch while overhearing the usual conversations.

"No he did*n't*."

"He need to decide who he gonna be sleepin' with."

"If he don't take care of his other kids, then he ain't gonna take care of any kids that he be makin' with you."

I made eye contact with a girl at the snack bar. She wore a Midwest Bank name badge, declaring that I was no longer the only Indian girl in the building. Arpita was her name.

"Are you two sisters?" The snack-bar employee asked.

We looked at each other and at the same time said, "I hate this place."

Arpita stopped at the table on her way out. She was carrying a Nutty Bar and a diet Dr. Pepper. "I just graduated from college. I don't plan on being here for more than a month."

I didn't have the heart to tell her that I had hoped the same for myself.

Three black men with bald heads sat at the empty table next to mine. One wore a Pacers jersey with "Miller" across the back, and the other two wore Peyton Manning jerseys. They stared at me as I pulled out the chair to sit down. I unwrapped a turkey sandwich with Havarti, a cheese that Jackie got me hooked on. My lunch also had a sandwich bag of nacho-cheese Doritos and a sandwich bag of three Chips Ahoy cookies. I pressed the loose chocolate chips with my index finger and put them in my mouth before eating the sandwich.

The three men checked out a group of women in jersey dresses as they purposely strutted by. "Mmmm, I'd like to get me some of that. What that girl got is off the chain."

I felt the three men staring at me throughout lunch and noticed one of them trying to initiate conversation. I focused on the Channel 8 news, my eyes glued to Patty Spitler.

He was suddenly at my side, pulling out the chair next to me and bumping my arm in the process. I gave him a dirty look.

"What up, girl?"

I ignored him, finding him unattractive physically and mentally.

"Did you see me checkin' you ova there?" He yanked down his oversize Colts jersey. "You probably noticed me noticin' you."

I was confused by the pickup line. Usually men thought I was checking them out when I wasn't.

I pursed my lips in displeasure and took a bite of my sandwich.

"Did you notice me checkin' you? My name's Bobby. Ya know, like Bobby Knight."

I ignored him, watching the end of the news, waiting for *The Young and the Restless* to begin.

"Shawty ain't speak no English, huh? Where you from?" He waited for me to answer. "I ain't normally into foreign dimes, but girl, you look good. Where you from? Are you Ethiopian?"

"*Ethiopian*?" I squinted my eyes. "I'm *Indian*."

"Ah, okay." He leaned back in his chair as if the situation were comfortable. "I tried to get with an Indian girl before. Oh wait, I mean she was Pakistani. Yeah, she was Pakistani."

"It's not the same."

"Are you a red-dot Indian? Where's your nose ring?"

I scowled.

"Well, you look Ethiopian."

"No, I don't!" I felt my upper arms tense. "I look Indian!"

"Well, Ethiopians and Indians are the same," he said confidently.

I had never heard that one before. I snappishly turned my head at him. It was the most play I had given him. "*What*?"

"You didn't know that?" he asked in disbelief. "Ethiopians and Indians are the same."

I put the Doritos in my purse for later.

"Anyways, you saw me checkin' you, right? I'm new to the job. Maybe you could show me around Midwest Bank."

"No."

"You wanna sit together at lunch sometime?"

"No."

"Why?" he asked. "Oh. Is it because of the Ethiopian comment?"

I didn't answer.

"Well, if you change your mind I'll be ova there. This ain't my only job. I work in a parking lot, too. Ya know. Holla."

*

I put my leftover takeout box of mushroom ravioli in the produce drawer of the fridge. I smiled at a co-worker on the way out, as I had been doing all day. They were all strangers even though introductions had taken place with several of them. They talked about oil and gas, stated their credentials, then frowned or became silent when they found out I didn't have oil-and-gas experience. My co-workers seemed to go by their last names in person, on the phone, and in e-mail. My co-workers with southern accents pronounced "oil" like "ol." I had wondered where all the white people were in Houston. They were at the office of *Petroleum Insight* magazine.

"I'm Zach," he said as he filled up a large Ozarka bottle of water at the dispenser. "I'm the drilling editor." He was younger, in his late 30s or early 40s. His blond bangs were swept to the side, revealing a forehead the size of a junior legal pad. He wore black-metal rectangular-rimmed eyeglasses, khaki pants with no belt, and a short-sleeve shirt with an orange, blue, and rust-colored abstract pattern.

I introduced myself.

He stood up straighter after filling the bottle. "Were you listening to Warrant this morning? You drove past me in the parking lot when I was walking in this morning. I thought I heard *Uncle Tom's Cabin*."

I laughed, caught off guard by the subject of my musical choices. "Yeah, I like Warrant."

He looked at me for explanation.

"Older-sister influence. She was a teenager in the '80s and I thought she was so cool. When my friends were

155

listening to Stone Temple Pilots and Nine Inch Nails in high school, I was always listening to Great White and Britny Fox. I know there are other people like me, but I just haven't met any other twentysomethings that are into hair bands."

"I've never met any either. I don't know about a singer named Jani, though. A guy named Jani frontin' a rock band. I don't think so."

I laughed. "That's not his real name."

He looked at me as if I shouldn't know such an intimate detail about an '80s rock star. "I know, but still … I saw Warrant when they were up and when they were coming down. Playing in smaller clubs. They're really good live."

"I was always too young to go to the concerts," I said.

We walked out of the break room and stopped in the hallway before going in opposite directions.

"Well, I hope you like it here. Just refer to the manual of style to help you out. Oh, and what was that you were driving?"

"A Vigor."

"Hmmm."

I walked back to my office, posters of LNG terminals fluttering as I passed them. As soon as I sat down, Max was in my doorway.

"We're putting together our weekly newsletter and I need you to write up this news item." He handed me the press release, somewhat aiming for my hands, causing my lip balm to roll off my desk. "Okay." It was about Husky Energy and Axens and a contract. I read it four times and did not understand what I was looking at. I was unfamiliar with the terminology. I couldn't identify the units of measure. I wrote the story, looking up every little detail in the electronic version of the manual of style that was in my inbox when I returned from lunch. Our editorial assistant, Nara Fowler, had sent it. I e-mailed the story to Reese for feedback after working on it for almost two hours. It was a rough draft that couldn't get any rougher.

I worked on shrinking the six stacks of press releases throughout the day, walking back and forth between my office and Max's, my shoes and questions making the most noise in the freakishly quiet working environment.

I had accumulated a long line of sticky notes across the bottom of my computer screen with tips from my co-workers, questions and contact information from readers, and random information I didn't understand. I had black pen marks across my fingers from smearing the ink across some of the sticky notes.

At 2 o'clock, I entered the conference room for the staff meeting. They all stared at me as I sat in a black chair against the wall away from the table. I was the new girl. Alyssa waved to me from across the room, giving off an exaggerated vibe of happiness.

I recognized most of the staff but could not recall their names. Reese led the session, speaking knowledgeably on shale gas. I looked around the room as several of the older men fell asleep during the discussion. I was wide awake but still did not understand the subject matter.

I focused on the press releases after the meeting again. The *PI* newsletter popped up in my face at exactly 3 p.m. I scrolled down, reading over the eight headlines. I had also learned throughout the day that there were two refineries in Indiana: one in Mount Vernon owned by Countrymark Cooperative Inc. and the other in Whiting owned by BP.

Reese knocked on my door while walking in. "Make sure you read over those stories. It will help with your education. You'll also need to look at those to see if we need to include them in our next issue."

"Okay, thanks." I printed them all just in case.

Nara entered, placing a plastic wine glass on my desk. She wore a pale yellow, sleeveless linen dress with a tie around the waist. I had noticed the popularity of linen around Houston. She held a bottle of red wine in her hands like a waitress. "Would you like a glass?"

"Uh, okay."

Nara poured to the rim.

"What's with the wine?"

"It's from a press kit. I can't remember who sent it. Weatherford, I think."

She looked around my office. "I'll order you a desk calendar."

"Oh, I don't need that. I just use my Outlook."

"Yeah, I guess I'm just used to doing everything *old* school around here."

*

I left work at 7 p.m. to attend the Houston Gas Processors Association shrimp boil at Woodrow's because Reese and Max could not attend. I parked the Vigor in the gravel lot and, while walking to the bar, halted at the sight of a traffic cop in an orange vest wearing a cowboy hat.

I passed through the outdoor section of tables and party lights. Inside were pool tables, foosball tables, long, wood-finished tables with green chairs, and wall-to-wall neon-lighted signs with Houston Texans and Bud Light logos.

I signed in with three women at the front, slapped on my name tag bearing my first and last name and my publication, and held on to my raffle ticket. TV screens were permanent fixtures, making me more comfortable. They were an escape during quiet moments between mingling with more strangers.

There were five younger people—all men—in a bar full of mostly gray-haired oil-and-gas-affiliated Houstonians. It was my first shrimp boil. I had never heard of the social event until I moved to Houston.

I ordered a Bud Light while standing next to a barstool. The man next to me ordered the same. He looked at my chest and read my name out loud. "*Petroleum Insight* is my favorite magazine. How long have you worked there?"

I looked at the name tag on his white Enterprise Products Partners L.P. polo-style shirt. Bill Richards was his name. "It's my first day, actually."

"Oh, it's your first day." He laughed. "Well, I'm sure you have a lot of experience, landing a job at such a prestigious publication." He spoke in detail about midstream construction.

I had no idea what he was talking about but threw in "yes," "okay," and "right" to create the illusion of a discussion. One of the sticky notes on my computer reminded me to look up the definitions of "upstream," "midstream," and "downstream."

I joined the line for shrimp. I added a boudin ball and fried alligator to my plate. I was proud of myself for knowing what the items were and what they tasted like. I scooped shrimp onto my plate. I selected a table with two women and sat a seat away from them. My fork clattered on the table as I sat. I introduced myself and hoped they wouldn't ask me questions about oil and gas. I dipped the shrimp in sauce and took a bite. There was a loud crunch.

The women laughed at me.

"Oh honey," said the woman diagonally from me in a sleeveless blue rayon shirt. "You need to peel the shell first."

I looked at the woman's plate of discarded shells.

"Oh, I've never eaten it like this before."

"You haven't? You've never been to a *shrimp* boil?"

"No."

"How's that possible?"

"I'm from Indianapolis—"

"Oh," she said quickly. "You're from up North. You northerners don't realize we have a whole different culture down here."

*

I went to Cyril's after my first day at *Petroleum Insight*. My jam-packed day of work, almost like an accelerated college course, brought back brain cells that I had lost throughout the years.

Cyril had just arrived from a business dinner with two potential clients at Pappasito's. He kissed me hello, an icy mandatory lip brush of obligation. "The waiter dripped strawberry margarita on my new Sean John. I just got the shirt cleaned. I mean I just took it off the hanger and put it on."

I watched him wipe the already-deep stain spot on a white shirt with a baking soda-dabbed cloth. I leaned forward on his couch, elbows placed near my knees, chin resting on intertwined fingers. I watched his face bleed angry about a mindless stain. He blabbered on about the new shirt. He didn't even look up at me once or ask about my day.

"I'm thinking about taking on this other job that I heard about. This business is sucking me dry. It only pays six figures, though. That's not very much money."

I rolled my eyes. I wished I made six figures.

He walked over to the coffee table and picked up two DVDs. "I haven't taken these movies back yet. I still haven't paid my other late fees."

I wondered why I was with a guy who had late fees. I would never have late fees and waste money. I didn't understand how he could turn down a six-figure salary. I watched him dab the stain again with the cloth. I looked at his protruding stomach. Then I watched him reach for his phone.

"I don't want to see you anymore," I blurted.

"What?"

"I don't want to see you anymore." I stood up.

"You don't mean that, Mala."

"Yes, I do!"

"Hold on, I have to take this call." He held his index finger up. "This is Cyril, how may I assist you?"

I went into the bathroom and looked at the overnight necessities Cyril had purchased for me. I looked down at the black rug in front of the sink. There were three bleach spots on it from my upper-lip-hair remover. Cyril had gathered my scattered bobby pins into a Smith & Wesson hearing-protection bag. I took only the lip balm and 3.5-ounce bottle of lotion and left the bobby pins, toothbrush, blow dryer, and hair spray. I grabbed my Indianapolis Colts coozie and Hoosiers travel mug off the kitchen counter. I threw my purse over my right shoulder. I'd lost track of how many times I had walked out but knew this was the last.

CHAPTER 11

My Husky story was on my chair when I arrived for my second day of work. The black type of my story was barely visible through all of Reese's red-ink pen marks. The words "passive voice" were scribbled all over the story.

He also wrote, "Did you check the manual of style?"

"Refer to the manual of style."

"You missed the point completely."

"You will lose the readers on this."

"These are major flaws."

"This is overuse of passive voice."

At the end of the story, he wrote, "We're going to have to scrap your story. It's not good enough."

I read the comments, one after another, wondering how it could've been so poorly written when I worked so diligently. My voice-mail indicator light was on. I had 14 new messages, several of which were OTC party invites. The others were questions from subscribers. My inbox was flooded as well, containing several e-mails in different languages.

I left the office at 10 o'clock for the Offshore Technology Conference. Max was in the lane next to me but looked away when I waved. I took the Kirby exit off 610 and parked in the blue lot. I jotted down a description of the area in case I forgot where I parked the Vigor.

I walked a long trek in black pointy heels to Reliant Center and blended into the crowds of people. The arched soles of my feet burned as soon as I passed the stadium. I carried a black tote that secured my wallet, cell phone, lip balm, writer's notebook, and, most important, a digital voice recorder I'd purchased on the drive to work. I was assigned a topical luncheon on upstream construction. I wasn't in denial. I'd have to record it in order to write the story and remember the details—the newsworthy information and the key points.

I picked up my press badge from the pressroom. There were several tables with reporters from end to end on their laptops. I looked at some of their press badges, not realizing there were so many other oil-and-gas publications.

My press badge read "Mala Thomas" in bold black letters. It also read "Petroleum Insight" and "Houston, TX USA." The title of the year's conference was in orange, and at the bottom the badge read "PRESS" in black letters highlighted in purple. It was attached to a blue ribbon that also read "PRESS" in silver lettering. It was my first press badge. I noticed piles of them clipped to customized lanyards, hanging in offices and cubicles of my co-workers. I attached it to the collar of the suit jacket I had purchased the night before.

I had attended work conferences in the past, usually consisting of claustrophobic booths lined up in a navigable room and simple people in suits or professional attire going through the passive motions of business-card distribution and exchange. But I had never seen anything like OTC.

Sexy salsa dancers performed at a booth on a sizable, personalized, red, square dance floor. The couple wore red and black complementing costumes with multipanel ruffles at the waist. The male dancer's shirt was unbuttoned, pants skintight and hair in short, greasy ring curls. He distributed winks to the audience but never focused on anyone in particular while baring his ripped chest.

Rotary tables and various rig equipment were monstrous displays. I discovered they were rig equipment only after reading the exhibit descriptions. A group of girls pranced around in cowboy hats, boots, and mini-jean skirts promoting their company. I sipped on a glass of pinot grigio at a wine bar in a company's booth and devoured a halved sausage breakfast burrito with spicy salsa and potatoes at another while watching a demo on underwater repairs on drilling equipment. There were shoe-shine guys and food for sale. OTC had everything.

I looked at the tall topical luncheon signs near the exhibit hall to find the location of my luncheon. I took the escalator to the second level, where there were round tables throughout the floor covered with black tablecloths. People conversed or lunged their faces at laptops while waiting for the next technical session or luncheon. Even in a crowd of thousands, there were still a limited number of women. I passed some familiar faces but could not remember my co-workers' names.

The line decreased as attendees handed in their tickets for the luncheon. I didn't have to purchase a ticket, because press got in free, though we weren't allowed to eat. I stood in line and watched as other luncheons opened up throughout the floor.

"I'm press." I flashed my badge.

"Press has to wait until everyone else with tickets gets in," said a tall man with white skin and black hair wearing a black suit. "Wait to the side. And if there are empty seats, you can eat."

I stood next to a young woman who was also a journalist. She worked for World Drilling and had just graduated from college. "You must be really into the industry," she said. "Working at *PI*."

"I'm fairly new to it. It's only my second day on the job."

"Your *second* day?"

"I'm also from up North," I said as if that would be a good reason for being unknowledgeable about oil and gas. Then I realized that I had referred to my hometown as "up North."

"Oh, I'm from up North, too," she said uncomfortably as if it shouldn't be called that. "I went to the University of Wisconsin."

"I went to IU. I'm from Indy."

"I'm from Fort Wayne. I haven't lived here very long. I'm looking forward to moving back after I get some experience."

"Move back?" I cringed at the thought. "Move back to Fort *Wayne*?" I flashed back to a memory of a white-trash pregnant girl dancing on a platform in shredded Daisy Duke jean shorts and a tight white cutoff tank top unable to restrain her breasts. I had visited a college friend from Fort Wayne and we had partied at a club that was five clubs in one.

"Fort Wayne is home," she said. "Unless I meet some boy in Houston, fall in love, and get married."

"Well, it was nice meeting you." I went in the other direction when I entered the luncheon. I sat at an empty front-row table to the left side of the keynote speakers' stage. There was a Southwest-style salad in front of me, garnished with corn tortilla chips. I looked around, happy that there were vacant seats so I was allowed to eat.

Two Canadian geologists, both named Rick, joined me while I forked the salad. I paid attention to etiquette by preventing each piece from dangling from my lips. The geologists were both at least 50 years old and wore matching yellow collared shirts with the Canadian maple-leaf flag emblazoned on the back. They asked about my work mostly. I provided the best answers possible. They talked about Houston and how much they love visiting every year for OTC and how they had been attending since the '80s. The only thing they did not like was the Houston traffic. They talked about their 10-minute commutes to work in Calgary and how they couldn't imagine driving in the Houston traffic every day.

The lunch consisted of tamales, green tomatillo enchiladas, green rice, and black beans. The geologists talked about Thai food during the lunch and asked me to recommend a place. I found the craving unusual and wondered why they didn't want Mexican or southern cuisine flavors of Houston. I recommended a place in Rice Village and a restaurant on Voss.

I cleaned my plate, rolling the rice in the sauce before spooning it into my mouth, fighting the desire to lick the remnants off the fork with the tip of my tongue.

I recorded the panel discussion comprising two CEOs from two contracting companies and two vice presidents of exploration from two upstream companies. I found a few terms recognizable and was impressed with myself for possessing a grain of knowledge on my second day of work.

I jotted down the notes on the screen, almost barbarically, as if I were fighting for them. I did not understand what I was writing and, while looking at my penmanship, realized I might not be able to decipher my handwriting when returning to the office to write the story. I was suddenly overwhelmed with relief that I had purchased the digital voice recorder.

After the luncheon and wishing the Canadian geologists a pleasant Houston visit, I headed back to the exhibit hall to browse more booths. There were plenty of women limping compared with the morning. I noticed three or four barefoot or hosiery-clad, carrying their heels in their hands. There were also a few women wearing sneakers with suits.

I took in the chaos of OTC and the abundance of elaborate booths, listened to a mixture of accents and languages, learned about new products but didn't quite understand them, and swapped business cards with everyone I spoke with. I overheard conversations of topical luncheon schedules, opinions on keynote speakers, menus of industry breakfasts, and thoughts on the best panelists. I seemed to be one of the rare young people at the conference, feeling striking in a crowd of thousands. I ran into Alyssa, who was very excited to see me and pointed out again that it was great to have a young person in the office. We agreed to meet up at a reception later for young professionals in the industry, ages 35 and under.

I flipped to the back of the conference program to locate our booth. Reese was sitting at a round table with a fanfold of magazines in front of him and two salespeople. I briefly chatted with them, learning that there were snacks and drinks in the back area of our booth. I opened the door to find a woman on her laptop, sitting on a couch, in an all-white skirt suit. Her name was Dawn and she worked in the U.K. office. She congratulated me on my new job.

I ate a package of Cool Ranch Doritos and drank half a bottle of room-temperature water. I sat on the opposite couch and pulled my feet out of my heels. The toes and soles of my knee-highs were ripped. I took them off, threw them into a trash can on top of a chocolate and cream wrapper, and walked back out to the exhibits.

I crossed paths with an Indian guy in my haphazard excursion through Reliant. He was very tall with dark, murky skin. He was the tallest Indian I had ever seen. My press badge was around my neck and attached to a Halliburton lanyard. I acted oblivious to his presence the first time while picking up a pen at the ABB Lummus booth. I pretended to be engrossed with the exhibit. I smiled flirtatiously when bumping into him again at Saipem's exhibit. Forty-five minutes later, we met up at the Tenaris booth.

"Stop following me," he joked. His smile was cheesy and even.

"Don't flatter yourself," I said half-jokingly. Then I laughed to cover up the partial seriousness. I put a small tin of Tenaris mints and a blue cover of sticky notes in my Mustang Engineering bag, knocking a tin to the ground.

He picked up the mints and put them in his pocket. His name was Vincent Abraham, but he told me to call him Vince. He worked as a subsea engineer for J. Ray McDermott and told me that *Petroleum Insight* was his favorite magazine. He told me he was a member of SPE, and when I reacted blankly he said, "the Society of Petroleum Engineers."

His face was round and gained inches closer to his chin. He had groomed eyebrows, a practically sheer goatee, and big eyes that stayed open as if he were about to get hit by a semi. His hair part was subtle and blended. His tie was pink and purple striped against a light pink shirt under a black suit jacket. The broad laces of his radiant black dress shoes did not seem to be the original set.

I knew by his name that he was Christian. I was pleased to meet a guy with potential, an Indian Christian—a rare find in Indianapolis but so common in Houston. I didn't feel physically attracted to him but needed to replace Cyril immediately. I couldn't stand the thought of being alone even though I had been alone for so long before Cyril.

Vince and I instinctively wandered around OTC together, straying from exhibits and walking as if we were on an open street.

"Brisket?" asked a woman at a booth in which I didn't pay any attention to the company name.

I immediately thought of Cyril and our Texas barbecue meals together. He had introduced me to brisket, another food item I had never heard of until I moved to the South. "Sure." I rarely declined free samples. The heat of the tender meat sparked my tongue. I looked at Vince. "Are you going to take one?"

"Oh no," said Vince in mild disgust. "I don't eat meat."

I stopped in midchomp. I was confused, unsure of Vince's religion.

I limped to a parking shuttle with a bagful of gadgets, pens, stationery, business cards (including Vince's), and the OTC conference program. The woman sitting next to me was barefoot, wearing her pumps in her lap. "I've been going to this for nine years and I still don't learn."

I had forgotten to turn down the radio after I had parked. The loudness of Journey's *Girl Can't Help It* startled me as I clicked my seat belt. I suddenly realized it was over with Cyril and cried the whole drive to the young professionals party.

*

I leaned the airplane seat back and closed my eyes. I was tired from the long day before. I had attended a rig christening party in Port Arthur with Zach and Alyssa. They had become my work friends and the co-workers who were familiar with my non-work life. I got to know them better on the two-hour bus ride to Port Arthur. Zach and Alyssa were both late for the 8 a.m. charter bus leaving from behind Williams Tower. I stalled for them, talking to the public-relations lady about hairstylists, the rig, the weather, *Petroleum Insight*, while ensuring her that Zach and Alyssa were almost there. I eventually said they were parking their cars at Macy's when they had actually just exited 610.

Alyssa was hungover, swallowing ibuprofen and wearing sunglasses on the bus. They weren't quite as open as Reese but divulged information about their families' places of employment, cities, and ages. They commented on my age difference with my sisters. As usual, I was silent.

It was a rig jacked-up adjacent to a construction yard. I laughed at the sound of a rig christening party, but no one else on staff found such a party out of the ordinary. When exiting the bus, we were given a pamphlet laying out the itinerary and describing the rig. The tours were from 8 a.m. to 12:30 p.m. The christening was at noon. The barbecue lunch was from 11:30 a.m. to 2 p.m. And more rig tours were scheduled after until 4 p.m.

Alyssa and I headed straight to the bathrooms, discussing our disgust at the thought of using the Porta Potties. To our shock, the portable toilets were not in blue plastic outhouses. They were full-size, air-conditioned, portable bathrooms with sinks and wooden toilets. Two wooden stalls were in each bathroom. Deep-pink sword lilies were in glass, flute vases to the right of the sink along with soap, paper towels, lotion, and hand sanitizer. To make the circumstances even better, men had their own bathrooms. Alyssa and I talked about the portable luxury restrooms throughout the day.

The three of us picked up souvenirs from big white tables—a book about the rig, a mini-rig replica, and a key chain. We toured the rig together. I listened to Zach, as he was my personal tour guide, the drilling expert. The rig was packed with people in casual wear—linen pants, tank tops, jean shorts, tennis shoes, sunglasses, and fanny packs. There were families with little kids who seemed to be committed to the rig as if they were roaming Disneyland.

I snapped pictures of the rotary table and top drive. I posed next to the rig welcoming sign, reading the maximum and minimum water depths and the rated drilling depth. I also posed with a rig worker who wore a uniform shirt tucked into bulky jeans and a hard hat that shadowed dark sunglasses. His moth-colored mustache was thick, trimmed carefully to detach it from his nose. Alyssa stood on his other side. He yelled, "She thinks my tractor's sexy!" when Zach took the picture. The rig worker told me that he was a roughneck. I laughed and as usual no one else did.

"That's what rig workers are called," said Alyssa. "They're called roughnecks."

"Oh. I didn't know that. I can't understand a lot of their southern accents. It seems worse here than it is in Houston."

Under a big white tent was the barbecue lunch: brisket, chicken, sausage, pork chops, ribs, ham, shrimp, crawfish, corn on the cob, pots of dirty rice, macaroni salad, potato salad, coleslaw, pecan pie, and bread pudding. I was proud of myself for knowing about the food items. There were no mysteries on my plate. I even knew how to eat the crawfish, having learned from Cyril at a business crawfish boil.

The christening ceremony began with *God Bless America* performed by a family member of an employee. The chairman and CEO of the rig company spoke, and after that a priest from a local Catholic church blessed the rig. I realized that it was time for me to go to church. I attended randomly every few months to revive my Catholicism and to see if I could get something out of the homily but never did. I had goofed on the words to the Apostles' Creed at my last church appearance. I thought about checking out Joel Osteen at Lakewood for a change.

I recorded the ceremony and then accidentally erased it with the slip of a finger. Zach had also recorded it and offered to lend it to me. He referred to my mishap as a "rookie mistake."

I brought my seat upright in the plane. I could not sleep. The Indian woman sitting one seat over had not initiated conversation. I wondered if she knew anyone in Indianapolis—friends she had kept in touch with when first coming to America or family. Or maybe she had a layover in Indianapolis. The sides of her hair were pulled back to the middle of her head with an off-black barrette. She had no gray hair, but the wrinkles near her mouth aged her face. Her husband was four rows ahead of us. His reading light was on even though the plane was lit with natural light. He had a valley of dark hair on his head, with macaroni-shaped spirals of gray injected continuously.

The Continental Airlines flight was two hours and 17 minutes, enriched with a miniature turkey sandwich, carrots, and a snack-size package of M&M's. I attempted to tear the mustard packet but it would not open.

The Indian woman reached over the empty seat between us, snatched it from my fingers, tore it open, and handed it to me. "Do you live in Indianapolis?"

"No. I live in Houston now, but I'm from Indianapolis."

"You are a Malayalee?"

"Yes."

"We are, too," she said, speaking for a husband she had not mentioned. "My sister lives in Indianapolis. We first moved to Indianapolis from Kerala, but it was hard to find a job there. It is white collar."

"It's easier to find a job in Houston," I said.

"Yes. It was easy for us. Houston has a lot of blue-collar work. We don't have education. We give that to our children. We both work in a factory." She tore open her mustard packet. "Our children live in Dallas. Two sons. One engineer. One lawyer. Dallas is very white collar. What do you do?"

I held up *Petroleum Insight*. "I work for a magazine."

"You're white collar. Houston is a nice place, but watch out for the blacks."

I stopped in midbite.

"There are 40,000 blacks from the hurricane. They are not white collar. Watch out for them. When you go somewhere, don't carry a purse. Keep your money and ID on you."

*

I looked out the airplane window at the distant structures of downtown Indy while attempting to tongue out food jammed in my wisdom tooth. The Circle looked like a disc. My lips pursed in repulsion at Midwest Bank even from a view so high in the sky. Working there seemed like a lifetime ago. I owned a completely different existence now—a phone number with a 281 area code, a Texas Discover Card, and Texas plates on the Vigor. I was a writer for an international news source in the fourth-largest city in the U.S. I was happy. I closed my eyes and thanked God for my life-changing epiphany and for the consistent job rejection in my hometown.

The airplane taxi to the gate was the longest taxi ever—at least 10 minutes. The plane coasted by Aviation Plus and I laughed at the site. I reread a text message from Vince. It said to have a good visit home. I listened to a new voice mail from

Cyril about the imperativeness of getting together to discuss our relationship. I deleted the first one when I boarded after listening to it 12 times. I then deleted Cyril's text message on the same subject. There were words misspelled, and I was offended that he didn't proofread his text message. I saved a voice mail from Audrey in case I would never hear her voice again. I also had a new text message from a white boy I had met at Sherlock's about getting together for drinks.

Sara picked me up from the airport. It was her idea to fly me home to surprise our parents. I had been back to Indy for Thanksgiving and attended the Circle of Lights on the night after to look at the fake Christmas tree created by lights and garland on the monument. My mind had drifted to my co-worker who grew up around oil rigs that were decorated with lights around Christmastime. I was bundled up in a puffy coat from college that I had found in my parents' closet, gloves with fuzz balls all over them, and a scarf-and-hat set I could no longer wear, because of my Houston residency. My friends laughed at me because it was 47 degrees outside—not cold in Indy but freezing in Houston. I could no longer handle the cold. They also made fun of me for saying "y'all."

I had been to Indy for Christmas, too, but flew back to Houston for New Year's to spend it with Cyril. It was that same eagerness I felt during breaks in college. My parents had told me details about Krupa's death when everyone went home after opening presents. They told me that Krupa was dead on the scene and that my mother carried her into the house hoping she was alive and that I was in the next room and Jency and Sara witnessed the accident. They told me that they did not press charges against the teenager who killed Krupa and that she cried, too, in the doorway of the house, her bright white face red in the cheeks as she apologized over and over while my mother screamed.

Sara and I threw our arms around each other in front of the baggage claim. Her hair was longer and stick-straight and shredded her shoulders. She wore a new color on her lips, probably chosen on an unexpected trip to the makeup counter, an event that I would've been present for if I had not lived so far away. Sara's eyebrows were freshly threaded. Her skin was darker—a summer tan created during weekends with Fred in their in-ground pool. Those weekends used to include me. I would lounge around on a honeycomb-foam raft with a full-circle pillow and raid my sister's fridge. When I would get darker, my mother would reprimand me, telling me to stop going to the pool, because the dark skin would decrease my chances of finding a husband.

"You look great," Sara said. The expression on her face revealed the extent of time that had passed between us.

We headed straight to the Def Leppard concert in Noblesville. Foreigner and Styx were the opening bands. I always wanted to go to the rock concerts with my sister when I was little, like Ratt's *Out of the Cellar* tour or White Lion's *Pride* tour. Jency listened to Madonna, Paula Abdul, and similar artists. I somehow latched on to Sara's love for rock, appreciating the instruments and developing crushes on lead singers.

"Too bad we don't have time to surprise Mom and Dad right *now*," I said.

"Yeah, there's no way." She merged onto I-465. Def Leppard's *Rock! Rock! (Till You Drop)* was blaring. "We'll be sitting in traffic on 69 forever."

"I don't really know any Styx songs." I hollowed out my purse for my lip balm. The remnants of the stick popped out onto the floor mat. I lunged for it, my right breast smashing against my thigh, seat belt slicing my face. "Five-second rule." I caught a glimpse of Sara's ZZ Top keychain in the ignition. She got it on the *Afterburner* tour and complained about how it was different from the keychain in the videos. The long part of the "Z" was on top in the videos, and the one she purchased at the concert had the short "Z" on top, so it looked as if it were upside down. She then justified the difference, claiming that the one she bought looked better.

"You do know their songs. *Babe, Come Sail Away, Renegade.* You definitely know those." Sara sang the chorus of *Babe.*

I cut her off. "Oh yeah! I do know that one." I recapped the stick and put it in a side pocket for uncomplicated access. "No Lou Gramm tonight, though. Do you know anything about Foreigner's current lead singer?"

"I'm not sure who he is. Probably some young guy who grew up listening to Foreigner." Sara sighed. "God, I miss the guitar solos."

The traffic on I-69 inched along in two lanes and then merged into grueling singularity on the exit ramp even though we'd left three hours before the concert. Sara didn't want to miss any of it.

The usher had a body-builder physique but a face like a little boy, with big blue eyes and rosy rounds on pasty cheeks. "My name's Chuck and I'll be your host for the evening!"

Sara and I followed him to our seats in the last row. I turned around and looked up and down the chaotic lawn scene. I focused on a group of teenagers dressed in all black, with black hair and mud-covered legs. Most of the people spread throughout the lawn fell closer to my age group, although there were 40-year-old men lined up in the front rows of the lawn with rented chairs and big beers. They had to have been there for at least three hours. "I've never even been to Deer Creek," I said.

"It's Verizon now." Sara slouched comfortably in her seat.

"Oh *yeah*. I always do that." I looked up and down at the lawn scene again. "It's just too white."

"What is?"

"The people."

"You said that the other times you were here. You grew up here. It's nothing new."

"I know, but I'm just not used to it anymore. I really appreciate the diverse cultures of Houston."

Sara pointed at the roof of the tent. "The last concert I went to here was Kiss. Gene Simmons flew out to the top. It was so cool." She took a sip of beer, the condensation from the cup dripping onto her gray Triumph shirt with black sleeves from the 1985 *Thunder Seven* tour. "Ah." She shook her head dreamily. "Oh how I miss the guitar solos."

"We got a great show for you tonight!" Chuck animatedly pointed to the stage, trying not to jump up and down. "Def Leppard rocks!" He swung his arm under and pointed to the stage. "Foreigner rocks! Styx rocks! Three great bands! What more could you ask for? Enjoy the show. I know I will! And let me know if you need anything."

We didn't recognize Foreigner's lead singer. He had hair like Stephen Tyler's and wore sunglasses and a flowing red blouse with tight jeans. "He looks young!" yelled Sara over the music. "He kinda sounds like Lou Gramm."

The person in front of us turned around. He had long hair and wore a black Foreigner T-shirt. "It's Kelly Hansen from Hurricane!"

Sara pointed at Mick Jones. "He's the only original member!" she yelled over the music.

"I know who he is!" I watched Mick on guitar. He wore dark sunglasses and a white long-sleeve shirt with the cuffs rolled and the first few buttons undone.

Foreigner walked off stage as if the show was over. "They'll come back and play *Hot Blooded*," laughed Sara.

Hansen began singing *Hot Blooded*.

"Yeah, it didn't seem like it would've been over yet," I said.

"I bet Styx and Def Leppard will do the same. They'll come back and play *Renegade* and *Rock of Ages*."

"No *Waiting for a Girl Like You*, though," I said. "I love, love, love that song."

"Yeah," said Sara. "I lost my virginity to that song." We sat down as Styx's roadies set up. "That sax player during *Urgent* was badass."

"Excuse me." A short man in a Trixter T-shirt tapped Sara on the shoulder until she turned around. "Excuse me." He popped his head between us. Dark chest hair gushed out of his shirt and climbed his neck. He held a cup of beer, the foam bouncing around the rim. Alcohol dripped from his hand. "Can you give us your stubs so we can get in and sit in those empty seats next to you? You can go ahead and meet us at the end. We'll give them right back to you."

There was a woman with him who wore what looked like a self-made pink Bon Jovi halter top. The stitching was busted from the stress of the tight fit even though she was very thin. The threads dangled from the waist. Her nipples poked through on descending breasts. Blond hair and black roots ended at the top of her ears. The couple looked about 45 or 35 years old with a high trans-fat diet.

"No, we can't do that." Sara rolled her eyes. She turned to me. "Basically they want to steal our seats and we'll have no proof that these are our seats."

"I tried to get them tickets, honey. I tried."

The woman sighed, her breasts falling even lower. The man put his hand on her ass as they staggered away toward concessions.

I didn't recognize most of the Styx songs. I liked Tommy Shaw's long velour jacket in the summertime. Lawrence

Gowan played on a platform with a spinning keyboard, hitting the keys behind his back, snapping photos of the band, and throwing out Polaroids into the audience.

"Oh, this is a good one!" Sara sang along to *Too Much Time on My Hands* and rocked her head back and forth. "This song came out when I was like 10!"

I thought of Krupa and wondered if it was a song they'd liked together.

"Excuse me." The man pulled on Sara's shirt. "Can we have just one stub?"

"*No!*" Sara shot back around and started head-banging as if nothing had happened.

I stared at them, bothered that they had the nerve to come back. The man pulled on Sara's shirt again. "Hey, girl, what's your name?"

Sara was oblivious, head-banging and screaming the words.

I was uncomfortable with the couple standing behind us. I watched, waiting for them to leave.

"What a bitch!" the man said.

I gasped.

"They need to go back to where they came from!" shouted the woman. Her face dropped when she realized I'd heard her.

"Ooh, that's original!" I tipped the bottom of the woman's beer cup. Alcohol spilled onto her chest. "We've never heard *that* one before!"

Sara was still head-banging and screaming the words to the song.

The woman slurred curse words as she swabbed her halter top with her hand. "You Puerto Ricans need to go back to Puerto Rico."

Sara turned around.

"What is going on?" asked Chuck. He motioned for a police officer to come in closer.

"They keep coming up to us and demanding our ticket stubs so they can sit in the seats next to us."

"That's bullshit." The man stumbled a bit. "That little bitch is making that up."

I gasped.

"We told them we weren't giving them our tickets," said Sara. We are trying to watch the concert." She turned halfway around, attempting to be discreet about watching Styx on stage.

"She spilled my beer on me," said the woman while pointing aggressively at me.

"You are not supposed to be standing here," said the police officer.

The man stumbled backward. A thin white joint of karma tumbled to the ground out of his pocket. "That, that, that's not what it is." He reached down to try to pick up the joint.

The cop cuffed him. "We are going to search you too, ma'am. Come with me."

"You should've told me what was going on earlier," said Chuck. "I like to fight."

I laughed. "It would've been hard to get your attention."

Chuck told us to start screaming and yelling for him next time. "Just flail your arms and I'll be at your side."

"All right. I will."

"Are you ABCD?" asked Chuck. He crossed his arms confidently. "ABCD, aren't you?" His cheeks became rosier as he smiled.

"What?"

"You know. ABCD. Another Born Confused Desi."

I laughed. "Yes, I do know what you're talking about. I ... I guess. How do you know about ABCD?"

"You're a desi," he said. "You're a desi, all right." He smiled goofily. "I'm always looking out for my desis." He hit his chest twice with his fist. "I got much love for my desis."

"So how do you know about desis?"

"I have a lot of Indian friends."

"You *do*?"

"Yeah, I'm from Chicago."

"I see."

"Well, you let me know if anything else happens. I like to fight and I got much love for my desis." He turned around after he walked away and hit his chest with his fist again. "I got much love for my desis," he mouthed.

CHAPTER 12

I placed a copy of *Petroleum Insight* on the kitchen table in front of my mother, who was drinking morning tea out of an old chipped coffee cup from the '70s, refusing to consume the senior coffee from McDonald's that my father purchased after his trip to Menards. Her hair looked calmly greasy from an after-shower baby-oil application. Her eyes were lined with kohl. She'd been so surprised to see me the night before. "I heard your voice," she said as she hugged me, an embrace that lined up our short bodies. My mother had just slipped under the covers, going to bed for the night. "I heard your voice."

She planned on making my favorites—beef cutlets, chicken biryani, chappatis, sambar, idli, and egg curry. I had learned how to make everything (except for idli and chappatis) on my Christmas trip to Indy. I had brought back to Houston jars (labeled by my mother) of coriander, turmeric, chicken masala, egg/vegetable masala, mustard seeds, cardamom, cinnamon, cloves, and moong beans. I made egg curry once a week in my studio. The first time I had cooked the favorite, I added too much turmeric powder, creating large orange chunks I had to scrape out of the pan. I had accidentally made extra servings of moong beans and had to use them as dressing on sandwiches and toppers on salads.

My father had been stunned when he opened the front door. He hugged me, glasses off, wearing an old Hanes T-shirt and a drab gold lungi with white squares. He laughed in surprise, a string of dental floss between healthily wrinkled fingers.

"Here's my first major article." I had e-mailed it to my family and friends but wanted them to have hard copies, too. I was so proud of it, scooting the issue over, centering it in front of my mother as I almost stubbed my toe on the large potted curry plant. On the cover was a natural-gas pipeline with engineers in hard hats and dirt tracks left from CAT excavators. "It's an international piece." I was so impressed with myself, knowing that people not only in the U.S. but in France, Saudi Arabia, Yemen, Nigeria, Japan, Angola, Mexico, Peru, Norway, and other countries could be reading my article at that moment. I kept an issue on my kitchen counter and on the fridge, since I had no coffee table in my studio, and looked at my name in print several times a week.

I handed an issue to Jency. She hadn't changed since I last saw her. She was fashionably conservative as usual, in a short-sleeve white cotton blouse with pinlike ruffles above her breasts and loose-fitting pastel-blue Bermuda shorts. She owned flat shoes in basic colors to match everything. Her husband, Eric, was at work, performing a root canal on a Saturday morning. Their three children were present, Lily, Ty, and Noah. The kids were surprised also and had been kept in the dark about my visit to prevent any slipups.

I also handed an issue to Fred. He was wearing a Skid Row T-shirt that he rarely wore, because Sara always stole it from his closet for her own use. Sara snatched the issue from him and then they kissed—a small, playful peck. They didn't want children. They were content as a twosome, a couple who got to have fun whenever they wanted. They did not have to attend school functions, go to parent-teacher conferences, or save money for college tuition. My mother was in denial about their decision—a choice that Sara and Fred both agreed and bonded on in the early stages of their courtship.

"That is so cool." Sara combed her fingers through her hair, sinking to the carpet. She leaned against the couch, legs under the coffee table, feet sticking out. "Look at Aunt Mala's picture next to her article." I wore a hot pink suit in the photo with a white shirt underneath. It was nicely airbrushed, the zit on my chin smoothed into my complexion, and the redness on my left nostril from a runny nose blended.

Lily, Ty, and Noah gathered around Sara.

"Cool!"

"Neat!"

"How'd you get your *picture* in there, Aunt Mala?" asked Noah as he pretended to make his trains fly. I couldn't believe how tall he was. His face was starting to grow into his big, brown, snuggly eyes. He was a perfect mix of Jency and Eric, with dark brown hair, a prominent chin, and a large nose.

"She wrote it," said Lily, speaking in a tone spoken by adults to children. It was a tone that was new or maybe just new to my ears. Lily did not possess any Indian traits and could easily pass for a white girl, with her summertime sun-kissed hair and watermelon-colored tan. Her ninth birthday was in a couple of days. I watched Lily smile and took note of her mannerisms, understanding what Krupa was like at the exact, young age of her death.

"How did you *write* that?" asked Ty. He played with his DiGi-Draw on the carpet. Ty was the only one with black hair. His eyes were golden brown, with eyelashes that women hoped to achieve every morning in the mirror. His skin was white, and he looked the most like my mother, with black hair and a light-colored body. He had taken up art classes at the YMCA, of which I was aware through our 30-second phone conversations. He had also recently gone on a field trip to Conner Prairie.

"That's what I do at work." I plopped onto the couch, both hands in my zip-up hoodie pockets, catching a glimpse of Krupa's photo on the fireplace mantle. I scratched the inside of my arms. I developed a skin rash during each trip to Indy, and when I landed back in Houston it would disappear within days. I looked down at the floor at the Connect Four game, Chutes and Ladders, trucks, stuffed animals, and Polly Pocket dolls. And when I looked at Lily's Cinderella DVD, I thought of the *Nobody's Fool* video, with Tom Keifer's pouty lips and Jeff LaBar and Eric Brittingham's guitar neck swing, instead of fairy godmothers, glass slippers, and evil stepsisters.

"Awesome!" Ty submerged his hand in his bowl, scooping breakfast into his mouth, oatmeal gushing from his hand and face.

"Ty!" Jency got up to get a towel. "You can't eat with your hands. I've told you this before."

"But Grandma and Grandpa do it. I want to eat with my hands, Mommy."

"Use the spoon." She held the stainless steel spoon firmly by the handle in her left hand.

"Don't use your left hand, Mommy!" yelled Ty. "Grandma and Grandpa say that's evil."

My mother swept the issue off the table and handed it to my father, who had just read the *Manorama* in the old periwinkle recliner, failing to show any interest in reading my article. "Look at Mala's article." He had just moved the recliner to the family room that morning. Other things were different in the house as well. My mother had changed the linen colors of the upstairs bathroom to white. There were new framed photos of my niece and nephews on shelves, presenting recent changes in face structure and smiles with more or less teeth. New turquoise-rimmed white plates were in the cabinets, a round Oriental rug in the living room replaced a rectangular mass of fibers, and a new soap dispenser in the master bathroom did not match the toothbrush holder and soap dish.

I leaned over and flipped to Page 8. "Here's my article."

My father flipped back to the cover. "Fifteen *dollars*? That is ridiculous. Who would pay that much?"

"People do," I said coldly.

He looked up and down the pages silently before reading. "Aren't there supposed to be two spaces after a period in an article? You don't have two spaces. You did this wrong."

"They need to make it fit, Dad. It doesn't matter how many spaces there are." I glared at him even though he wasn't looking. "That's not my job anyway. I don't do the layout." I leaned back on the couch, disappointed for attempting to uselessly defend myself.

He kept reading. "This picture is kind of blurry." He lifted it up to show me.

The photo was crystal clear, an aerial view of LNG tanks. *Petroleum Insight* used only high-resolution photos.

"It's ridiculous that they have blurry photos. What a crappy magazine."

I leaned back on the couch and looked away.

"You have Tulsa here with no state. You forgot to put Oklahoma."

"That's our style, *Dad*," I said, not really hiding how annoyed I was with him. "There's a manual of style."

"Well, you put Sohar, Oman, here." His voice rose. "You were supposed to put Oklahoma with Tulsa. It's wrong."

"It is not *wrong*. Everyone in the oil-and-gas industry knows Tulsa. We have a certain *style* that we follow. There are other people that read over my work. I'm not the only one." I rolled my eyes in one long whirl.

He took a few minutes to read the rest of my article and then closed the magazine. "That was a good article, but no one reads magazines anymore."

I laughed, and then Jency laughed. Sara rolled her eyes.

He broke out the last bite of a banana and dropped the peel on the closed issue, covering up a section of the pipeline.

"Well, *we* love it, Mala," said Fred.

I slid the issue out from under the peel when my father walked away. I brushed it off and gave the magazine to my mother for safekeeping with my previous awards, scholarship certificates, and kindergarten projects.

*

"The food court looks different." I looked out into the sea of white people, the eating area in brighter light than the rest of the mall. The concentrated food area appeared to be more spacious, with new restaurants, higher-quality tables and chairs, and fresh signage on the original restaurants. The janitor looked familiar, and I slowed my walk to get a better look. It was Lucas Ward.

"They did some remodeling." My mother carried her long-strap purse like a clutch under her arm. She unwrapped a Nutri-Grain bar.

"No more Taco Bell," I said. "Where's Penn Station?"

"Both gone." She handed pieces of the bar to Lily, Ty, and Noah before feeding herself.

"Luca Pizza?"

"It's Pizza di Roma now."

"Ooh I want pizza," said Noah. He swung Jency's hand back and forth.

"We just ate lunch, little boy."

"Maybe we'll get cookies later," I said, my eyes growing in exaggeration for my nephew. I realized that the cookie place I grew up with had changed to Blondie's Cookies.

"Yummy!"

I looked at all the teenagers. Greenwood Park Mall was the hangout for the kids on the south side. I used to go there every weekend with my friends or to Movies 8, finishing the night off with a steakburger with cheese and everything and fries (with cheese on the side occasionally) at Steak N' Shake on Meridian and Stop 11.

I had smoked my first cigarette at the mall near the food-court exit next to a Dumpster. I was with Shannon, who had recently been suspended from school for smoking a cigarette in the bathroom. Also at the Dumpster were 15-year-old gang-member wannabes from local township schools who listened to Bone Thugs-N-Harmony, shoplifted, and told tales of hittin' it and quittin' it with flocks of teenage girls. I held the cigarette between my fingers.

Shannon lighted the cigarette with a Zippo she stole from a music store on County Line and 31.

My lips barely touched the butt.

"You have to suck on it," instructed Shannon. "Then exhale."

I blew out smoke, wondering why I didn't cough on my first time like I had seen on TV and heard about from others.

"You didn't inhale." Shannon rolled her eyes and lighted her second cigarette. One of the guys complimented her baggy khaki cargo pants. Then he told her he liked her necklace. Shannon touched the wood beads of the hemp choker as seductively as she could and informed him that she'd stolen it. She took a puff off her cigarette and told him she liked his hair. It was bleach blond with spikes like skewers. There were dandruff flakes on the shoulders of his black patch-adorned coat. He stuck his tongue down Shannon's throat and put his hand up her shirt, pushing her against the wall, almost running into the Dumpster.

I watched them as a cigarette burned between my fingers. I was wearing a flannel shirt, loose jeans, and powder that was too light for my skin—more evident in photos. My braces were coming off soon. I wondered when I would even have my first kiss.

One of the gang-member wannabes approached me. "You got another cigarette?" He had struggling white skin, sunken, heroin-addict cheeks, bloodshot brown eyes, and stubble that blushed around his face in the shape of an upside-down rainbow. He had a shaved line through his left eyebrow and chapped lips, with skin peeling around the corners of his mouth and in the center of his lower lip.

"No, but you can have this one." I liked the attention. I couldn't believe a boy was giving me attention.

His middle finger skimmed the palm of my hand as he took the cigarette from me. He pushed his sleeve up while he smoked the cigarette. His coat was two sizes too big, as was the black hooded Ecko sweatshirt underneath. His jeans fell around the middle of his thighs, and on his feet were a dirty pair of white K-Swiss. A massive gold herringbone chain hung down his chest. "Where you from?"

I froze. "From around here."

"That's not what I—"

I cut him off. "My parents were born and raised in India."

"They *only* speak two languages in India," he said. "Spanish and Portuguese. Those be the official languages."

I laughed in his face, then laughed again when I noticed how confident he was in his statement.

"Many languages are spoken in India." I did not tell him that Hindi was the official language. I didn't tell him about Malayalam or Konkani or Tamil, Gujarati or Telugu or Marathi.

"Well, I *knew* someone that lived there and spoke these languages," he said arrogantly. He paused as if he were expecting me to admit I was wrong.

I laughed in his face again. I didn't believe him. "Maybe the person you *knew*"—I did the quote sign with my fingers when I said "knew"—"lived in a colony or something." I looked at Shannon, who was still making out with the gangster wannabe.

"Do your parents have an accent?"

I rolled my eyes. "*Yeah.*" I thought it was a stupid question. I couldn't imagine it getting any worse.

"How could they still have their accent if they live in America?"

I ignored him.

He looked at his feet while dragging them. "I have a Mexican friend. He'd probably date you."

I pulled out the pack of Marlboro Lights that I held on to for Shannon. I lighted one and took a puff, coughing several times, causing my upper body to shoot forward.

"Can you understand your parents since they have an accent?"

My eyes grew. "*Of course* I can understand them."

"But ... but how?"

"They're my parents!"

There was a long silence as he looked as if he was trying to understand. I dropped my cigarette to the ground and stepped on it.

"So you're Hindi, right?"

"It's Hin*du* and no, I'm not Hindu. I'm Catholic."

"Oh. So why don't Hindus eat meat?"

I braced myself. "It's a religious thing."

"*Well*, if they'd eat the cow they wouldn't starve."

I gasped.

*

The bubbly purple and green flowers faded out on the sheer fabric as the tank top became wider at the bottom. I held the flowing tank to my chest as I turned to my mother. "What do you think of this shirt, Mom?" I would need a white tank top to wear under it. There was summer clothing on clearance to be replaced by sweaters, fleeces, coats, and corduroys for a cold and snowy October, November, December, January, and February. I could still wear the summer clothes during the so-called winter months in Houston.

"It's nice." Her hands sifted through a rack of clothes, the hangers banging against each other.

"I love it!" Lily put her hands on the shirt and twirled around.

Jency, Sara, Ty, and Noah stayed in the mall area and took turns sitting in a massage chair while they waited for us to finish shopping.

My cell phone rang and I sent it to voice mail as Cyril's number flashed on the screen. I had deleted his phone number but had it memorized.

"Yesterday," my mother began. "He got angry because I forgot to bring a coupon when we went to the grocery store. He told me to pay him the dollar when we got home."

"Mom, it's time for you to get the divorce."

"Then he said that he didn't want the money and I told him that he shouldn't have asked for it in the first place."

"You need to just get a divorce. You sold your wedding ring. You might as well get a divorce." I peered at my mother's bare left ring finger. She'd thrown it in the trash in a rage. Then dug it out and sold it.

"You always say that. I'm not getting a divorce."

"What are you guys talking about?" asked Lily.

"Nothing," we replied at the same time.

Lily and I got in line to buy the shirt. The cashier's hair was bright, an unnatural red that looked as if it were dyed on a weekly basis. Spins of black eye makeup devoured her pupils with every blink. She had a silver cheek piercing on the right side of her face, the barbell jewelry post moving in and out. She did not blend with her co-workers.

One sales associate beamed as she suspended swimsuits on hangers. She tossed her headband-managed auburn hair. It settled at a perfect edge on her back. Her bangs were curled under across her forehead. A sand-colored blouse was precisely tucked into dress pants with buttoned back pockets. An even amount of fabric showed all the way around her waist. Another sales associate was putting away return clothes, smiling as well, in a short-sleeve blouse with egg-shaped pearl buttons to the top of her neck. Her knees down to her ankles were exposed but shielded with beige hosiery.

The cashier smiled at me as she scanned the price tag. When she turned around to get a bag, I noticed black fishnets on her pasty white legs, a deep fringe line around the bottom of her dress, and short black boots with no heels on her feet. She bagged the shirt. "*You* people are so beautiful." She glanced at my mother. "With your dark hair and your dark eyes and your dark skin."

Lily giggled.

I spun and looked at my mother. She was looking through a rack of crotch-covering mini-jean skirts, disapprovingly.

"Does your mother speak Indian?"

I looked back at her again. "I … *guess.*"

The cashier leaned forward against the counter. A smidge of black eye makeup had fallen next to her nose. Her eyes intensely locked on mine. She recited a phrase to me that wasn't in English. "Do you know what *that* means?"

I looked to the side then looked at her blankly. "*No.*"

"That means 'hello' in Indian."

CHAPTER 13

My entire family went to the movies together in one car while I hung out with my friends. I said a prayer that they wouldn't die in a car crash, because I couldn't handle being all alone. I wanted to be dead before all of them. I didn't want to live without them.

I hadn't been back to Indiana University since accepting my diploma in Assembly Hall, wearing a jean skirt and blue cotton V-neck beneath my gown, and under my cap black roots fused into burgundy-tinted locks.

Energy levels rose on the car ride south on 37. Police officers lined the interstate, busting college students speeding by with friends from a weekend trip or racing through with trunkfuls of homemade favorites, processed food, and clean laundry. Laughs and conversations lacking moments of silence passed the time as Tom drove me, Audrey, and Jackie to Bloomington. We planned on playing Sink the Biz at Nick's English Hut, shopping for posters or matted photos at Greetings while strolling down Kirkwood, driving past the arboretum, and, on the morning drive home, stopping by Oliver Winery for indoor wine tasting and bottle sampling by the pond with baguettes and cheese.

Students, mostly in sweats and with messy ponytails or disheveled hair under baseball caps, walked near Briscoe

Quad and McNutt with their fingers on their chests over backpack straps or hung out with friends after dinner at the food courts, holding bottles or fountain drinks.

"The Virgin Vault!" Audrey tilted her head back, off the seat, at Foster Harper. "Let's go in!" She took a sip of water from a tall drinking glass she brought from her kitchen cabinet.

"Do we *have* to?" Tom pulled the car in front of Harper without waiting for an answer.

"Maybe we can stop by Gresham and get Potato Oles from Taco John's," said Jackie. "Remember how we used to eat those almost every day freshman year? Remember how fat we were?"

"Freshman 15." My mouth watered. "What if they don't even *have* Taco John's anymore?"

"Freshman 20." Audrey folded up a package of peanut butter-and-cheese sandwich crackers she couldn't finish. She took off her glasses, which were filmy and needed to be cleaned. She pressed in her contacts.

"Freshman 25," said Jackie.

"My poundage was all from beer." Tom patted his stomach twice.

"I want to see our old room," I said as we passed two young men who neglected to hold the door for us. Audrey and I roomed together on the fourth floor and Jackie stayed on the fifth floor freshman year.

"God, think about all the roommates I went through in this building." Jackie spun in a half-circle as she looked around and cringed. "There was that girl that stayed for the day and moved all of her stuff out because she was scared to be so far away from Kentucky. Then there was that athlete with braces who always made her boyfriend sleep on the floor. Then there was Dani from Marion Catholic who always had sex with her trailer-trash boyfriend while I was in the room. Then there was that goth chick who used to eat all my Ramen noodles then lie about it. And she did that weird voodoo with carrot sticks."

I laughed. "You did have it rough that first semester." My phone beeped twice. Then it beeped twice again. One message was from Cyril, asking me to call him. The other text was a "hope you're having fun" message from Vince.

A young woman who appeared to be a junior or a senior manned the front desk. Her face was fresh and her hair brown, brushed straight but with missed strands of waves. "How can I help you?" She planted her elbows on the counter, forcing her chin to plop through her palms. There was puffiness to her eyes and a temporarily wasted structure to her features. She snatched a pack of cigarettes off the desk as if they demeaned her professionalism as a front-desk associate and pulled one out from behind her ear and put it in her pocket. "Do you plan on staying at Foster?"

We all glanced at each other.

"Yeah!" Audrey threw her arms up.

"Okay, well I can give you a tour of the model room."

I remembered viewing the fictitious dorm room the summer before freshman year. It was every mother's dream, with crisp sheets on a made bed, coordinating pillows, and a bedspread with a blanket folded on top. The spotless carpet and the textbooks neatly lined up on a bookshelf and stacked on a desk were the biggest fantasies. An unmade bed with Febreezed sheets, piles of clothes on a floor stained by beer and Easy Mac, illegally purchased cheap alcohol, and zipper bags of marijuana on the desk would have been a realistic replica of a college dorm room.

"Yay!" Audrey clapped her hands.

"Do you know which building you'll be staying in? This is Harper, the largest building. It's co-ed."

"It's co-ed now?" I asked.

"Well, it has been for some time." She sifted through a ring full of keys and moved out from behind the desk. "Then there's Jenkinson, Magee, Martin, and Shea."

"No, we don't know which one. We just know that we are staying at Foster." I giggled at my own lie.

"Well, *you'll* be staying at Shea." She adjusted her bra strap, yanking it on top of her collarbone. "That's our international dorm."

I was speechless. I frowned as my chin tilted downward, with my eyes on the front-desk associate. I didn't speak with an accent. I was not dressed in a sari. There was no bindi on my forehead. My hair wasn't in a braid that reached my lower back. My jeans were tight and flared at the bottom over tall black heels. My shirt was blue and low-cut, revealing cleavage. I didn't understand how she could even consider me to be an international student. I was standing there with three white, American friends.

I did have a brown friend at one time in my life at IU whom I met my freshman year in economics class at Ballantine Hall. Shazia was a Pakistani Muslim who was tall and skeletal yet still very beautiful, with long, black sunny hair that moved fluidly like the hair of women in hair commercials. She had full lips on a trim face and a brass-colored mole wedged in at the edge of her nostril. It didn't steal her prettiness but would look ugly on someone else. Shazia's birthday was on Saint Patrick's Day, but she officially declared the day before as her date of birth to prevent the St. Patty's Day hype from stealing her special day. Her parents were very strict. She owned an open closet full of strapless and stomach-revealing tops and hoochie shorts and skirts but had to hide them at a friend's place when she went home to Evansville for the summers.

Shazia introduced me to her Indian and Pakistani friends, always mentioning that my sisters married white men. Shazia was acquainted with the small group of Indians and Pakistanis from Evansville. They ridiculed me for not knowing that "FOB" stood for "fresh off the boat" or because I didn't own Indian clothes or know the Indian girls from my hometown. I did not like any of Shazia's friends, but I did like the cultural connection of our friendship. Shazia understood my upbringing.

Then I caught Shazia with my first boyfriend. We had only dated for 3½ months, but he was still mine. It should have been no surprise, as Shazia routinely messed around with her RA's boyfriend. She messed around with other girls' boyfriends even though she was dating someone, too, a townie busboy at Scotty's Brewhouse. She never seemed to feel guilty. She always blamed the boyfriends, saying that they were jerks for cheating on their girlfriends and that she would never actually date any of them.

"Mala." Shazia attempted to sound remorseful as she cocked her head to the side. She was completely naked, going down on my boyfriend with her hair pulled back in a ponytail. It was the first time that I had ever seen her hair pulled back. "I'm so sorry."

I never wanted to see Shazia again, but I did—at a department store on Third Street at the start of junior year. I needed to return a 99-cent package of hair things and purchase double-sided tape to mount a full-length mirror to my room door at Willkie. I pushed a cart around in case I wanted to buy other things. I entered cosmetics. I perused the lip glosses and then somehow fell into eye pencils, then powders, blushes, and mascaras until I was conducting full price comparisons with all the brands. I was too cheap to buy anything from the makeup counters at the mall. "Copper Coral" was an appealing color out of the rows of lip-gloss tubes in the glaring lights of the aisle.

"I like that color," said a shopper in the aisle with me. She was a cute girl and, without speaking more words, revealed a bubbly personality. Her hair was medium length and intense blond. She wore a tech vest with a neon-green, skin-hugging Abercrombie & Fitch shirt underneath, tucked into jeans, exposing a white, jewel-studded cloth belt. Her eyelashes were encrusted in black mascara, and her foundation looked chalky on a pimple between her eyes.

"Yeah, me too." The color in the tube always looked different on my lips. I squeezed the tube. A bit of product oozed out. "I like darker colors, though."

"Yeah, I like dark nail polish." She tossed her rosy-white hands up, palms in her face, then back onto the cart. She sauntered on until she reached the bronzers.

"I mean like these Mexicans, they all stare at us. Like they all lay bricks," said a loud girl behind us in the aisle talking to a friend. They were young, probably sophomores, and skinny with tight skirts and matching short blond hair and white flip-flops.

"Yeah. Mexicans are everywhere now," responded her friend.

"That is derogatory and offensive," said the shopper in the Abercrombie shirt. She looked over at me. "What you are saying is racist and you should not be saying it." She looked at me again. "You are offending someone that is not speaking up for herself." She looked at me again.

"Whatever." The two girls walked out of the aisle.

"I was defending you," she said to me.

"Defending me?"

"Well, yes. You weren't defending yourself."

"I'm not Mexican."

"You're not? Wow. You look so Mexican."

"No. I don't. I look Indian."

"You're *Indian*? My roommate's Indian." She stopped what she was doing, clutching the cart handle with both hands. "Her name's Rima. Do you know her?"

"No."

"So have you been to India a lot?"

"A few times."

"My roommate seems to go a lot. If she's not getting an 'A' in a class, she drops the class. She says her parents will be mad at her."

I raised my eyebrows.

"Rima never goes out and does anything." She wobbled her head. "She's always studying." She smoothed her hair into a fake ponytail and then set it loose around her shoulders.

"My *mom's* part-Indian."

I looked up from the lip gloss at the blonde with the popping blue eyes. "Do you mean Native American? You don't have anyone in your family that's from India, do you?"

"No."

"So, she's Native American, not Indian."

"That's what I meant." She giggled innocently. "I'm *so* bad with that stuff."

I left the aisle, lip gloss in cart, and casually browsed the store, stopping by all clearance end caps. I bought a tube of lip gloss that I found on clearance and a roll of double-sided tape and put them in my purse with the receipt. I pushed the cart toward the corrals at the front of the store and then I saw her. Shazia.

"Mala," she said in that same fake-guilty voice from years ago.

It bothered me that I remembered her voice, that it was still familiar. The sound of my own name stabbed the air and echoed in my head. I never really told Shazia off as I thought I would tell someone off in a dramatic situation.

Audrey had cussed her out at the Bluebird one night when Hairbangers Ball was performing. I had stood to the side and watched as Audrey screamed in Shazia's face and shook her by the shoulders. Audrey also left messages on my ex-boyfriend's voice mail, calling him a loser and telling him I was too good for him. She relayed the same message in e-mail format as well. Jackie wasn't as hard-core as Audrey but flipped her off several times throughout the night.

I pushed the cart toward Shazia. The images of Shazia's mouth on my ex-boyfriend flashed through my mind. I ran at Shazia with the cart, heart racing, calves pumping, wheels of the cart squeaking against the hard-tiled floor. I heard Shazia call my name out again but in a more panicked tone. Then I heard a loud booming sound as Shazia buckled at the knees, her head flying back but her hair still streaming flawlessly. I took off running, ramming my elbow against the edge of the cart, with no shopping bags to slow my speed.

"Mommy!" A little boy cried out.

I didn't look both ways when running to the Vigor. I added extra scratches next to the keyhole as I fumbled with the lock. The car alarm went off. "Damn actuator!" I turned the key to the right to turn it off while catching a glimpse of a traditional mint, split in half, in front of my feet. I calmed down as I felt safe in the Vigor. The scent of my perfume lingered in the car, a combination of orchids and pink grapefruit. My keys dangled manically in the ignition. I caught a glimpse of the Valvoline oil-change sticker in the left corner of the windshield and my precisely shaped eyebrows and naturally thick black lashes in the rearview mirror. I fastened my seat belt and rolled the windows down, the rear windows both stopping at a swanky slant, as I turned right at the light onto Third Street.

*

The tall shot glass dripped of beer as I pulled it out of the bucket. I sank the Bismarck.

"Throw it back!" Tom poured more beer into his glass.

Audrey and Jackie chanted my name. Two of Tom's acquaintances, grad students at IU, chimed in. I was disgusted, drinking out of the bucket with people I did not know. I never thought twice about it during my college drinking days at Nick's. I checked them quickly from across the table for mouth sores.

I gagged slightly as the shot glass touched my lips. I dropped my thoughts of Tom's friends' possibly infectious backwash and threw it back. I couldn't finish it in one gulp. I blamed it on being full from a Nick's burger when in reality I couldn't handle doing shots anymore and I was tired from partying the night before at Rock Lobster.

"Save room for Rockets pizza," said Audrey. "Or Aver's."

"I don't want any freaky-deaky pizza," said Jackie. "No Aver's."

"I'm supposed to get Bob Evans with my parents sometime tomorrow, too," I said. "Sunshine Skillet with biscuits. It'll be a restaurant full of white people and me and my parents." I felt ill as I thought of all the food I had eaten in the short time I had been in Indy—White Castle, Rally's, Steak 'n Shake, Penn Station, and Hardee's. I wanted to eat at all the restaurants that were not in Houston. With my sisters, I also dined at a Mexican restaurant we'd frequented, but because of the Mexican restaurants in Houston, it was no longer tasty.

The game started back up again around the table. Each person poured beer into the Nick's-emblem shot glass from their drinking glass. The shot glass bobbed around in the beer-filled bucket. Tom poured his beer into the shot glass until it sank into the bucket, purposely sinking the Biz. "Oh, damn," he said sarcastically. "I sank the Biz."

"I have to pee." I banged my knee on the table when I stood up.

"Ha ha wasted," said Tom.

I looked at Audrey and Jackie. "Don't you have to go?"

"No." Audrey tapped her glass, a drop of beer landing in the shot glass as she poured.

"I'm not breaking the seal," said Jackie.

"Are you kidding me?" I laughed. "No one else has to pee?" The bathroom was an uncomfortable size but not as incommodious as the bathroom at Upstairs Pub. I looked in the mirror wondering why no one told me I looked so hideous.

I made my way back, noticing Seth Harris sitting with a group, laughing, talking, and drinking. He was my classmate at St. Agnes and Marion Catholic. We made eye contact, and he slid out of the booth when I came closer to the table.

"Hey Mala. How are you?" Seth didn't have any friends in grade school or high school. Kids made fun of him for being smarter than average and stuttering while speaking. I ran into him every once in a while on campus. We always acknowledged each other but never conversed.

Seth introduced me to his friends in the booth, all IU graduates.

"Wow. Houston," he said. "That's far." He dropped his hands into his pockets and leaned against the wall, indicating a platform for extended conversation. He was confident, more outgoing. "I'm in med school."

His friend grabbed my arm, pulling me down to look at my earrings. They were gold chandelier earrings, caked in circular sections of rubies and diamonds connected by pearl clusters.

"Where did you get those?"

"My parents got them for me in India."

"Cool." Her eyes were glazed over. She sent my arm flying and then leaned over her beer with her head in her hands.

"I'm actually here with Audrey and Jackie and some other people," I said, focusing back on Seth. "We're all playing Sink the Biz, of course."

"Audrey and I were two really quiet people in grade school and high school," he said.

"Audrey *was* quiet around people that she didn't want to talk to." I smirked as I thought of how much Audrey hated that comment.

"I see Marion Catholic people all the time."

"Yeah. I did when I lived here." I suddenly had one of my "what if I'd never left Indiana?" moments. "I actually just threw away my high school yearbooks this morning. I was going through some random bins in my room for Goodwill. I didn't want the yearbooks to take up space at my parents' house, and I definitely don't want them taking up space at my place in Houston."

Seth was silent.

"Well, we'll be over there if you want to say hi." I pointed in the direction of our table, being insincere in my invitation, as a means of ending the conversation.

I sat in my seat. "Guess who I ran into."

"Oh God," said Jackie, rolling her eyes. "Who?"

"Seth Harris." I turned to Audrey and laughed. "He said you were really quiet in grade school and high school. He said the same thing about himself."

Audrey rolled her eyes. "I wasn't quiet with the people that I liked."

"Marion Catholic people are everywhere," said Jackie. "I mean, seriously. You can't escape them. Snobs."

I dived back into the game, drunk from one shot of beer and the breezy sips from my drinking glass.

"Hey guys!"

Seth startled me. I couldn't believe he took the invitation seriously.

"I thought I'd come by and say hi," he said. He sat in the empty seat next to me.

I introduced him while I tapped a drop of beer into the shot glass.

"So you're going to India?" he asked.

"No."

"I thought you said something to my friend about going to India."

"No my earrings are from India."

"You're Filipino, right? Aren't you Filipino or something?"

The alcohol froze my furrowed eyebrows longer than usual. I spaced out at him, missing Jackie sinking the Biz. Then I looked at Audrey. Her two different-colored eyes glowed the same color. "Fili*pino*?" Everyone at school knew me as "the Indian girl." "Or *something*?"

I heard laughter from Audrey, Jackie, and Tom.

"I mean, are you Filipino?"

"I'm *Indian*."

"I remember that you had pictures from somewhere when we were in third grade. I thought they were from the Philippines."

"No, I'm *Indian*," I said in disbelief. "I'm not Filipino." I wondered how he could remember the third grade but not my ethnic background.

He laughed, not the slightest bit mortified by his mistake. "Do you still live in my neighborhood? Do you still live on Rahke Road? Your parents, I mean."

"Yeah. But they're moving to Geist in a couple of weeks."

"My parents still live on Rahke," he said.

"Oh."

There was an awkward silence.

"I'm going to play with you guys," Seth said as he poured himself a glass of beer and tipped some into the shot glass. He slouched in the chair.

Audrey's mouth dropped. She and Jackie left to pee, failing to be discreet about their dissatisfaction with Seth's self-invite.

"So you're Audrey's husband," he said as he watched Tom pour his beer into the shot glass.

"That's fuckin' right, dude!" Tom purposely sank the Biz again.

"Audrey and I were really quiet people in grade school and high school," he said.

"Audrey is always quiet around people she doesn't like." Tom's eyes had thick red chunks surrounding his irises, and his lids dropped lower when he spoke certain words.

Seth poured for the second time. "Well, I think I'm going to get back to my friends." He stood up, leaving a full glass of beer.

"Take that with you, man," Tom directed. "Don't waste beer."

Seth looked at me. "It was good seeing you. Enjoy Houston and tell Audrey and Jackie bye for me."

Tom told me, trying to whisper, that Seth was a douche bag.

CHAPTER 14

I dangled on the line between drunk and trashed after two beers at the Astros game. I imagined myself in the stands with Cyril, cuddling and eating jumbo dogs.

"My friends are going to meet up with us at Kenneally's," said Vince. "Have you been there before? They have this really good pizza. It's thin crust."

I hated pizza on crackers. My favorite pizza places in Houston were Fuzzy's Pizza and Star Pizza. "Sounds good," I lied, trying to control words that sounded slurred even to me. Anything fattening seemed appetizing. Then I realized he would order it meatless, and the visual of the naked pie depressed me. I would have to go through the Taco Cabana or Whataburger drive-through and order my usuals.

Vince had all the time in the world for me. It was our third date, and so far I had learned he was a dedicated vegetarian. He was disgusted by shrimp, referring to it as the "cockroaches of the sea," and also hated beef tacos. He cringed at the mention of the foods. His father was a Marthoma Christian and his mother Hindu. He abided by his mother's Hindu eating habits, while his brother and sister loved cheeseburgers and calamari like their father.

Vince was unexpectedly tall, 6 foot 2, in a family of parents and siblings who were 5 foot 4. He lived with them, which was a turnoff to me, but I accepted it as part of our culture. I was a Houston resident. The city was practically Little India compared with Indianapolis. He claimed to love living at home; while his parents paid the bills, he could do the grocery shopping and pick out the cookies he wanted. Their home was in Sugar Land. He told me that a lot of Indians lived there and that there were also large populations in Missouri City and Stafford. I informed him that I was aware of the cities and their inhabitants. I was proud I knew about the cultural fun fact.

Our first date was at Balaji Bhavan on Hillcroft, across the street from the salon where I had my eyebrows threaded every two weeks. I didn't tip on my last visit. My usual threader, an Iranian woman whose younger sister also worked in the same salon, was sick. I chose a random woman who was sitting clientless in the waiting area. She yelled at me for having ingrown hairs and told me I had horrible skin. Then she asked me why I had pimples. I responded that I was about to start my period.

Vince had talked the restaurant up, promoting the food's authenticity. It was my first time eating at an Indian restaurant, sampling masala dosa, idli and sambar, and vadas, internally declaring that my mother's was better. I sneaked a peek in the back of the restaurant to find a slim Indian woman in a tightly wound blue and gold sari with a dingy, graying black braid down her back stirring big pots of rice and chicken curry. I browsed the mini-bakery even though I didn't possess a great love for Indian sweets. There were men walking back to the restroom with their hands held up, fingers covered in sambar and other food. I liked how customers were eating with their hands as if they were at home. When Vince got up to wash his hands, a patron approached me and said that I was very impressive and that he worked at the Bollywood Theatre at Richmond and

Highway 6 if I ever wanted to see him again. He slipped me his e-mail address on the back of a receipt from an Indian grocery store.

On our second date we had glazed pottery with a bottle of shiraz-cabernet, a wedge of Havarti, and a dark chocolate candy bar. I brought Dixie cups instead of wine glasses, and he frowned at my decision of convenience. Vince rushed through, glazing a cowboy-hat candy dish with a moon-and-stars stencil and a single color. He told me he wasn't creative but liked doing something out of the ordinary on a date. I glazed a coffee mug, alternating three shades of blue for the vertical stripes and running a wide violet horizontal line through the center. I glazed attentively, concentrating on evenly spacing each stripe and applying an equal amount of glaze for an end result of magnificent color. Vince told me I needed to loosen up a bit as he watched, already finished glazing the cowboy hat, his Adidas hat tipped down. Vince's favorite brand was Adidas. He wore a black Adidas watch on his left wrist and black Adidas sunglasses across his eyes on our dates.

He invited me to the Astros game at Minute Maid Park for our third date. I had been to one other baseball game—an Indianapolis Indians game against the Louisville Bats. Jackie had tickets from the real estate company at County Line and Meridian where she'd landed a receptionist's job (which she hated) after college graduation.

We met up with Jackie's co-workers. Peggy was a personal secretary for a realtor at the agency. She was 20 years old and tied the knot at 18 with a husky guy she had dated since she was 12. She carried a photograph in her wallet of him on his motorcycle. It was scissor-cropped unevenly to fit in her wallet. Peggy also worked at the mall part time, passing out perfume samples to pay off wedding bills. Her teeth were tortuously crooked. Her round freckled cheeks looked as if they could blow up with laughter. She eyed me as Jackie introduced us.

"So Jackie had mentioned something about you being Indian."

"She did?" I looked at Peggy skeptically.

"Well, she has this really cool vase on her desk and she said that it was from India. She said that she had an Indian friend."

"Oh."

"How long have you been in America?"

I coughed on a bite of nachos. "I was born and raised here." I sipped my Zima and watched a batter run through first base.

"Well, what do you call yourself? You're not Indian, because those are the ones that have tribes and tepees. The Indians and wagons. Those Indians and wagons."

"I'm Indian." I rolled my eyes up. "My parents were born and raised in India." I didn't know what to think of the weird wagon comment. "You're referring to Native Americans." The seat scratched the backs of my knees as I stood and leaned against the seat bottom to let a woman in our row, carrying four fountain drinks, walk through.

"No. You're a Native American. You were born in America."

I was speechless, perplexed by Peggy's level of confusion.

"Why did your parents come to America anyway?" she asked. "Did they come here to have you?"

"To have me do what?"

"To give birth to you."

I frowned.

"Well, why did they come here?"

"Why did they come *here?*" I held my nachos away from my body. "That is *the* dumbest question."

"Well, sorry," Peggy said abrasively as if I had offended her.

"This is America. They came here because this is America."

*

Vince opened the door of his X5 for me while pointing out highlights of the Astros game. The Beamer had tinted windows and curb rash on the right back rim. The front interior seemed untouched, free of gas receipts, parking-garage access cards, and watered-down fast-food drinks in the cup holders. Papers on the floor in the back interior fell from a discolored stack on the driver-side rear, and CD cases spread like fallen dominos across the seats. There was a white Adidas water bottle in the middle backseat and a black Adidas duffel bag that stretched across the back floor. He asked me about my car.

"A Vigor," I said.

Vince fidgeted behind the wheel, taking his eyes off the road. "A Vigor?" He glanced at my bare legs before fixating on my face.

"It's an Acura," I said seriously. "It's like a Legend."

"Never heard of it." He curved his right hand halfway around the steering wheel. "What year is it?"

"'94."

Vince was silent. It was a stillness I interpreted as snooty. He *was* a Malayalee, but I would pick the Vigor over him any day. "It only has 108,000 miles on it," I said defensively. "It's in great condition. It's been maintained. It has new brakes, a new timing belt, and a new blower. It has a five-cylinder engine. It's in-line."

"Those *are* low miles," Vince said as if it were the only positive thing about the Vigor.

"So," he said, changing the subject, "when are you going back to Kerala for a visit?"

"I'm not."

He shot his head to me. "You mean … not this year?"

"No. I mean I'm not going back. Ever. I'm pretty sure I'm done with India. My relatives all have e-mail addresses. They like to e-mail and ask for money."

"Well … yeah."

Things were silent for a while before we got into a discussion about high school. Vince had attended a multicultural high school with a large Indian population.

"I couldn't imagine that. I was the only Indian in my grade school and high school. I wanted to be white when I was little."

He looked at me in disappointment. "Not me. I was really proud of it. I felt bad for the white kids because they never had anything to wear on Culture Day."

"You had a *culture* day? I wouldn't have anything to wear either. I didn't own any Indian clothes in high school. If we had something like that at my school, it would turn into a day full of racist comments."

He was quiet.

I fiddled with my Texas-shaped dangling earrings.

Vince handed me his iPod. "Pick a song."

I flipped through his music. I couldn't find a single '80s rock track. I put the iPod down and looked out the window. "Whatever is fine."

It seemed to bother Vince that I didn't select a song. "*Well*, what kind of music do you like?"

"Eighties mostly."

"Oh, me too. Didn't you see anything that you like? I love Depeche Mode."

"No. I mean I like Queensryche and Van Halen and those bands."

"The hair bands?" He stopped at the light at the intersection of Westheimer and Chimney Rock, braking a foot away from the black Pontiac Fiero in front of us with a "for sale" sign in Spanish on the rear windshield over broken sections of tint. "You like the *hair* bands?"

"Yeah, older-sister influence. I thought she was so cool when I was little and I always tried to be like her." I looked at a couple cuddling at a bus stop. The man was wearing a suit and the woman a maid's uniform. The man next to them was in orange shorts and a light blue T-shirt. He wore earmuff-size headphones while gloriously playing an air harmonica.

"Well, I do like Van Halen," Vince said.

"Really?" I was thrilled, interest sparked. "Who do you like better? David or Sammy?"

"David or Sammy?"

"Yeah. David or Sammy?" I tortured him by asking the question again, knowing that he would not have an answer. "David or Sammy?"

"Uh. I don't know."

"David Lee Roth. Sammy Hagar. They were the lead singers of Van Halen. Roth was the original lead singer."

"Oh."

There was a mean sense of dead air, a notification of incompatibility. I watched a plastic bag blowing around on Westheimer. "Do you at least like Led Zeppelin?"

He looked out the window.

"So you don't like any real rock?" I asked as if I were stating it.

"Real rock?"

"You know. Musicians who can handle a guitar solo."

"That beer made me feel a little full." Vince rubbed his stomach. "I usually don't drink beer."

I frowned uncontrollably. I thought it was feminine when men got their nails done and did not drink beer, own tool sets, or watch sports.

"Why'd your parents name you Mala? Your name means necklace."

"They liked the name," I said squarely.

"Krishna is pretty cool," he said. "My friend. Krishna's girlfriend is Malu. I don't think she's Catholic, though."

I burst out laughing. "Krishna?" I toppled over, laughing, in the passenger seat. I told myself I would not have drinks at the bar.

"Yeah. Krishna."

"That is … ," I said through the laughter. "That is hilarious!"

Vince wasn't laughing.

I wished I had eaten more than half a mini bagel for dinner.

"Well, what's his girlfriend's name?"

"Dorothy."

I erupted with laughter again. "*Dorothy?*"

Vince laughed. "Yeah, you wouldn't think an Indian girl would be named Dorothy." He shrugged.

We laughed hysterically together. I wiped my tears away and took a long look at his lips, trying to imagine kissing them. I could not form the image in my head.

"Dorothy is really cool. She's so cool. You two are going to get along great. She doesn't really hang out with any Indian people either."

Vince bought me a gin and tonic at the bar. I was tanked and it was only 10 o'clock. I knocked back the entire gin and tonic and told Vince I'd be right back. I took what seemed to be the longest piss ever. My thighs hurt from squatting so long over the toilet. I looked down at my panties—cotton underwear with big pink and green flowers. They were not sexy. I did not want to touch Vince. I talked to myself in the mirror, speech slurred. My incisors stuck out more than usual. My curls were frizzy on the left side of my head. A faint stain of gloss was on my lips. A random welt on my cheek, covered with foundation, broke free through the makeup. I couldn't believe how hideous I looked through in-and-out blurred vision. I realized I was over-the-line intoxicated. I knew there was no turning back.

A couple stood with Vince. I ducked behind people at the bar to get a good look before meeting them. The Indian girl was very pretty, unoriginal, clear and unadorned, with straight, sleek black hair that ended at the middle of her back. The larger side of her hair part rubbed against her eyelashes. She wore a basic, cotton, long-sleeve red shirt. A clunky red bag, inappropriate for barhopping, was over her right shoulder. She gripped the strap with her right hand, her forearm slamming into her right breast.

The Indian guy's white baseball cap sat backward on his head, the stitching ruptured and woolly near his ears. His sideburns were messy. There were needlelike hairs forming a rectangle in his chin and whopping diamonds in his ears. I found him attractive in a street-dancer kind of way.

Krishna and Dorothy introduced themselves. I laughed when hearing their names and then took a drink of the newly ordered gin and tonic from Vince. I blanked during the first few words of conversation, learning only that Dorothy and Krishna both worked for Deloitte and lived with their parents.

"How's your date so far?" asked Dorothy.

"It's good." My eyes followed Vince to the bar. My attention was diverted back to Dorothy as if a spotlight illuminated her long black hair and clunky red bag. I watched Dorothy's lips sway back and forth, her fingers clutching the purse strap tighter and tighter, left hand falling forward while she spoke. The chipped red nail polish on her curling fingernails stood out to me the most. I couldn't get over her name being Dorothy.

"Vince is a nice guy," cooed Dorothy. "He's like a big teddy bear."

The next thing I knew, I was sitting at a table with Vince, Dorothy, and Krishna, another glass softened into the curve of my hand. I scanned the three of them as they chattered among themselves. I was part of an Indian couple socializing at a table with another Indian couple. It was the first time in my life. I suddenly longed for the comfort of my white friends and conversations about white wedding dresses and getting kicked out of the house at the age of 18 and references to parents by their first names. The bar dimmed darker, and the waterlike taste of gin and tonic flooded time. I looked past Dorothy at a couple leaning into each other at the bar. They were both tall, in knee-length jackets, with cigarette smoke streaming from their fingers. The woman wore dark green flats, obviously chosen to avoid towering over her date. They were new to each other, evident by their beaming exchanges and modest touching of arms and upper back only.

"Are you okay?" asked Krishna. "You look really drunk." He pulled on his earlobe, the diamond earring tumbling into the cuff of his ripped jacket sleeve. He slammed his arm on the table and retrieved the earring. It was a clip-on.

"Yeah," I slurred. I giggled as my chin slid down my fist and arm, my head landing on my bicep, halting further movement. I silently called him Clip-On Krishna and laughed out loud at my own joke.

They all stared at me and then looked at each other for an explanation of my behavior.

"Any*way*." Dorothy tossed her hair. "We've been together for five whole months." She made a kissing face at Krishna, puckering her lips near his.

I wanted to gag and wasn't sure if I accidentally did.

Krishna took his jacket off. He wore a short-sleeve Gandhi T-shirt underneath, revealing a tattoo that read, "WHAT IT DO." I laughed at it, wanting to ask him if his other arm read "Thug Life."

Dorothy pulled her clunky red bag off the table by the strap and flipped open her cell phone. The screen lighted up the center of her chin. "How did you guys meet?" She kept her face in the phone, her thumb moving across the keypad.

"OTC," said Vince.

Dorothy looked up at Vince. "O-T-C," she mocked as if we had met at a brothel or a crack house. She heaved her head back ferociously, discharging one colossal cackle into the smoky atmosphere.

I raised my glass but set it down when I tasted vomit in my mouth. My eyes spun through Vince, Dorothy, and Krishna. I picked up the gin and tonic and downed half of it. I was disassembled, unable to contribute to or even trail the conversation. I craved the freedom of the Vigor, wishing I'd driven separately like I usually did. I felt confined, held prisoner by my decision to plummet into a drunken stupor. I was also held prisoner by three brown people, three Texans whom I had a feeling I would not get to know after the night was over.

"I send Vince these really long text messages when I'm bored at work," said Dorothy. She kneaded Vince's wrist and hand in a downward motion.

I gasped and looked at Krishna. He was unmoved by his girlfriend's affectionate behavior toward Vince. My jaw dropped at Krishna.

Dorothy removed her hand from Vince's as she looked at me. "I *like* your hair."

I was startled by the compliment. "Thanks." Never had an Indian girl liked my short, curly hair. They told me to grow it long and straighten it so I could look more like them. My opinion about Dorothy changed with that single flattering remark.

Dorothy leaned in, her eyes sweeping through my curvaceous locks. "You look like a 10-year-old."

I initially felt my cheeks sink into my gums. I clenched my teeth. My mood crashed. I'd had problems with Indian girls for as long as I could remember. It began at Malayalee parties where my parents forced me to be present. Little Geeta told me I wasn't cool because my belly pooched out and I didn't eat chicken curry that was cooked by anyone but my mother. No one would play with me and I'd have to watch Malayalam movies with the aunties in the living room. The cold dismissal carried over into college when Shazia would drag me to Indian events at IU. There was always some North Indian girl with long, sleek hair that would ask me why I didn't wear mine straight and long. Then she would shun me for not wearing Indian clothes to Diwali.

I touched my hair, fingers together, as if I were shielding it from Dorothy. I scooted away from the table, windy in movement, to use the restroom. I loudly cursed Dorothy on the way there, feeling like the panhandlers at Richmond and Voss who talked to themselves. I always turned away from them, pretending to play with the radio, hoping they wouldn't come to my window.

I scrutinized myself in the bathroom mirror. My supershort curls were suddenly a vision of perfection. There was no frizz. I couldn't tolerate anyone thinking otherwise about my populous swirls of black hair. Fuming in the mirror, I heard Dorothy's comment again, replaying the smirk on her conventional face. I firmly planted my hands near the wet sink, elbows bent, and looked directly into my bloodshot eyes. "Who the hell does she think *she* is?" Two women in the restroom cautiously stared at me.

I shoved the door open and casually walked past Krishna and Dorothy. I noticed them staring at me through the corner of my eye. I snickered at the sight of Vince at the bar ordering more drinks. I sat at an empty table across from Krishna and Dorothy. My own table. I didn't have the Vigor to take me home, so I was to have my own table instead. I crossed my legs, left on top, and glanced at Dorothy and Krishna through blurred vision. Although it was an obstructed view, I could see they were appalled.

Vince came back with two drinks, turning his head back and forth between me and his friends. He turned his back to Krishna and Dorothy. He soared taller in height than he had before. Vince's cheeks were plumper. His eyes were open wider as if he was going to get hit by two semis instead of one. He stood behind me.

I tilted my head so far back to make eye contact that it felt as if it could fall off.

"I got you another gin and tonic," he said while putting the drinks on the table.

"Oh, Jesus Christ," I said. "I mean Krishna." I toppled over, laughing at my religious joke. A snort slipped out that tickled my throat and the roof of my mouth.

Vince laughed, too, pulling the chair around and sitting next to me. His leg relaxed against mine.

"I want to go home." I pressed the send button on my phone to report the hair comment in a text message to Audrey, Jackie, and Sara.

"You want to go *home*?" Vince asked, concerned.

"I got a text from Alyssa, my friend from work, and she's at Armadillo Palace right now. We could go there. We could go to this '80s glam-rock bar that I like." I couldn't stop thinking about Cyril.

Vince looked away, unsatisfied with the choices I was offering. "You should stay. How about we go to Deco? I'll just tell them that we're going home."

"Oh, okay." I was fine with a change of scenery just as long as it excluded Krishna and Dorothy. I was surprised that Vince was so quick to ditch them.

I could hear Krishna's frustration.

"Take her home and come back. Take her home, man. Hang out with *us*."

"We're going home," lied Vince.

*

I was startled by the crowd. Deco appeared to be an Indian dance lounge. I took it all in, the sea of young Indian men and women, shoulder to shoulder, in the classy, dimly lighted lounge. I spotted one white guy sitting on a couch with a group of Indian girls. He had to have been dating one of them. There were white bartenders and the valet was white.

"Krishna and Dorothy were saying bye outside, but you just took off to the car."

"Oh sorry. I didn't really notice. I was just ready to go."

"Isn't this great?" Vince skimmed the room. "To be around your own people."

"I've never seen anything like this before. I've met quite a few Indian people since I've been in Houston, and they weren't all they're cracked up to be."

He rolled his eyes. It was the first time he showed how annoyed he was with me. We didn't make it to the bar without being stopped by someone. Vince was Mr. Popular, knowing practically everyone at Deco. Each Indian glorified Vince, pointing out that he was a "good friend" and a "sweet guy."

One of them was named Vivek. He was hammered, condensed in height and dark in surface tone. His lips were raspberry-colored and wet-looking, as if he had just eaten a Fla-Vor-Ice. There were bottomless moon shapes under his eyes. Smashed perspiration speckles were revealed by an unbuttoned shirt with midnight-blue, cobalt-blue, black, and white vertical stripes. Vivek's chest appeared to be solid and muscular through his shirt. His hair was buzzed, creating a naturally rectangular forehead.

The alcoholic scent of his breath became heartier with the increased intensity of his voice. He told me he was a friend of Vince's from his Indian baseball league. He patted Vince on the back repeatedly, holding himself up while grabbing Vince's shirt. "He's a great guy," he told me. "He's such a good guy. He'll treat you right."

Vince and I finally made it to the bar, hand in hand, but not before being interrupted by more people. I would never want to be that popular. I put my hands on the bar in front of the bartender, arms taut. Vince slipped his arms through the gaps created between my sides and arms. I leaned against his chest and rubbed his forearms in one single motion. I didn't do it as a natural instinct but because I felt I should give some encouragement to a guy who was Malayalee and marriage material.

Vince kissed me. It was a graceless kiss, awkward and cramped, with no inkling of tremors or waves, craving or sufficiency. I avoided him when it was over, darting my eyes over to the DJ and sucking on the double straws in the gin and tonic that I suddenly realized I was holding. I wished it was Cyril kissing me. We went outside, holding hands, to say goodbye to people on the patio.

*

Without inviting Vince in, he entered my place. It had become home. On my fridge was a magnet that read, "I'm not from Texas but I got here as soon as I could." Almost everything in my apartment was from IKEA, including the dish drainer, dish towels, scrub brushes, oven mitts, can opener, pizza pan, frying pans, pots and pans, baking pans, cookware sets, spatulas, measuring cup, food savers, and 20-piece fork, knife, and spoon set. I had replaced my paper plates and Styrofoam cups with real plates, side plates, bowls, 59-cent coffee mugs, and a drinking-glass set. I didn't know that household items could be so cheap. I was willing to deal with the construction on I-10 every day for two weeks after I discovered IKEA, and I also enjoyed their Swedish meatballs.

He carried a plastic HEB grocery bag containing what he said were a few of his favorite DVDs. He bent down until the bag touched the floor, releasing the handles.

I pulled the bed out of the wall, instigating an unwanted, instinctive sexual invitation. I looked to the corner of the room and along the wall. I decided that I did have space for a couch.

Vince lunged for the bed, landing on his back. He kicked off his Adidas casuals to reveal white Adidas ankle socks.

I tossed two pillows onto the bed and crawled up next to him. The pillow was doughy against my cheek, the used, stained mattress almost up to pillow-top standards.

Vince rubbed my head, transitioning to my scalp and massaging vigorously with his fingers as we watched an infomercial on R&B love songs. I wished Cyril were holding me.

"Krishna and Dorothy told me to just drop you off and come back," he said.

I laughed. My eyes were half-shut. "Yeah, I heard Krishna." I recalled his argumentative face, attempting to persuade Vince to get rid of the bitchy Catholic Indian girl who sits at her own table.

"Wouldn't that have been funny if we saw them at Deco?" Vince rolled onto his side and looked into my caving eyes.

"Yeah." I would have found it entertaining but found it bizarre that Vince would've thought it was funny.

"She just meant that you were cute," he said as he rolled onto his back, the power of his scalp massage losing force.

I sat up, my right hand landing on my left knee as I turned to him. "What?"

"She just meant that you were cute like a schoolgirl, like a 10-year-old."

I furrowed my eyebrows at him as I began to tell him how ridiculous he was being. I was too drunk to complete the sentence and crashed on the bed, face up.

"Are you self-conscious about your hair looking like that?"

"What? I like the way I look. I look good."

"No, I don't mean. That's not what I meant."

We were both silent.

"Dorothy's really cool," said Vince.

I rolled my eyes. "Yeah," I said sarcastically.

"She *is*. Krishna is going to *marry* her," he said. Vince kissed me. I was more drunk than I was at the time of the initial kiss at Deco but not enough to create a desire for his kiss. Maybe it was the stark white lighting from my apartment floor lamp or his sloppy hand movements over my breasts and stomach. I really did not want to see Vince naked.

"I have something for us." He took his hands off of me and pushed himself forward off the bed. He reached for the HEB bag. The bottom of the red "B" was hollowed out.

"You want to watch a *movie?*" I was too confused to feel relieved.

He dumped the bag, DVDs scattering in front of the mattress.

I tilted my head to the side, looking to the floor, the top of my ear resting on my shoulder. Two nude women with groomed, hairy crotches were on the cover of one of the DVDs, posing in a hammock with their tongues in each other's mouths. I stood up and looked at the DVDs on the floor. I didn't blink. Each DVD had naked men and women on them. "*Porno?* Porn!"

"Yeah," he said lightheartedly, as if I should be breaking out my own collection.

"You brought over a *bag* full of porn?"

"Well, I thought we could watch it while we have sex tonight." He knelt, sitting on the backs of his heels.

"Sex? Right now? I'm a freakin' virgin!"

"Virgin?" He laughed for a brief moment. Vince rolled up onto his feet, scrambling for the movies. He looked like a little kid cleaning up his toys so he could hurry and watch *SpongeBob SquarePants*. "I'm going home." He mumbled something about virgins and his luck with women.

It bothered me that he was leaving without being kicked out. I bolted to the fridge, remembering that I had a package of ground beef for quesadillas. I chucked it down the stairs, and it beat him to the bottom of the staircase. "Have some beef! You're the fattest vegetarian I've ever met."

Vince looked at the meat on the ground and then up at me. He looked horrified.

I wasn't sure which terrified him more, the sight of the meat or that I was loony enough to throw it at him. "Go ahead and go," I said as he was already out of my sight. "I can pick up another guy just like that." I snapped my fingers. "You should be grateful that I even agreed to go out with you!"

I crashed onto my bed and cried into my comforter. I didn't know why I was crying. I lay down, rolled over, and opened my cell phone, pressing it to my ear as I listened to Cyril's phone ring. He answered, disrupted in his sleep. I hung up like I had several times before. The most recent was earlier in the night before my date with Vince. I waited less than a minute before calling again.

"Hello?" Cyril paused. "Hello?"

I stayed stone-cold silent, wondering if he knew it was me, listening to his endurance on the other line. I would've hung up if I were on his end. I pictured him in bed with his shirt off, gun under his sturdy pillow, and a single white sheet draped over his chest and under his arm.

"Hello?"

"It's me."

*

Cyril was at my studio in 20 minutes. I imagined him blaring chopped and screwed mixes in the car while racing down Beltway 8. I changed into sexier underwear and popped a red Life Saver that was over a year old while I waited. I was too uncoordinated and lazy from the alcohol to brush my teeth.

He wore a faded white T-shirt that read, "It's a Texas Thing, Y'all Wouldn't Understand," and Sean John jeans with needle-detailed back flap pockets. "There's ground beef down there." The spice of his cologne disseminated in the air and down my throat as we hugged.

I pressed my head against his soft set chest for a long moment. I felt at home, in the presence of someone who truly knew me. "Ground beef. Huh, that's weird."

"Wow, your breath. You've had a lot to drink."

"I went out with friends."

"Okay, what guy were you out with?" Cyril sat on my bed and looked around as if he had never seen my place before. A Winger poster hung above my mini-television, and a framed photo of me, Audrey, and Jackie at the Rathskeller lay on the floor near the TV. I was deciding on a place for it. I thought about Krupa as I looked at the three smiling faces in the picture and how she never had the chance to experience a lifetime of real friendship.

My '80s rock-ballad CD played softly in the background. I made the CD a week before my nervous breakdown on the Circle. I had no love prospects at the time but wanted to have all my favorite '80s rock love tunes together when I noticed a rock-ballad CD on sale at Borders.

"What song *is* this?"

"It's Tesla. It's called *Love Song.*"

"*Your* music." He shook his head.

Cyril rolled on top of me like he had many times before. His boundless lips swept mine solid. My watermelon-flavored lip balm seeped into his taste buds. I slipped my hands under his shirt back, my fingers stirring upward over soft and rough skin until I pulled the shirt over his head. We kissed intensely.

I was not nervous. "Let's have sex," I whispered.

He reached into his jean pocket.

"That's not expired, is it?" I asked as he tore open the condom. I didn't question his preparation, why he had a condom with him, his wishful thinking, and precaution.

The array of attire on the floor flickered as I came around to him. I trusted him. The matchless scent of his scalp, the natural aroma, overwhelmed me as I remembered the first time I breathed it. And the first time I smelled it on my shirt after staying the night at his place. When Cyril would sleep at my place, I never changed the pillowcases until after the scent faded away. Circumstances were no longer the same. His skin smelled clean, as if he'd applied a light lotion all over his body. It was a scent I did not recognize. I noticed he had lost weight, a line of muscle in his chest distracting me.

Cyril kissed the faint trail of hair descending from my belly button. He kissed the blemish above it—a scar from a drunken, spring-break piercing incident.

My legs formed a V-shape around him, calves flexed yet jiggly and the soles of my feet deeply curved. Cyril was inside me with delicate yet overpowering grace.

I lay there in his arms, glad I had no sexual expectations. I wasn't 16 anymore, naïve in thinking that rose petals would be on the bed and candles lighted around the room while I had sex for the first time. My virginity was finally gone. I wondered what I'd spend my time stressing about as a non-virgin. "So that counts, right?"

Cyril laughed. "Yes, it does. So I guess we're back together."

I jerked my head off his chest and tilted my head to the side to look at him.

His cheeks were rosy, glowing in the room, lighted by the crack of dawn.

I was silent, inarticulate, and misunderstood.

The luminosity drained from Cyril's face. "Okay, fan*tast*ic." He hurled the comforter off of him with one hand. He put his jeans on and, with them unbuttoned and shirt grasped in hand, he looked at me as if he couldn't bear to look at me. "I hate that I ever fell in love with you."

CHAPTER 15

Tom and I advanced in line to board the Stadium Express. I was on my way to Magazine Reporting class at Ernie Pyle. I wasn't sure what class Tom was going to at the HPER but thought it may have been a sports elective course. Tom's eyes were droopy. He wasn't very talkative. He had a fight with Audrey around 3 a.m. I could only hear the muffled sounds of their heightened voices through the wall and then complete silence five minutes later.

It was 29 degrees, a sharp contrast to the 65-degree weather of the previous day. Tom wore cargo khaki shorts and a white short-sleeve T-shirt. His skin looked frosty, arm hair rising from his body. His ears were protected only by his long red hair when the wind wasn't gusting through it. He looked like a fool. Tom had spent the night at our place and did not have a change of clothes to meet the needs of the cold day. Audrey snoozed deeply in her bed while we left. She didn't have class until 1 p.m.

I felt as if someone was paying close attention to me, watching me as if he didn't care that I noticed. I made eye contact with a student farther down in the line. He wore a long, muddy-gray coat. He dug his hands into his coat pockets as if he were trying to keep warm. A sooty-cream knit scarf circled his neck loosely, tapped his chin, and created a waterfall down his chest. I caught glimpses of a green shirt through gaps between the button loops of the coat. The right side of his shirt collar projected out of the scarf like the pointy tip of a paper airplane. I looked away.

One by one, students loaded the bus, wearing heavy, puffy coats, pea coats, and leather jackets, gloves and mittens, winter hats and scarves, backpacks, and single-strap satchels. Tom sat near the window, while I occupied the aisle seat next to him. We both put our backpacks next to our feet.

The student who was staring at me took the seat in front of us and slid all the way to the window. Curly light brown hair settled softly on his head like a wig on a mannequin. There was a light black mole on the right side of his jaw that seemed out of place, as if it had been surgically moved from another part of his face, and was shaped irregularly like basil leaves. He turned halfway around in his seat and stared at me.

"What class are you going to?" I asked, trying to ignore the staring.

"Archery," Tom replied unenthusiastically while looking at the young man who was staring.

He looked fixedly at me as if I were an exotic species that had been captured and being transported through campus. He couldn't keep his eyes off me while I spoke.

I looked at him sharply with the purpose of breaking his rude stares through his dark-brimmed, round glasses that washed out his skin. I tried hard to ignore him, turning to Tom as if he wasn't even sitting in front of us.

The student turned his body to Tom. "Her English is really good."

Tom looked at me and smirked. It was the most emotion he had shown all morning. The comment seemed to wake him up like a cup of dark roast or a morning Red Bull. He knew what was happening.

The student shifted his attention back to me as if I had appeared out of thin air. "How long have you been in the country?"

"I was born in this country," I snapped.

He leaned away from us in shock.

I jolted awake in bed, gasping for air, digging my fingers into my collarbone, the soles of my feet in contact with the mattress, forcing my knees to drift to the side. The fitted sheet had slipped onto the left side of the mattress. My sheets and comforter were twisted, so I could not tell which side was up. The television remote had fallen to the floor. It was my racially recurring nightmare. Only this time it was different. I woke up feeling pissed off at the world. I felt different, more alone than usual. I was always so disturbed by the dream that seemed so real. It was a regular part of my life, like brushing my teeth or securing the door locks at night before bed. It could've easily happened in real life, only I wasn't in college anymore. I was working at Midwest Bank.

I realized the hours of the day ahead. The punishing, mundane hours at Midwest Bank. I cried when I thought about wasting another day in my dead-end job, withering in my cubicle. "I'm so frustrated. I'm just so frustrated." I sat up even more in my bed, dreading another day of wasting my career dreams. The lack of fulfillment was paralyzing. I rolled off the bed and onto the floor and cried dramatically into the soft carpet in front of the dark cherry-wood nightstand. "I'm so frustrated. I'm just so frustrated."

*

I watched the phone as it rang. I didn't care to answer it. My hot-pink nail polish had just dried. I stared at the empty, undecorated walls of my cube. My extreme hate for my dead-end job was reflected in the actions that consistently lacked any sort of work ethic. My phone rang again. It was Christy. She was always rude, never smiled, and consistently had a supersize fountain drink on her desk. She was a fairly large woman with upper arms that looked like butt cheeks.

"I don't think my phone works," she said. "I've been calling this lady and she never answered. You *need* to put in a request for me so they can fix my phone."

"That doesn't mean your phone doesn't work." I started to call her a jackass but refrained. "You are on it now, dammit! It's ringing and we are speaking. She doesn't want to talk to you! Get a clue, lady! Oh, and I didn't hear a 'please' in there anywhere. And I don't *need* to do anything." I slammed the phone down, the cord free of twists courtesy of a detangler, irate that I had to deal with Christy.

I pressed "play" on Windows Media Player, as *We're Not Gonna Take It* had been paused.

"Mala, girl, can you turn that down?" asked Rakisha, although it was in a demanding tone. "I'm listenin' to Lil' Flip. I can't hear my music."

I turned to a knocking sound on the outside of my cubicle.

There was an Indian woman standing in the opening. I flinched, caught off guard by an Indian person at Midwest Bank other than Arpita.

"Hello. I'm Susheela."

"Hi," I said uneasily. I looked her up and down.

Susheela's shoulders cradled her black hair, which was partially frizzy on the sides and ends. She wore black, loose-fitting dress pants, hems landing on top of black loafers with dull buckles exposed. Her dress shirt was postal blue, tucked in yet unable to reveal her shape. Susheela's eyebrows were groomed as if they were from a sketched pencil drawing, strays blended into her tea-colored complexion. The skin near her mouth was free, becoming trapped when she spoke. "I'm new here. I work in HR. I noticed you yesterday and wanted to come over and introduce myself. I've met Arpita already."

"I'm Mala."

"I think I know your parents."

I tried to smile.

"Your sister's dead, right?"

I think my eyes stayed open for an eternity. I looked away, then back at the computer. I had never heard it put so insensitively.

"Well, that happened 20 years ago. Do you even remember her? I'm sure your parents are past that."

My cheeks felt hot. I got out of my chair and sidestepped Susheela. Then I turned around. "It doesn't just go away." I almost slammed into another unfamiliar woman who was short with coarse black hair that ended at her chin. Her dress shirt was long, past her behind, a colorful combination of seascapes and desert drawings.

"I'm Keely." She stuck her hand out.

She was my new boss, the woman who would be taking over the position I'd been screwed out of. Susheela looked at me as she walked away and then turned back to look at me one more time.

"Word around is that you're really smart," said Keely, carrying the Midwest Bank handbook and other paperwork against her chest while the long strap of her black leather purse hung wildly at her elbow.

I looked around at my co-workers. The compliment was embarrassing.

"How's your job search going? I know you are looking for something to fit your degree."

"I apply and search for jobs all day while I'm in my cube."

Keely laughed uncomfortably. She used her knee to bring up the handbook and paperwork that were slipping from her arms.

"It was nice meeting you," I said.

"Oh. I'm implementing a new rule. When you arrive in the morning and leave for lunch and come back, send me an e-mail. Also send me an e-mail when you leave for the day. This will help me keep track of attendance and create a more pleasant working environment. So I will need a total of four e-mails from you per day."

My eyes expanded as I stood in silence.

"Oh. Where are you going?" Keely asked unassertively.

"To the restroom."

"Okay. Well, when you come back I'll need your help. I don't know how to use Word."

I turned away. "Wow," I said under my breath. I sauntered through the hallway of the lower level of Midwest Bank. The framed photographs were smiling portraits of Midwest Bank employees taken in the '80s or possibly the late '70s. A history hallway. One woman stood out like a weed in a vase of flowers. An unflattering hairstyle, though probably flattering at the time, billowed over her face with waves of curl and bangs that appeared to be crunchy in texture and lined with flakes from aerosol hair spray. Her eyelids were smothered in powder blue, making my eyes feel heavy. Her flower-pattern dress was like a garden of excessive, tacky florals that added 20 pounds to her figure.

Elise from human resources was inserting coins into a vending machine near the women's restroom. She was tall and slender and always wore her short hair in a ponytail, a stub poking out of her head.

"Hi, Mala," she said cheerily.

I smiled at her with a closed mouth, a pathetic, forced expression. I could always spot Elise a mile away because of the bright green nylon jacket she wore every day over a long, light or dark jean skirt. Even in 80-degree weather, I would see Elise in the green cover-up and long jean skirt strolling around Monument Circle.

"Mala, may I ask you," she began. "Where do you hail from?"

"Hail from?" I had never heard that one before. "You mean where are my parents from?"

She leaned down to retrieve a Snickers bar from the machine.

"My parents were born and raised in India." I put my hand on the door of the women's restroom.

She furrowed her eyebrows while looking me up and down. "Really?" She gave me a time-consuming look. "I would've never guessed that."

I pushed open the bathroom door.

"Maybe because you don't have one of those dots on your head." Elise tapped her forehead where the bindi would be and laughed hysterically.

"Moron." I entered the restroom, not waiting for Elise's reaction.

Rachel was washing her hands in the restroom. She was a customer-service representative who started a lot of her sentences with "I'm not racist but … " Her hair was sleek, blond, and iron-straightened, with neglected wavy pieces that adhered to her neck. Her makeup applications were colorfully thick, painful to look at, and reapplied every two hours. "Hey, girl. I made tortilla soup last night for dinner and brought the leftovers for lunch today. I wanted you to try it so you can see if it tastes authentic."

"What do you mean?"

Rachel looked at me as if I were blockheaded. "Well. Since you're Mexican. You can see if it tastes like how your mom makes it."

"I'm not Mexican. I'm Indian."

"You're Indian. Oh my God. You don't look Indian at all. But you eat a lot of rice. Don't you?"

"I ... I guess."

"You don't look Indian at all. I mean most Indian people all look the same."

I walked out as Rachel was in the process of speaking her next sentence. I needed to get out of Midwest Bank for a few hours. I thought about catching a movie, browsing through the spinning displays of earrings at Parisian, or going for a walk on the Canal. I headed back to my cube to retrieve my purse. I passed a man on the way who introduced himself as Tyler.

"I just joined the IT staff." He smiled proudly as if he had landed his dream job, wearing a black Midwest Bank-logo laptop bag across his chest. He took a sip from his Midwest Bank travel mug. "I just love it here."

I gave him a dirty look.

He flinched a little. "What do you do here?"

"Well, let's see here, *Tyler*. I come in late and leave early. I take hours of breaks. While I'm here I surf the Internet all day, usually searching for jobs or applying to them while having to deal with the obnoxious people that work here."

"Oh, uh ... "

I sneered, cutting him off. "Get out while you can."

As I grabbed my purse, I felt as if I could cry. I had a nasty taste in my mouth, raunchy samples of my day. I headed straight for Monument Circle, where I hunkered on the steps facing East Market Street. I looked up at Chase Tower. Then I looked at the Columbia Club. Then I looked at myself. My clothes were vivid, as if they were my only outfit. It was a new fitted black shirt with fluttering sleeves, new jeans that looked fashionably destructed, and new black kitten heels that had thicker openings in the third holes of the ankle straps. It was a summery day with a perfect breeze. It was a day that did not match my mood.

I pressed my fingers into the area slightly above my temples and cried. A storm of tears devastated my eyes and shattered across my face. I broke down. "I'm getting out of here," I said confidently even though I was crying, having an epiphany. "I'm getting out of here. I'm done. I'm done. I'm done. I'm done." I repeated it over and over uncontrollably. I noticed a couple staring as I talked to myself like the homeless people who lived on the downtown streets. The couple was drinking Starbucks, the man up a step higher than the woman, with a green straw in his drink and his long legs limp over the steps.

I stood and wiped my face with my tear-streaked hands. Something was different. I didn't know what it was. "I just can't take anymore. I just can't take anymore. I'm getting out of here. I am getting out of here." I noticed Elise coming toward me in her bright green nylon jacket. I ignored her when she waved.

I looked up Houston online, an affordable big city with warm weather. It was everything I wanted in a city, and it was far, far away from my hometown. I remembered Audrey's brother mentioning a friend who lived there.

"We need to speak with you."

I turned around to Christy and Mr. Brown.

Christy had a smirk on her face, her chin disappearing even further into her neck than usual.

"We've been waiting for you," said Mr. Brown. "You are not supposed to take more than a 15-minute break. You were 138 minutes late for work this morning. You will have to stay an extra 138 minutes this evening. Mala, I really don't want to have to write you up."

"Write me up for *what*?" I huffed.

"Christy here said that her phone isn't working and that you refused to put the request in."

"Her phone is working! She called me on it."

"Mala, I don't appreciate your disrespect. When you disrespect one of us, you are disrespecting the Midwest Bank family. You'll never be employee of the month if you keep acting like this."

"Well then write me up," I snapped with a little bit of a head swing that I learned from my co-workers.

I packed up my belongings—lip balm and 3.5-ounce bottle of lotion. I sidestepped Christy and Mr. Brown, my shirt sleeve skimming the wall as I squeezed by them. "The Indian girl is leaving her crappy job! The Indian girl is leaving her crappy job!" I threw my purse over my right shoulder and walked out of Midwest Bank.